Edge
of
Piracy

Books by Donald Barr Chidsey

Edge
of
Piracy

a novel by

DONALD BARR CHIDSEY

WILDSIDE PRESS

To Bunny

Edge
of
Piracy

Chapter

1

Ezra held the glass to his eye for a long while, in no hurry to commit himself. It was about six bells of the late watch, full light.

"Guns?" asked his uncle, the skipper.

"Ports anyway," Ezra answered. "I can't see for sure whether there's anything been run out. But she looks fast."

"Um-m. A sloop. I could make out that much myself."

It was a lovely morning, the sea a hundred million bright blue choplets, the sun a great gay burst of gold.

"Well?" said the skipper, and he sounded a trifle testy, edgy, which was not like him.

Ezra Bond lowered the glass.

"That she's alone in these seas, and a racer to boot," he said carefully, "that makes it look like she's maybe a mail carrier, a royal packet, you know?"

Captain Hart took the glass, which rightfully belonged to him, but he did not raise it. He nodded.

"That's just what I'd figured," he said, "but I wanted younger eyes to put an amen to it."

Stung by the swarm of privateers that had emerged from various mainland American ports, and especially those of New England, Great Britain in this the fifth year of fighting would not have permitted any vessel to take to the high seas out of convoy—except, of course, a warship or a mail carrier, which was much the same thing, since the mail carriers were properly a part of the Royal Navy and manned by regular R.N. mariners.

The *Forbearance*, also sloop rigged, out of Saybrook, Connecticut, was not a full-time privateer; she had not been built for that purpose; but she did carry a letter of marque, a genuine one issued by the Continental Congress itself, not one of the forgeries and fakes that floated about. She had a legitimate cargo, mostly dried eels and barrel staves, but she had an armament considerably more formidable than was the custom for such small vessels —six wide-mouthed carronades, three on each side, and a long brass bow chaser. The *Forbearance* crew was large for the size of the sloop—forty-two officers and men. Her owners did not expect her to go cruising in search of enemy shipping, but they did think that if anything juicy fell, as it were, right at her feet, she might at least pick it up.

A royal mail packet would be a rich prize. She would carry no cargo, but she'd be heavy with powder and shot; and besides the mail—which itself might be of interest to General Washington, since it would consist largely of official dispatches—she would almost certainly have a treasure chest of gold coins for the soldiers stationed overseas.

Captain Hart put the glass under his left arm and started to pace the poop, which was not large.

"Well, shift course two points of easting and keep everything cracked on, the way it is now."

Ezra looked at him in amazement. He had known his Uncle Hart since babyhood, but this was the first time that they had sailed together. Ezra was the first mate.

"You're going to run away?"

"Huh?"

"Sir."

The skipper was unabashed.

"Tarnation right we're going to run away. Ezra, didn't anybody ever tell you that those vessels carry sometimes up to twelve guns, besides marines for boarding? We're in no shape to bump heads with such as that. Our business is carrying goods, not fighting. Sure, we'll fight if we have to, but we'll pick our opponents."

"I see."

"Well, what's the matter? Give the orders."

"Aye, aye, sir!"

An hour and a half later, off watch now, Ezra Bond saw that the British vessel looked a little nearer. He studied her, shading his eyes, for the morning was getting long. She too had changed her course.

He ran to the poop deck.

"My God, sir, I believe *she's* chasing *us!*"

"Please mind your language, Ezra," the skipper said coldly. "I wouldn't want your Aunt Bessie Hart when you get back thinking that you'd picked up words like that on a ship of mine."

Deliberately, without hurry, he raised his glass, and he studied the mail carrier for some time. He lowered the glass. He sighed.

"Yes, I do believe she is. And what's more, she's going to catch us before sundown. Well, don't just stand there, Ezra. Run out the guns, bring up the match tubs, pass around the cutlasses and the pikes, sand the decks, string the boarding nets. And after that fetch my Book. I want to read a few passages to the men before we go into action."

Chapter

2

There was plenty to do, and this helped. Ezra Bond had been at sea almost continuously since he was twelve—that is, for ten years—but though he had known some scrapes and near-things he never yet had been engaged in a real slam-bang fight. He wondered how he would act when things got hot. He hoped that he didn't show his uneasiness as he walked about among the men, barking orders. *They* were uneasy too, most of them, but they felt no call to conceal it. A majority were local lads, from Saybrook, Stonington, New London, Lyme, many known to Ezra personally, a few even kin of his, but about a quarter of them, perhaps as much as a third, from their talk were English and in all probability deserters from the British Navy. These latter men had even more cause for fear than the others, and Ezra could see that fear reflected in their faces when they looked back at the pursuing vessel, which they quietly cursed. They knew what would happen to them if they were caught. It was better not to think of that.

It was hard to refrain from glancing now and then at the mail packet, and in admiration. There was no longer any question about her intent: this had become an out-and-out chase. Even at that distance it could be seen that the Britisher had exceptionally sharp lines and was exceptionally low-cut, with long sticks and wide spars. She might have been Bermuda-built. She looked like something out of Chesapeake Bay, and with a bone in her teeth she was overtaking *Forbearance*, though *Forbearance* was at her best point of sailing. It was exasperating; it galled a man; but the fact was, the gap was being closed. The mail packet came on with the inevitability of time. Ordinarily, those aboard the *Forbearance* with reason believed that they could show their heels to anything afloat except maybe a ship of the line or a frigate with a high wind squarely behind her; but only a freak squall, it would seem, could save the sloop now; and the sky was as clear as a baby's eyes, the air balmy.

Most of the work needed no thought, being familiar, for they had held many drills on the run down from Saybrook, but there was one new job, a hard one. With time to spare, they set about shifting the Long Tom from its bow position to the poop, where, with something like this in mind, a platform had previously been built. The carronades threw a tremendous ball but they were not reliable at any appreciable distance, being good only at close quarters. The Britisher had a bow chaser—they could see that much from the *Forbearance*—and doubtless she would open up with it in a little while. The obvious tactic for the Americans to employ was a sudden yaw when the two vessels were close, so that she could bring a broadside to bear—this would be a broadside fight, of course—but meanwhile they might as well make full use of their artillery by converting their own bow chaser into a stern piece. It was a big weapon, made of brass, and they would not have dared to shift it in seas less mild, for in the event of a blow it could break loose and take over, smashing legs and bulwarks and whatnot. However, the weather held.

"Might give us a spurt of extra speed, we start firing," Tom Garrettson offered. "The kick of it."

Tom was the second mate. A middle-aged man—he must have been thirty-five—he had been in more than one sea battle; and anyway, he had no imagination. Tom was the only other mate, the skipper standing a watch just like one of them.

He, the skipper, was a mountain of strength, that imperturbable man, that veteran. He supervised the preparations without any show of nervousness, almost casually. It was not that he did not take this affair seriously, for he took everything seriously, being indeed a very serious old man; but he showed no twitter, no twitch, and never so much as raised his voice, except when he read from the Book.

" 'The Lord is a man of war: the Lord is his name,' " he read to the men assembled for that purpose in the waist. " 'Pharaoh's chariots and his host hath he cast into the sea: his chosen captains also are drowned in the Red sea. The depths have covered them: they sank to the bottom as a stone. Thy right hand, O Lord, is become glorious in power: thy right hand, O Lord, hath dashed in pieces the enemy.' "

Afterward, and after he had seen that the work was well under way, he went to his cabin, perhaps to pray, perhaps to read some more, for the Book still was in his hand.

A few hours later—it was a little after noon—Ezra sought him out.

The cabins of the *Forbearance* were tiny, dollhouse chambers. One, to starboard, was a one-bunker for the captain. Opposite this was a similar one, only it had two bunks, and this was shared by Ezra Bond and Tom Garrettson. The corridor between them was so narrow that two men might have had trouble passing in it.

The skipper's door was ajar, as Ezra could see, and the skipper himself, in his bunk, on his back, was sound asleep. Ezra paused, marveling. He had thought that he knew his uncle well, but such coolness passed all understanding; it was almost showing off.

Lemuel Hart was a small tough man, wrinkled, leathery, light brown. He looked as if sparks would fly if you scratched him, he was that flinty.

14

Suddenly he opened his eyes. They almost *clicked* open, with a popping sound, and there was no filminess in them, no rheum. He was instantly and all over awake, a good trait in a seafaring man.

"They shooting yet?"

"Not yet, sir, but I expect they will soon. They're still closing on us."

"Thought I'd've heard it if they had. Well, don't answer them unless you really think you can reach. No sense wasting powder and ball."

"Yes, sir."

"What you got there?"

Ezra held up his burden, a captured Union Jack.

"I was thinking that maybe if we broke this out—"

"No good. They come this far, altered course this much, they'll be bound to have a good look. Nobody believes in a flag any more anyway."

"Yes, sir."

The skipper closed his eyes, but opened them immediately.

"Ezra, you know where everything is?"

"I—I don't understand."

"Course you do. In case I'm killed you'll be the captain, and I just wanted to be sure you knew where the ship's papers were and all that."

"Oh, yes, sir."

"All right. Wake me up when they start banging away."

He closed his eyes again, and went back to sleep. It was his custom to take a nap like this in the afternoon, and he saw no reason to change it.

Chapter

3

The first shot was like a cough, a burpy hollow sound that might have emerged from the throat of some notably bad-tempered man. They saw it before they heard it. The pinpoint of glitter at the nose of the mail packet abruptly was covered with grayish smoke that soon strung out in streamers, pushing ahead of the vessel that had emitted it as though impatiently seeking to make the capture by itself. Then came the sound.

They did not see the ball, but they saw its splash, sending high a column that the breeze fragmented into scintillant specks of color, specks that twisted as they fell.

It was closer than might have been expected. It was more than a warning, an order to heave to: it was a shot fired in anger, meant to hurt.

Ezra ordered that the *Forbearance*'s brass piece be loaded, and then turned to wake his captain.

The old man was up anyway, and as he came across the poop he was buckling a sword about his waist. The sword looked rather silly; it looked too big for him; and surely he could not have used it with any degree of skill, for the cutlass was the weapon for a sailing man, not a slim steel toothpick from out of the court. All the same, it was fitting for the captain of a vessel in action to wear a sword, and Lemuel Hart was nothing if not fitting.

"You know you must stay right here on deck, and on your feet. You know that, don't you, Ezra?" he said in a low, corner-of-the-mouth voice, for after all he was a relation.

"Well, I suppose so."

"You probably feel like ducking behind the captain or behind a bulwark or something, or if you don't feel that way now you will almighty soon. But you mustn't. It's important that the officers stand up and pretend there's nothing dangerous happening. Important to the men. That makes us handsome targets for anybody up in the crosstrees with a musket, but it's the way it's got to be, understand?"

"I expect so."

"See that you do."

It seemed a sin to grapple in conflict on such an afternoon. They were down near the Tropic of Cancer, and the rolypoly white clouds loafed across a sky as blue as the water below, where some of the innocent small seas, possibly one in twenty, were topped with a chalk mark of foam. The sun shone indefatigably.

"Here it comes again."

There was the same grayish blob of smoke, the echoing boom, the splash; but whereas the first one, though the direction was good, had landed several hundred yards astern, this second one, equally accurate, came so close that for a wild moment Ezra Bond thought that they had been hit, that their rudder was smashed.

The geyser was mountainous, blotting out all sight of the mail packet, rising, it looked, mast-high. The man at the helm stood fast, though he had to keep his back to the enemy, but the gunners unashamedly dived for the scuppers, and Ezra himself, feeling his knees go greasy, was afraid that he would slide into a faint. The spray stung him like a cloud of iridescent polychromatic pinpricks. Then everything astern was clear again, and he was able, cautiously, to let out his breath, while the gunners got to their feet.

The skipper nodded to the chief gunner.

"Can you reach it?"

The gunner studied the situation for half a minute.

"I can try," he said.

"All right."

The gun had been loaded. The gunner already had a match, lighted at both ends, around his neck. With his twister, a worm-like wire made of iron, he worked some of the powder out of the touch-hole, holding his hand behind it to keep it from being blown away. From a flask in the other hand he sifted out some of the priming powder, which was much finer, dumping it into a groove on the muzzle side of the touch-hole. He lit this priming powder, standing there leaning over the touch-hole, which his cupped hand shielded against the wind, until he was sure that the powder from the gun proper was ignited. Then he stepped back quickly, and to the left.

The explosion was terrific, not only at the muzzle but at the touch-hole, where a fan of flame fringed with sparks soared for several feet. This was, of course, because they were firing squarely into the wind, always a perilous procedure.

Instantly they were swathed in smoke, and when this had cleared they could see no splash; but a seaman stationed aloft for that very purpose sang out that the ball had fallen in a good line but at least two hundred feet astern of the vessel that pursued.

The skipper sighed.

"Well, that thing don't look to me like a swivel, does it to you, Ezra?"

"No, sir. It looks like the same kind of a gun we've got right here, that can be laid but not aimed."

"Except the way the sloop itself is aimed."

"That's right, sir. Except with the sloop."

"Um-m-m. . . . You at the helm."

"Aye, aye, sir."

"Put her over two points to starboard. Or *about* two points. You don't have to steer small."

"Aye, aye, sir."

Ezra saw what the captain meant to do. With their fore-and-aft rig and with such a fine following wind—granted too that the seas stayed tiny—it would not be difficult to zigzag. This course, however, would lose forward speed, for air would be spilled out of the main and the jibs alike at each tack, either way; and unless the Britisher tried to match each tack with a similar one of her own—which was unlikely—she would overhaul her prey in half of the ordinary time. He pointed this out to Captain Hart, who grunted.

"That's just what I'm doing it for. She's going to catch us up anyway, and the sooner the better. It'd only make 'em perkier if we keep running away. And besides, I suspicion that some of our boys are feeling kind of nervous—a fight'll be good for them."

"There goes his flag, sir. Should we break out ours?"

"Yes. The correct one."

"Aye, aye, sir."

It gave Ezra a thumping feeling at his chest—a feeling that was in no way connected with the fear that he also felt—when the Stars and Stripes, as they were already calling it, was hoisted to the masthead. The flag itself was not familiar—the very design had been made only a few years back; but already the sight of it was giving him confidence, together with a clean conviction that at least there would be no deceit, not even a momentary show of deceit. Ezra himself had proposed the running-up of a British flag, a legitimate *ruse de guerre*, but he had done this only out of a sense of duty, on the chance that his uncle had not thought of it. Uncle Hart was right, though: the mail-packet skipper would not be put off, at this stage of the game, by so flagrant a fraud. And that was just as well. There was

19

bound to be a battle anyway, and let's have it an open, honest battle.

Nobody cheered when the flag was raised, perhaps because most of the men were too busy watching the chaser; but it made Ezra Bond feel better. It stood out from the mast, snapping angrily, as though in defiance.

Once the *Forbearance* had started to zigzag, the shooting ceased. The Britisher came straight on, seemingly delighted, her skipper no doubt taking this to be what in fact it was—an admission that further flight was futile and an expression of eagerness to get the business over with.

The distance between the two vessels shortened rapidly now. This was almost eight bells—four o'clock in the afternoon. It had been a stern chase.

Captain Hart checked all preparations once again, nodding approval. He might have been a watchmaker, so precise was he. At last he said: "All right."

Ezra Bond, the skipper's mouthpiece, shouted the agreed-upon orders.

The helmsmen—there were two now, for safety's sake—put the sloop into a long, wide larboard yaw, so that she shushed sideways through the water, a reproachful sound.

The mainsail was struck and firmly furled, though the jibs remained in place, just enough to keep some way on the vessel. A sail can catch fire, especially on such a sunny day, and all the rigging, of course, was tarred, which would make for a frightful flame. The deck already had been wetted down, as it had been sanded.

The three larboard carronades already had been shotted and run out. These were the only *Forbearance* guns that would take part in the action. They were manned by double crews.

The British skipper proved to be another watchmaker, in spirit. As soon as he noted the yaw, which he must have approved, he put his own vessel into a similar movement, almost exactly matching that of the *Forbearance*. It was as though they were performing a marine ballet step, these two sloops, a *pas de deux* that they had rehearsed many times.

Now they were side by side, scarcely two hundred feet apart.

"All right," Captain Hart said mildly.

Ezra O-ed his hands at his mouth.

"Fire!"

Chapter

4

It was as though the whole world had blown apart. The tranquil sea, the tranquil sky, were blotted from sight. Ezra never had seen so much smoke—it made his eyes water and rasped his throat. Each time a *Forbearance* gun was fired there was a sudden flare of red, like the opening of a furnace door, that stung his cheeks as he stood there. The noise was continuous, a condition rather than a succession of sounds, a state of affairs, cacophony that would never abate.

If only he had been given some task, something to do, it might have been endurable. Tom Garrettson, fortunate fool, ran back and forth behind the gunners, shouting encouragement to them; and they had their assigned work. The hands were below, armed and ready in case of a boarding party, crowded just under the half-open hatches, a ring of heads, of popping eyes. But the first mate was expected through all of this simply to stand by the side of the captain. There were no orders, for orders could not have been heard anyway. It was each man for himself.

Alone, then, Ezra found himself thinking about Pastor Henderson back in Saybrook. This at first seemed absurd; but soon he reasoned it through. He had known this sensation before, this pandemonium. He had known it in church.

It was not Pastor Henderson, a kindly, mild-mannered man, who had delivered that sermon. *He* had sat on the platform beside the visiting preacher, at whom Ezra had not dared to peek, keeping his eyes, instead, upon the familiar face of Mr. Henderson.

The sermon was about Hell, a place described in detail and with coruscating eloquence. Here was a literal, orthodox Hell. The visiting preacher, an evangelist, made much of the flames, the searing heat, the smoke that swirled everywhere. He told of brimstone, the sharp, choking stink, and the shrieks of fiends, the war cries that Satan's minions emitted. He made the whole thing so vivid that you could smell it, you could hear it, and shrink timorously from it. You were there. You never had been anywhere else; for you had sinned, and were suffering the horrid consequences of that sin, which would last forever.

The boy Ezra had shivered at first, then twisted as though red-hot pincers truly were tearing off bits of his skin. He'd had all he could do to keep from screaming. The church was cold, and Ezra did not have a foot-warmer, since his father disapproved of spoiling children, but long before the sermon was finished—and it lasted three and a half hours—the boy was drenched with sweat, his clothes clinging to him.

Now, on the *Forbearance*'s deck, he had the same feeling that he had known in church, the feeling that this was the way the world always had been and always would be, that there could never be hope of anything else.

In the breathless moment before the firing started, Ezra had seen that the British vessel was larger than she had seemed from head-on, much larger indeed than the *Forbearance*. It was because she was so low in the water that she had looked small, but in broadside this distortion was corrected. The Britisher carried five guns on the side that she presented to the *Forbearance*, yet she did not appear to be getting as many balls thrown with the five as the *Forbearance* men were throwing with their three. Ezra

23

could see the flashes like tiny red lightning bugs at the mouths of the cannons, on and off, on and off.

Coming from windward, the Britisher inevitably got the weathergage. It made little difference in a duel of this sort—a slugging match without maneuver—except that it gave the Britishers a slight visual advantage, since the smoke from their cannonading immersed the *Forbearance* on its way to the open sea. Ezra from where he stood could see the deck of the other vessel only intermittently, but the top hamper was clear enough, rising above all smoke. The Union Jack still flipped and flapped there.

He looked up. The Stars and Stripes still was flying too, to be glimpsed now and then through gaps in the smoke. He grinned.

Then he was on his hands and knees. He could not remember falling—but there he was, blinking, doubtless looking foolish as he coughed, and his chest ached as though he had been punched there or even smitten with a maul. The backs of his hands, at which he was staring, were stuck with a multitude of woodsplinters. As he lurched to his feet, his head reeling, it came to his mind that a ball must have passed so close to him as to knock his breath out—for he was gasping—and hurl him down on the deck.

His arms stretched for balance, his hands flapping like the fins of a fish out of water, he turned.

"Are you all right, sir? Uncle Lem, are you—"

His hands met empty space. He went to his knees again, this time intentionally. He found the captain.

Lemuel Hart was on his back, arms spread out in starfish fashion, mouth twisted. The ball that had caused the trouble could not have hit him directly, but the splinters it had torn from the top of the gunnel had caught him full-on. These were big splinters, not the outside spray with which Ezra had been peppered. They stuck out all over the captain, like the quills of a porcupine, and one of them had gone right through his Adam's apple. He was bleeding from every one of many wounds, but there was little doubt that he was already dead—or fast dying.

24

Ezra tried to lift him, to get him to his cabin, but though the uncle was a small man the nephew still was dizzy from shock, and he stumbled.

A bosun's mate and one of the hands came out of the after-hatch and toted Lemuel Hart away.

Tom Garrettson ran up to Ezra, helping him to his feet, squeezing his forearm.

"They've *struck!* My God, look at it—they've *struck!*"

This was true. The British guns had fallen silent, no longer with red flashes at their muzzles, while smoke drifted languidly away; and down the masthead, glory be to God, came fluttering the Union Jack.

"Tell our men to stop firing," Ezra yelled.

Garrettson could hardly hear this, though it was shouted into his ear; but Ezra's gestures were enough. Soon the *Forbearance* carronades too ceased to speak.

It was eerie. It was like floating in some outside world, with no current, no life or movement, only vapor. Their ears tingled but did not ring any longer with noise that was gone. There were no echoes, for what could those bangs have bounced from?

Ezra took a few steps toward the rail. He was stiff, teetering a bit, and he bent forward from the waist like a man who wades through high water. Tom Garrettson rejoined him. Tom nodded toward the British vessel.

"They got a fire over there," he said, his voice unnaturally loud.

"Yes."

Smoke that was thick and black and greasy, not at all resembling the acrid gunsmoke with which the world had been filled a few moments before, was pouring out of a hatch amidships. The guns over there were deserted. No powder monkeys scurried across the waist. Only a single officer was to be seen on the after-deck.

"They need every man they have to control it," Tom opined,

"before it reaches the magazine and they get themselves blowed up to Kingdom Come."

"A lucky hit," said Ezra.

"Oh, a lucky hit, sure enough."

The British officer had a speaking trumpet at his mouth, and it would seem that he had been using it, but only now, like a spear piercing a sheet of wet paper, did his voice break through to them.

"Damn it, I said: 'Who's the captain of that vessel?' "

There was a trumpet as part of the equipment of the *Forbearance* too, but Ezra Bond was not sure where it was kept. He used his cupped hands instead. He had a very strong, carrying voice.

"I am the captain." It gave him a creepy feeling, to hear himself announcing this fact. "Have you surrendered?"

"Hear this, Yankee: We're having trouble here, and I am sending you a passenger for safety's sake."

"Have you surrendered?" Ezra called again.

"Damn you, yes. We had to. I'll send the captain's sword with this passenger."

"Why can't the captain bring it himself?"

"Damn it, because he happens to be dead."

Ezra turned. "Take the deck," he called over a shoulder to Tom Garrettson as he made for the cabin.

Propriety demanded that he too wear a sword when he received that of the defeated commander. A sword was like a marshal's baton, a king's scepter. It was a symbol of authority. To greet that passenger-envoy without a sword strapped around his waist wouldn't do at all. And Ezra never had had a sword of his own.

Lemuel Hart was indubitably dead. Already the blood was beginning to dry, turning brownish and crickly at the edges, though the cheeks still were warm. The skipper lay inert, like a doll with a broken spring, all crumpled, grotesquely askew. Ezra felt sharp hot brine at his eyes when he unbuckled the sword. He had to

26

pause a minute just inside the cabin door, to get control of himself. He could hear men groaning.

When he came up on deck again he saw that a gig was putting out from the British sloop. At the oars was a tar. Seated in the sternsheets, under a pink silk parasol trimmed with lace, sat the passenger who was to be rescued.

"My God," whispered Tom Garrettson, "it's a woman!"

Chapter

5

The *Forbearance* was not high in the water, being a small vessel, and the Jacob's ladder they put overside for the woman had only half a dozen rungs. Nevertheless she addressed herself to it with deliberation and care. She was smallish, young, trim, with large green no-nonsense eyes and a stunningly lovely natural complexion. So big was her bonnet that the men above, men who were seeing a woman for the first time in more than a month, could not tell the color of her hair; but Ezra Bond, for one, hoped that it would turn out to be either light brown or dark red—to go with those emerald eyes.

She was, then, by any definition, a beauty. She must always have been that. She was accustomed to being the center of masculine attention, and she had felt men's eyes upon her wherever she went. It would be no different in the middle of the Atlantic Ocean. Her brief perturbation, then, was caused by something else: it stemmed from her wish to get up that ladder in such a way that the sailor who held the gig close to it should not catch a look at her legs—or possibly something higher.

She closed the parasol with a snap. She might have been a merchant closing his till for the day. She surveyed the ladder. She measured the distance. She tucked the parasol high up under her left arm, where already there was a court sword complete with scabbard and belt. With her left hand she gathered both outer and under skirts close about her body, leaving the right hand free for the ladder. The sailor, for his part, pretended not to peek.

Quick as a squirrel, and as gracefully, she made it with one hand. It was to be doubted that the tar got much of a look.

Ezra himself gallantly helped her to the deck. She stood erect, still, small, but almost imperious in her manner, afraid of nobody. Her hair was powdered—a pity. She looked around. At last she addressed Ezra, who, it would seem, she had singled out as the least offensive of that sweaty, begrimed crew.

"Take me to your captain," she commanded.

Ezra made a bow. He never had been taught to bow—an act seldom needed in Saybrook, not at all at sea—but he found that it came easily enough. He just bent forward from the waist, holding his hat over his heart. He did not try to "make a leg," a refinement which, he reckoned, might call for practice.

"Ma'am," he said solemnly, "I *am* the captain."

She opened her eyes very wide at this, but all she said, in something of an undertone, was: "You Americans have curious customs." She might have been referring to African blacks.

Ezra said nothing. By this time he had sensed that the visitor was by no means as calm and collected as she made out to be. Scarcely twenty, by Ezra's estimation, she was far indeed from home. She had just witnessed, and lived through, a short but very loud and very messy action at sea. She had been taken off a burning vessel and deposited on one where she was surrounded by smoke-blackened barbarians, rebels to her, many of whom were gazing upon her with lust-loud eyes. It would have been a miracle if she was in truth half as self-possessed as she strove to appear.

"I'm instructed," she said slowly, "to give this to you."

And she handed him the parasol.

29

He laughed. He couldn't help it. The men too laughed, a great upsurging guffaw.

Ezra, his chest jerking, at last got control of himself, and he turned with the purpose of cursing the crew into silence; but by that time the young woman herself was laughing, and indeed it was several moments before she could regain her composure.

"La," she cried at last, still gurgling down giggles, "I got flustered. Here—here's the right one."

She handed him the sword.

He bowed again as he accepted it. He had a grip on his feelings by this time, and was already reproaching himself for such unseemly laughter when his uncle lay lately killed only a few feet off.

Smoke poured in even greater volume from the mail packet. The tar in the gig had made no move to return, but stayed clinging to the Jacob's ladder, willing enough to be far from a vessel he took to be doomed.

"Is it a bad blaze over there, ma'am?" Ezra asked.

"La, 'tis likely enough 'tis. They fairly *shoved* me off, without granting me a chance to snatch up any of my effects. I don't suppose that by any chance, captain, you happen to have any rose water aboard of this pirate ship?"

"We are not pirates, ma'am."

She tossed her head to indicate the vessel she had just come from.

"*They* said you were, over there."

"Well, they're entitled to their opinion, I guess, but in law we are not pirates—no, nor at heart either."

"Oh. Well anyway, the rose water?"

"I am afraid not, ma'am. I regret it."

"I could hardly have hoped . . ." Suddenly she gave him a smile, and his knees all but buckled under the flash. "I am Lady Helen Ashley," she announced.

He bowed yet again—he was getting to be a tarnation jumping-

30

jack, he reflected ruefully—but this time it was less in homage than to hide his face for a second. He had never before met anybody with a title attached, and he feared that he might be going red. Bowing, he was learning, could be a convenience. When in doubt, bow.

He still wished that she didn't pad and wire and pomade and powder her hair, so that it was impossible to tell what it once had been. He supposed that just about all of the women in England did that. All the ones that were ladies, at least. All the ones that had a title.

She did not seem conscious that she might have given offense by calling these wild men pirates, but she was not further disposed to talk, and stood looking about her with an expression in which there was a mite of expectancy, as though she was waiting for somebody to bring her a pillow or a cup of wine or something. She actually tapped her foot.

Ezra had no added time for her, just then. He checked his crew. Four gunners hurt, all by flying splinters, all painfully, none seriously. The British balls had been high. The *Forbearance* was not leaking anywhere, for it had not been hulled. The larboard gunnel was badly chewed, a few bits of standing rigging had been sliced, there was a hole in one of the jibs, and a sizable shred had been torn out of the furled mainsail, but there was no damage that could not be repaired within a few hours.

Ezra thanked the men, gravely praising their marksmanship, and he told them about the captain; and then he put them back to work.

The arms were checked, in case the British were playing a trick or would change their minds. The carronades were loaded and shotted once again, after a thorough swabbing. The deck was resanded.

All of this time the gig waited at the foot of the Jacob's ladder and smoke boiled forth from the packet's hold.

Ezra thumbed at the gig.

"Go over there with him for a closer look," he told Tom Garrettson. "Better take a pistol—here. And don't go aboard. Ask 'em how bad is it? Ask if they are ready to have us send over a prize crew. Or, if they're going to have to abandon ship, do they want to borrow our longboat?"

Lady Helen Ashley displayed impatience. Ezra Bond paid her no mind.

"Another thing," he called to Tom in the gig. "Tell them that when they see our flag come down it don't mean that we're striking. Oh, no! Be *sure* to tell them that."

"Eh?"

"I'm going to sew my uncle up in it," Ezra explained. "He has earned that much."

"Oh, aye. Aye, aye, sir."

"And mind that you get back in time for the funeral. We have a lot of work to do here."

"Aye, aye, sir."

Chapter

6

" 'Weep ye not for the dead, neither bemoan him: but weep sore for him that goeth away: for he shall return no more, nor see his native country.' Now all of you—'Our Father which art in Heaven, hallowed be Thy name—' "

He closed the Book without marking the place, and stared for a spell at the bundle by his feet. Small as Lemuel Hart had been, his body was a bit too long for the *Forbearance*'s flag. The feet stuck out at one end, and one of the weights was tied to the ankles there. The other weight, at the head end, was tied by means of a cord that passed through the halyard holes of the flag. It was a jury job, not handsome, but adequate.

Ezra dismissed his uncle in his uncle's own words.

"All right," he said.

Two men lifted one end of the plank, and the body slid, all unprotesting, into the sea. It made only a tiny splash.

As they stepped away from the stern they saw with a start that the British were beginning to abandon their packet at last.

For more than an hour after calling off the battle the British had been fighting their hold fire. Several times Ezra had sent over an offer of assistance. After all, the packet, *Dundas* by name, belonged to him, or at least to the owners of the *Forbearance*, of which he was one, having a mate's lay, a sixteenth. The *Dundas* was a prize of war, and Ezra as officer in charge of the *Forbearance*—he could not think of himself as the captain, anyway until the late captain had been buried at sea—was her master. He could have insisted upon taking charge. But the acting captain of the *Dundas*—*her* late skipper lay unburied on the deck—pleaded that there was no room for the Yankees where his men toiled. This Lieutenant Yale was the same who had shouted so insolently through the speaking trumpet, a squat, swart, thick, disagreeable young man, with great black eyebrows that met in the middle. "Damn it, man, they're fighting for their lives down there! Only so many of them can get at it, and what good would you do?" This made sense, and Ezra subsided, though he kept an anxious watch, never getting far from the mail packet, out of which smoke steadily rose.

Yale did bring his longboat alongside, as Ezra previously had done, in case the fire got altogether out of hand. And he sent thirteen sick and wounded over to the American vessel by means of repeated trips of the gig. Overcrowded to start with, Ezra put them up as best he could in the *Forbearance* hold. From them he learned, with amazement, that the *Dundas* crew, sick and well, numbered only thirty-one, of whom three, including the captain, had been killed. That captain, it appeared, had made the mistake of anchoring too close to shore when he stopped at the Azores for wood and water: almost half of his men had slipped over the side one night to swim to freedom.

"Y'see, we have a long tradition of desertion in the British Navy, captain," one of the men told Ezra, "and you can't go against tradition, now can you? Of course, I don't swim. Otherwise I wouldn't be here now."

Ezra nodded.

"Yes, I know. Why *do* you boys jump ship so fast, no matter where you are, whenever you get a chance?"

The tar, lips infolded and eyes squinched shut as though he

34

had a mouthful of lemon juice, did not hesitate before answering.

"Captain, if you'd ever been *in* the British Navy you would know why. That's all I can say."

"Bad as that, eh?"

"Worse."

Now, however, as they ended the funeral of the late Lemuel Hart, they saw that Lieutenant Yale had given up. His men swarmed out of the hold even faster than the smoke, which they somewhat resembled, and tumbled frantically into the longboat.

"Put the Moses over," said Ezra Bond. "I'm going to go there myself and see what I can do."

The Moses was a very small boat, a gig really, and was carried inboard, unlike the longboat, which was towed. It took only half a minute to launch the Moses, but by that time the *Dundas* longboat already was pushing off. Ezra hailed.

"Are you sure there's no hope?"

Yale, a dispatch case in his lap, was holding the tiller. He showed as besmudged and as weary as his men.

"Do you think I'd be leaving if there was, Yank?"

Ezra, doing his own rowing—for he had not wished to ask a hand to venture into such a place—passed him. Yale stood up, and bowed mockingly, and waved toward the burning packet.

"Go ahead, Yankee. Go ahead and commit suicide."

Ezra made fast the Moses to a line dragging astern, and hand-over-handed up that line to the deck. He could hear the crackling of the flames as he did so, and when he got up there the sheer heat of the fire caused him to stagger, for more than smoke was ripping up out of the hold now.

He stepped over the dead captain. Odd, that both skippers should have been slaughtered. This one, like Hart, was a small man, and old, and the gold braid on his tunic and tricorne made him look even more like a child's toy that had been smashed.

35

"I've got the ship's papers here, you Yankee," Lieutenant Yale shouted. "And if it's the mail and the money chest you're after, save yourself the trouble. They were pitched overside half an hour ago."

Ezra gave up, dropping into the Moses. He was sobbing as he rowed back to the *Forbearance*. Here was his first prize, one that should have made him rich, and all he was getting was a handful of official papers and a sword for souvenir—plus a pack of inconvenient prisoners. It did seem a shame.

They were all tired, and hungry, and crowded. They were short-tempered, these men who a little while ago had been shooting at one another. It was as well that the Britishers were outnumbered, for if it were otherwise there might have been another fight. The sight of the burning dispatch sloop, a splendid one, held their attention and helped to keep them from snapping at one another.

For just a little while there was some hope that the *Dundas* might have burned herself out, her magazine intact. The flames had subsided, and there was not even very much smoke, what there was emerging stodgily and without spirit. Ezra Bond's heart quickened; but Lieutenant Yale shook a glum head.

"She'll blow up," said Yale. "You'll see, she'll blow."

And she did. At eight bells of the second dogwatch, when the sun was fully down, the *Dundas* exploded.

Even though it was expected it made everybody jump. There was a vast, whistling, hollow upsurgence of sparks and burning pieces of timber, so bright that it blinded them to the actual sinking of the vessel, so that they never knew whether she had gone down bow-first or stern-first or had simply rolled over to die. For a full minute afterward they could hear hot fragments hiss as they dropped into the sea, some of them uncomfortably close.

With a weary shrug of graciousness, as though it thought it was doing the world a favor, the moon rose. But its rays revealed no sign of the *Dundas,* not so much as a spar, not so much as a ditty box.

They lingered thereabout all night, putting back and forth under jibs; and with the dawn they searched those waters diligently; but they found nothing.

Chapter

7

There was a power of folks aboard that vessel, so that a man hardly had room to move about. As Tom Garrettson put it, it fair gave a body the mulligrubs. Ezra grimly agreed. "We could cry with Isaiah: 'Lord, how long?' " Ezra observed.

These two kept their grievances between themselves, but elsewhere on the sloop the complaints were loud—and pauseless. The prisoners squawked because they were not given the run of the ship, the regular crewmen because they had to stand by for exercise periods, which they contended were too many and too long. The prisoners said that the bloody Yankee rebels were not respectful. The bloody Yankee rebels said that the prisoners ate too much and didn't do any work.

Because of this unanticipated influx of passengers Ezra found it advisable to ration the drinking water, something that the regulars did not like at all, especially as the weather grew warmer, for they were southing all this while, whereas the visitors were indignant to learn that they were to be allotted no rum.

"Rum, huh? Next thing you know they'll be demanding wine with their meals," was Tom Garrettson's comment.

Lady Ashley—Ezra thought of her that way, rather than as Lady Helen, though he did not rightly know which way was correct—gave them very little trouble, though from her manner it was clear that she was disappointed in the accommodations assigned to her, the late Captain Hart's cabin. If the place stank of tar and whale oil instead of the musk and bergamot to which no doubt she was accustomed, she refrained from pointing this out. Aboard the *Dundas* she had, like any passenger, supplied her own food, which it could be expected was a mite more delicate than ordinary ship's fare; but again she didn't growl. They allowed her to have the officers' messroom to herself: it was small enough at best, and Ezra and Tom, doing double watches at a time of great tension, ate, usually standing up, when and where they got the chance.

The lady's hair turned out to be a pleasing if unspectacular light brown, a brown with glints of gold in it. With no clothes but those she walked around in, and no boudoir supplies of any sort, she soon called for hot water—more of it than Ezra rightly should have allowed her—and washed all those foreign substances out of her head, which was a notable improvement, though it did serve to make her seem even smaller.

Only when Ezra proposed to lodge Lieutenant Yale in the cabin did Lady Ashley put her pretty foot down. She was emphatic about it. She forbade it.

Ezra's plan was to let Yale sleep in whichever of the bunks, his or Tom's, was not occupied at the time, since one or the other always was on watch. This would be inconvenient, but not intolerably so for a sailing man. Ezra proposed it not entirely because he thought that Yale rated such quarters as an officer, but also because he wished to keep a close eye on the man, whom he did not trust. But the lady said no.

"He's a lout," she declared. "And a lascivious lout at that. I'll not have it."

Ezra was not sure of what "lascivious" meant, but he could guess. There had been, then, an unpleasantness aboard the *Dundas?*

39

"It's true there's no latch on that door," he conceded. "Never felt the need for one before this. But—I could lend you a pistol."

"Which I wouldn't know how to use. You misunderstand me, captain. I am not *physically* afraid of Lieutenant Yale. I just find him obnoxious, that's all. Slimy. He looks like the sound that your heel makes when you pull it up out of the mud. No, I won't have it."

Ezra Bond had given in, he did not know why, and Yale was furious because he was quartered ignominiously with the common sailors.

Ezra had been brought up, of course, on Isaac Watts's moral jingles, many of which he had perforce memorized, and in particular he remembered:

"For Satan finds some mischief still
For idle hands to do."

It was axiomatic among officers that a busy mariner was a good mariner. Grumbling was to be expected—indeed, an absence of grumbling could be cause for alarm and might call for an investigation on the ground that quiet men were dangerous men—and no officer needed to bother himself about it, so long as the work got done.

They taught you that early, when you first expressed a wish to move aft from the forecastle. You learned it before you learned anything about navigation.

Here, however, the conditions were different, and usual rules of conduct did not apply. Two thirds of the men aboard the *Forbearance,* his own countrymen, really were overworked. All of the watches had been doubled. More food must be prepared, more firewood stacked; and that on a cut water diet. There were extra weapons drills, extra fire drills as well. In addition there was the duty—and an onerous one it could be—of guarding the prisoners when they took their deck exercises in small batches every morning.

On the other hand, the remaining one third, the prisoners themselves, had nothing at all to do; which was bad.

Ezra had taken every reasonable precaution against an uprising. As soon as he had time he caused all of the newcomers to be searched, right down to the skin; and though he didn't get much —some knives, a few pairs of brass knuckles—he felt better afterward. He even took Lieutenant Yale's sword, against the perfervid protests of that officer, who was insulted because Ezra refused to accept his parole.

"Damn it, you're no gentleman!"

"Never said I was."

The *Forbearance*'s powder magazine was kept double-locked, a guard on it all the time. The armory, consisting mostly of cutlasses and spikes, Ezra put into the chart locker in the cabin. These were passed out to the sentries at exercise time, and counted and taken back afterward, and locked up again. The men at the helm—always two at a time now—had cutlasses strapped to them all the while that they were on duty. Ezra himself always carried a brace of loaded pistols, as did Garrettson, and also the bosun, Shaw, and the bosun's mate.

All this was tiring, it wore him down. He did not get enough sleep, and he suspected that his eyes were rimmed with red. Often he had wondered, daydreaming, musing on a lonesome watch, what it would be like when at last he got command of his own vessel. He had waited long enough, glory knows! Ten years! Well, it was not like anything that he had imagined. He felt no elation. He didn't have time to feel any.

What made it even worse was the presence of the woman. Not that she was offensive! Though it was clear that she had no notable love for the company in which she found herself, in the circumstances, it seemed to Ezra, she was carrying on extremely well. At least she kept out of the way. And she agreed with him about the unreliability of Lieutenant (she pronounced it *Lef*tenant) Yale. But though she was no flirt, she was tarnation near at hand, of necessity. They had to squeeze against each other when they passed in the corridor, it was that narrow; and squeezing against this noblewoman with the green eyes was quite different from squeezing against Tom Garrettson or the late Lemuel Hart. She would leave her door open for air, and he could hear her in there, even when she was asleep: he could hear her breathing, and hear her when she stirred in the bunk, and he would reflect that she was probably naked or mighty close to naked. They were down near the Line now, and nights were all but as hot as the days. The tar bubbled languidly in the seams of the deck. The squeal of the timbers was somehow drier. Everything that you touched stung your hand. And when Ezra Bond did get a chance to catch a little of the sleep he so badly needed, he would hear her breathing in there, so close that he might almost have reached out and touched her. It was not a restful feeling.

This was the way things stood when five days after the fight they made their landfall.

Chapter

8

That was a Sunday, and Ezra, after some prodding by Garrettson, came up on deck soon after dawn. The sky was opalescent, the sea a riffle of gray-blue silk. There was God's plenty of breeze, yet the day would be hot.

Lady Helen Ashley was there, seated on the taffrail, ignoring as best she could the two helmsmen, who doubtless were wondering what she would look like with her clothes off.

Suddenly Ezra felt sorry for her. She was a damned nuisance, but after all she was hardly more than a girl, and her superior airs could well have been a natural part of her upbringing, and all unconscious, innocent of insult. She was, admittedly, going through an ordeal—a leering, all-hands lieutenant, no friends, far from home, a battle, noise, a fire, flight to a strange American vessel, which she had honestly supposed was manned by cutthroats, and worst of all, life without any change of clothing, without anything to work on, to read, to do.

On impulse he went up to her and made a slight bow, lifting his hat.

"Good morning, ma'am."

She granted him a smile, but it was a politeness smile, not notably toothy, made with the mouth alone, the eyes having taken no part in it.

"La, it *is* a good morning, now that's true enough, captain."
She showed as though downright chatty. "The men below there
though don't seem to glory in it. I've never seen 'em look so
sullen."

She nodded toward the waist, already half-filled with early
risers. It was tacitly agreed that she should keep out of the waist,
confining herself to the cabin and the afterdeck.

"They're sore because this is the Lord's Day and I've ordered
the regular watches, regular drills, and exercises, and so forth.
They don't like that."

"Don't sailors work on Sundays the same as any other day?
They did on the *Dundas.* I know that."

"Indeed they do, ma'am, on most vessels. There's even a saying: 'No Sundays off soundings.' And they have a little rhyme
about it:

" 'Six days shalt thou labor and do all that thou art able,
And on the seventh holystone the deck and scrape the cable.' "

The helmsmen chuckled, but Ezra brought them to attention
with a look.

"But Captain Hart, he used to let them take it easy, providing
that the weather was easy too. He was a mighty devout man, my
uncle, and he didn't believe in doing any work on the Lord's Day
that didn't absolutely have to be done. That's why they're sore
down there."

"Then, uh, why don't you pursue the same policy?"

"For reasons of my own."

She was all abasement.

"Oh, I beg your pardon, captain!"

"It's nothing," he said, meaning that.

He dismissed the helmsmen, telling them to leave their cutlasses; he would hold the wheel while they went for their relief.
He sounded the bells changing the watch.

There was some silence after that, the woman being maybe a bit embarrassed. Ezra Bond would have liked to ask her how she happened to be traveling from England to the Caribbean alone, but he feared that such forwardness might rile her.

"I wonder if you could tell me something, captain?"

"Will if I can."

"I wonder if you could tell me how much longer it'll be before we sight land?"

"Well, if my calculations are correct it'll be some time today, probably this morning. And they *ought* to be correct. They jibe exactly with Lieutenant Yale's as to where we both were when we had that fracas, and I've been able to shoot the sun every noontime since."

" 'Shoot the sun'—what an odd expression!"

"It's technical, ma'am."

"And would it be too much to ask where this land will be— or at least whether it will be St. Kitts?"

"Now why should I put in at St. Kitts, ma'am? Had you forgot maybe that our countries are at war?"

"I'm not likely to forget it, after what happened the other day when I lost all my possessions, now am I?"

"Well, anyhow, the place we're headed for—I *hope*—is Statia."

"Oh? I don't think I have ever heard of that land."

"It's what everybody down this way calls it—Statia. Its right name is St. Eustatius, and it's run by the Dutch. A very small island, and very ugly."

"I thought that all of the islands in the West Indies were beautiful?"

"Most of 'em. This one's an exception."

"Why is it ugly?"

"Because it isn't lovely, and you're used to lovely landfalls down in this part of the world. Almost anywhere."

"In other words, the company it keeps?"

"That's right, the company it keeps. But I guess it would be ugly anywhere else too. It's not much but one big bare rock that they call The Quill—I sure don't know why, because it don't look like any pen I've ever seen—and the fort and the town and a small beach, and back behind the town a few cane fields."

"You know, I've never seen a field of sugar cane."

"You haven't missed much."

"Now why, if this place is as unattractive as you say it is, then why are you going there?"

"Trade, ma'am. I may not enjoy the scenery at Statia, but I sure like the prices. Y'see, the Dutch I guess didn't know what else to do with it so they made it into a free port. And it's sort of in the center of things, down here. It's near so many other islands, larger islands where there are lots of planters that don't care too much for paying high tariff duties and so they skim over to Statia."

"Isn't that against the law?"

"I reckon it is. But it makes a good, lively market. That's why they call Statia the Golden Rock—not because it's pretty like gold but because there's so much money to be made there."

"I see."

It was pleasant, standing there holding the wheel and talking with this Englishwoman. He looked at her and grinned. He had been told that he had a striking grin. She smiled back at him, and this time it was something warmer than a politeness smile.

"Yes, I've heard of that place, I think," she said after a while. "Isn't it where the pirates stock up and afterwards sell their booty?"

"You have a great fondness for that word 'pirate,' ma'am. I guess there used to be plenty of them in the old days, but not now —not at Statia anyway."

"Well, privateers then? Is this vessel a privateer, captain?"

"No, we're not even that. We're a letter of marque."

"What's the difference?"

46

"A privateer's a man who's got a special license allowing him to carry on war on the high seas against an enemy that's the legitimate enemy of his own nation, and he fixes up a vessel with that and only that in mind, and he goes out looking for prizes. A pirate, of course, doesn't have to wait for war. He's *everybody's* enemy. He's what the lawyers call *hostis humani generis*."

"You are very learned."

He shrugged.

"Just as well to keep up with these things, the way I figure. But that's all the Latin that I do know."

"Go on. You haven't told me what a letter of marque is yet."

"Well, a letter of marque, he owns a vessel he's aiming to use in a regular trade, but he wants to be able to protect himself if he's attacked and maybe even take the other vessel. So he posts a bond and he's issued a letter of marque."

"I don't see any difference between that and a privateer."

"There isn't much really, I guess."

He grinned again, looking at her. She smiled back, and it was a real smile this time.

"And yet I'm disappointed, captain."

"Oh?"

"I had always hoped to meet a real pirate some day."

He rolled his lower lip between thumb and forefinger, as he regarded her sideways.

"Well, I reckon you could say that you almost had. Truth is, ma'am, sometimes we sail right along practically the *edge* of piracy, as you might say."

"Ah, that's better."

The new men reported, and started to strap on their cutlasses. Ezra hoped that they had not seen him grinning. A captain shouldn't do that. They saluted, and he turned the wheel over to them.

Their arrival made no difference to Lady Ashley, who, Ezra

47

reckoned, was used to having servants around. He himself would have dropped the talk right then, but she was not finished.

"You haven't asked me, captain, why I want to go to St. Kitts. Wouldn't you like to learn?"

"Why, I'd admire very much to learn, ma'am. And as far as Statia's concerned, you'll be able to get from there to St. Kitts on any clear day. Not very comfortably maybe, but it won't last long—and it won't cost much. Why, from Statia itself on a clear day you can *see* St. Kitts—see Mount Misery and Brimstone Hill —because they're perched right on the horizon like that, and you don't even have to have a glass."

"That's good."

"Planters going back and forth between St. Kitts and Statia all the time. No trouble at all. If you don't know any of 'em yourself I could introduce you."

"That's very kind of you, captain, to treat with the enemy like that."

He sniffed.

"Matters of trade, the enemy's pretty much the same as anybody else. And folks down this way ain't too fond of the government in England anyway, especially the planters. They've got a sneaking fondness for us Yankees—and sometimes it isn't all that sneaking either. They kind of wish they'd been in a position to do what we did."

"Um-m-m . . . That's something I'll look into when I get there."

"Bound to, ma'am. Practically everybody's a planter down there. You'll meet lots of 'em."

"Especially since I'm a planter myself."

"*Eh?*"

"That jolted you, didn't it, captain? Well, I am. I inherited a plantation on St. Kitts, near Basseterre. Now, I know what you're going to say: That a woman can't administer property. And that's

48

true, as far as it goes. They don't think we're intelligent enough for that."

"You sound a mite bitter, ma'am."

"Maybe I am. Anyway, the property's mine and it's the only thing that I have got in the world, and it's held for me by a solicitor who's as old as God and who has been trying for years to get me to go to bed with him."

One of the helmsmen sniggered, and Ezra stabbed him with a stare.

"I can do anything I want with the man. Twist him around my little finger. So I've got full authority—I've saved *that* anyway—" and she touched her breast "to do anything I want about my own property when I get there."

"Good thing. It takes half a year for a letter to get answered, sometimes longer."

"I knew that."

"Why not run the place through an agent, a manager? That's what practically all the owners do nowadays."

"I know. And that's what I did the three-and-a-half years I have owned this property, and every year the price of sugar goes up but the money the agent sends my solicitor for me gets less. There's *something* rotten in the state of Denmark, and I decided that if I'm going to find out what it is I'd better go myself—so here I am."

It was at this moment, with Ezra Bond O-mouthed in admiration, that the lookout aloft hailed.

"Land ho! Dead ahead! Land!"

Chapter

9

The Mariners' Rest was not for just anybody who could call himself that. Forecastle hands would not get past the front door, much less upstairs. It was not that the Mariners' Rest stood on rank as such: it was only that it was expensive, perhaps the frilliest brothel in the whole Caribbean area.

The Mariners' Rest was described in upbreath accents all over the world, for the most part by men who had never been there. It was a myth as well as a reality, both at the same time. Men in Calcutta and the Whampoa Anchorage, men along the Liverpool waterfront, along the Liffey, in the flea-bitten bistros of Marseilles and Alexandria, at the drop of a nor'wester would describe in glowing detail the crystal chandeliers, the velvet rugs, the tapestries, the plate and porcelain fit for a king, the incomparable dishes, the superlative French wines. Some, if you gave them a little liquid encouragement, might go even further and rave about the beauties to be found upstairs, where the real fun began. These were extraordinary, exotic females, they would relate, imported from Guadeloupe. They washed every day. They doused themselves in perfume. They never took off their necklaces and earrings, even when they were engaged in pursuit of their trade. Between bouts they wore exquisite French lingerie, or even, if their schedule permitted, beautiful and costly French gowns. Each was attended by a maid.

When the narrator reached this point it was as well to stop him, for obviously he was drawing on his imagination. He would not be sponging drinks if he was the sort of sailor who had been upstairs at the Mariners' Rest, Oranjestad, St. Eustatius, Netherlands America.

In truth, the Mariners' Rest was sumptuously furnished, though on the outside it was plain enough, if unexpectedly neat and even prim for that part of the world, a square white two-storied building without verandas, set back a bit from the lower end of Statia's one and only street, with a trim small garden before it and even a small trim white fence. Except for the flowers in the garden, brash tropical blooms, it might have been a cottage on Cape Cod.

Most of the ground floor had been knocked together to form one large, elegant taproom. This was paneled in teak, a wood suitable to the gravity of the business that was conducted there, commercial business of the highest kind. The girls were never allowed in this taproom. Indeed—and this was one of the reasons for the many stories told about them—the girls of the Mariners' Rest scarcely ever were allowed anywhere else but their own bedrooms, and even there they were expected to stay away from windows, lest outsiders get something for nothing but a peek. Occasionally, if the weather was fine, and there was no moon, they might be marched, late, when business had ceased for the night, up and down the little Oranjestad beach; but even then they were under the watchful eyes of a couple of formidable chaperones: Hendreck, a giant, and his light-o'-love Susette, who was sometimes called the Madame and sometimes the Queen of Upstairs. Either of these, single-handed, could have fought off any lecherous intruder.

Hendreck it was who let you in when you knocked. He recognized Ezra and even called him "Mijnheer Bond." Ezra softly corrected him, explaining; and Hendreck as softly congratulated him on his new title.

Hendreck took him to a corner. The place was almost half full. This was the middle of the day, and except for the Governor's mansion, the Mariners' Rest was the least hot place in St. Eustatius. Some of the men were alone, others were in pairs or trios, talking trade. Everything was quiet, respectable. Nobody dreamed of raising his voice, even to order a drink. The Mariners' Rest had little use for loudness.

Susette came downstairs, greeting Ezra with a metallic smile. She was almost as large as her lover, and her body was solid, no fat. Ezra once had seen her knock down a man with the back of her open hand. Yet when Hendreck told her about the death of Captain Hart real tears sprang to her eyes.

"What a pity! And no loot, either! He was such a gentle little man!"

"Yes."

Susette came from Martinique, where she would have been classified as a *mamelouque*—that is, halfway between an *octavonne* and a *sang-mêlé*, being fifteen-sixteenths white. They were fussy about these distinctions in the West Indies.

She rolled her eyes toward the ceiling.

"*Mijnheer* would—uh—well, you feel like that, captain?"

"It's been a long voyage."

"Of course. I'll arrange." She put a forefinger against her lips and rubbered them back and forth. "But I must ask you to wait a little while. Ten minutes, possibly a quarter-hour, captain?"

"That will be quite all right. No hurry. I'll have a sangaree, Hendreck."

"*Immédiatement, mijnheer.*"

Sangaree, or pack-punch as they sometimes called it, was spiced wine—a fancy drink, it might be thought, for a sailorman; but Ezra was conscious of his new rank, and also he was sick of rum, almost the only liquor you could get in Saybrook, except

52

applejack if you knew where. He never drank aboard ship, unless etiquette called for it—a visiting skipper, for instance.

Etiquette just now called for a visit to the Governor of St. Eustatius, an amiable Dutchman by the name of De Graeff, high on a hill back of the town, but De Graeff must have been bored by so many reporting skippers, and Ezra in any event was in no hurry: he could allow himself a drink and a little of something else as preparation. Pleasure before business, he told himself.

While he waited he was thinking about his English passenger. Each astonished to find himself enjoying the company of the other, they had gabbed at some length after that first pleasant session at dawn, and indeed they had all but talked the *Forbearance* right into her anchorage at Statia roads. There was no real harbor at Oranjestad—Orangetown, the boys called it—but the Dutch, who were clever at such things, had built a long and highly effective mole, making, as it were, an artificial harbor. There might have been as many as two hundred craft out there right now. Not all of those skippers would make a formal call on Governor De Graeff, but Ezra liked to do things right.

Hendreck brought the sangaree. Ezra sipped.

"Place hasn't changed much, Hendreck, from what I can see."

"No, sir. Not much. Only that we see more and more men from your country."

"Folks everywhere are going to be seeing more and more of us. Um-m. Last time I did some business on this rock it was with Abraham van Bibber. He still around?"

"Oh, yes, *mijnheer*. The same place, the same office. He's taken up with a man in Martinque, they're partners, a man named Richard Harrison. So you know him?"

Ezra smiled a mite.

"Yes."

"I thought that you would. Because he's a Yankee like you."

Ezra sipped.

53

"Not exactly, Hendreck. Not a Yankee. He comes from Maryland."

This was difficult for the drawer, whose brow crinkled.

"But—isn't that a part of your country?"

"Well yes, it is. Yes, I guess you could list him as a Yankee."

You never could explain the distinction, and Ezra had given up trying. He supposed that the passenger had thought the same thing that morning when he asked her whether she should properly be addressed as Lady Ashley or Lady Helen.

"Why, it doesn't make any difference, really. It's only a courtesy title, as they call them. I only use it when I want to impress people."

"Such as pirates?"

She had smiled.

"I know better now, captain."

Pressed, she said without sighing that she was an orphan who had no brothers or sisters, alone in the world.

"Not even any near cousins."

"But I still don't understand. Can just any woman call herself 'lady'?"

"La, no. But it's more politeness than anything else. It doesn't mean anything. The daughters of a peer, they're always called 'lady.' And my father happened to be an earl."

"Oh."

"It, uh, sounds like a lot, doesn't it?"

"Well, I guess it means that you're an aristocrat anyway?"

"Oh, la, no! A real aristocrat of England wouldn't even talk to the likes of me. No, my father bought that title. I don't know how much he paid for it, but I wish he hadn't. *I* would have got that money, eventually. And the title of 'lady' isn't worth all that. But I wasn't consulted. I was only ten at the time."

"Now if a man married you, would he become a lord?"

This had really made her laugh, so that she heaved and choked, and it was some minutes before she could speak again,

Ezra standing helpless by her side all the while. But she was genuinely sorry, and said so, putting a hand on his forearm, while those large green eyes still shimmered with laugh-tears.

"*Please* forgive me," she whispered.

"Sure."

"After all, I suppose that some of the things I say seem funny to you?"

"Well, some of them do—yes."

He was thinking of that talk when Susette came back.

"Everything's ready, captain."

"Thank you."

He finished his sangaree and went upstairs.

Chapter

10

In the rowdy-dowdy sunshine of outdoors Ezra paused a moment to take stock. It did not faze him that he was on his own now. He knew the workings well enough, and he had connections here in Statia, men like Van Bibber who could apprise him of the immediate commercial situation, putting him in touch with the right traders. The Dutch were easy to work with. Ezra had a "safe" cargo, a cargo he could dispose of without fuss. Barrel staves and dried fish were always in demand down here. Probably the chief question would prove to be whether to stay here and sell to some Englishman or the agent of such an Englishman, or to go to one of the French islands and trade the cargo for molasses. The French always had molasses to sell cheap: they would do everything but give it away. The only thing molasses was good for was to make rum, as they did with it in England and New England, but France had laws that would not allow for much rum, the fear being that it would hurt the sale of brandy.

However, in any event a call on Governor De Graeff was the first item on the agenda, an explanation of the late unpleasantness to be delivered before the British got in *their* say. Uncle Hart always had been punctilious about the arrival visit, and Uncle Hart's precedent should be respected. Ezra started up the street toward Government House.

The Street of Oranjestad—it was always spoken of like that, as though it was spelled with a capital "S"—nobody seemed to know whether it really did have a name—was a little over a mile long; but such a mile! It was broad, and paved with cobbles on which iron-tired wain wheels and the iron-shoed hooves of horses clunked angrily. It was lined with two solid rows of office-fronted warehouses, so that a stranger's first thought would be: Where do the regular residents sleep? A large part of the crowd—and the Street was very crowded indeed today—slept on the ships anchored out there. Perhaps the others did not sleep at all? Just now all of them, trader and sailor alike, were furiously busy.

It was dusty, it was deafening, it was hot. Men shouted into one another's faces and flipped their hands and popped their eyes as they haggled. Men wheeled goods in barrows, dumped goods into piles, stacked goods in warehouses, carried goods on their backs. And these goods were of all conceivable sorts, from various parts of the world. There were fruits of all kinds—guavas, alligator pears, melons, pomegranates, oranges, pineapples. There was a great deal of "clayed" sugar—that is, semi-refined sugar; and there was even more muscovado, as the raw crushed cane was called. There were spermaceti candles from Providence, nutmeg from the Dutch East Indies, Jesuits' bark from Peru. There were osnaburgs, ticklenburgs, lead, twine, flints, paper, rhubarb, cinnamon, silver, mirrors, sadirons, jeroboams of claret, blankets that could be bought for four-and-six if you bought big enough batches, and there was Bristol beer and Dutch beer and beer that was not identified.

This was but an overspillage, the stuff displayed outside of the shops for a quick sale, or the stuff for which no room could be found indoors and which as a result was standing in the Street itself and along the beach and on the quay. Tarpaulins could be tossed over some of it in the event of rain. The more valuable materials—the gunpowder, the beef, the brandies and fine wines, the Russian duck and Russian sheeting, the tapestries, the iron

57

hoops and rivets—were stored out of sight in the warehouses themselves. All of the warehouses were crammed to overflowing, and for the most part they were large two-storied stone buildings.

The men who handled these goods, who sold them or bought them—whether with sterling or Continental paper, or with Surinam guilders or Amsterdam guilders, or with francs, or by barter—were, like the goods themselves, of every imaginable sort and from every corner of the globe. There were Spaniards with rings in their ears, Jews with little square black-silk skullcaps, lank slab-sided Yankees, Chileans, Frenchmen, bisque-faced Italians, Englishmen who looked down their noses, here and there an utterly black Ashanti or Dahomean slave, or an East Indian the color of well-waxed mahogany. The din was terrific, and pauseless. Babel, Ezra reckoned, must have been something like this. " 'So the Lord scattered them abroad from thence upon the face of all the earth: and they left off to build the city,' " he murmured to himself as he squirmed and was buffeted through the crowd. " 'Therefore is the name of it called Babel; because the Lord did there confound the language of all the earth: and from thence did the Lord scatter them abroad upon the face of all the earth.' Oh, excuse me, sir. I'm sorry I stepped on your toe."

This was by no means Ezra Bond's first visit to St. Eustatius, but the place never failed to fascinate him. He had acquaintances here, but he did not, this first day, seek them out.

He started to climb. The ascent was gentle in the beginning, scarcely noticeable, but it became steeper, and then the Street ended in the lower of two flights of wide stone upleading steps. This was what was known as the Bay Path, and it led to the Governor's house and the fort. There were massive breast-high retaining walls on either side. The view, as he got higher, was magnificent, and more than once he stopped to admire it.

The mountain on his left, beyond the fort and the Governor's house, the Quill, sometimes too called the Punchbowl, looked enormous from this close. It was a volcano, extinct these many years, and on a previous visit Ezra and a party of seamen had climbed its side and dropped into the crater, which was rife with the wildest kind of vegetation, a veritable jungle, in startling contrast to the rest of the island.

It was on his right, however, that the more interesting view was to be had—the town itself, looking toylike down there, and beyond it the vessels anchored in the roads.

Ezra had never seen so many vessels in one place, not even at Boston, not even the time when he had visited Philadelphia. Like the goods again, and like the men, they were of all kinds and came from just about everywhere. Without any difficulty he spotted the *Forbearance*, one of many sloops. There were schooners and brigs and barks, a few full-rigged ships. He even saw a pinkie that might have come out of New London. There was a frigate of the Netherlands Navy and several naval cutters, no doubt here on a flag-showing mission, for Holland was at peace with the world. In and out among these vessels, and between them and the shore, there darted with a skimming motion dozens of gigs that looked from this distance like waterbugs. Some of these were dowdy, but others were very smart, varnished, their flags flapping. The air was a mad medley, audible even from where Ezra trudged, above the jabbering of the merchants ashore: bells, trumpets, squealing capstans, rattling cables, even, once, the boom of a saluting cannon. It was all very colorful, and it did a sailing man's heart good to look down upon it.

Farther out there was a more ominous sight, a British frigate named *Thisbe,* so Ezra had been told. She would not come in; she could seize nothing in this neutral haven, and the formalities of appearing would have taken too much time; but she was prepared to snap up any American or French vessel she could find: France had recently declared war on Great Britain as an ally of the new United States. Meanwhile she would prowl among the Leewards, now and then, no doubt, sending ashore press gangs

59

that would comb the towns and villages for Navy deserters or for able-bodied but unattached waifs who might be branded as such and taken in. The *Thisbe*, like every British war vessel, assuredly would be short-handed.

"*Wie gaat daar?*"

"A friend," answered Ezra.

He readily identified himself to the lieutenant who was called, and he passed into the fort, smiling a little at the absurd precautions.

He smiled again at the sight of the guns along the wall, ancient twelve-pounders, most of which had not been fired in years, though a few must have been kept ready for purposes of signaling sunrise and sunset and returning the salutes of war vessels.

He leaned on the parapet near one of those old pieces, and again he gazed down on the roads and on the town. He could easily see the Mariners' Rest far down there at the other, lower end of the Street, and he saw all of the tumult between these two tranquil places. It was curious, he reflected. Being *physically* above all that ado made him feel almost as though he was *spiritually* above it as well, which he guessed really he wasn't, for after all he too was in the business of making money.

"Quite a town, isn't it, captain?"

He knew who it was before he turned. He gave her a grin.

"Well, it's sure different from Saybrook, Connecticut. I'll say that for it anyway."

Chapter

11

She was accompanied by both Lady and Governor de Graeff, a fact that jolted Ezra, who bowed to the one and shook hands with the other, an acquaintance. Thinking fast, while his face was averted, Ezra marveled that anyone, much less a castaway like Lady Helen Ashley, should be so honored. The De Graeffs were ordinarily accessible, but they were by no means democratic. It was true that female arrivals were not common in this part of the world, where white men outnumbered white women as emphatically as Negroes outnumbered *them*, and true too that this visitor had beauty, presence, charm. All the same, the Governor was a very busy man, and his wife was a snob; nor was either a fool who would be taken in by an unbacked story of distress. Ezra began to believe, again, that his English passenger was a lot more important a personage than she pretended to be. It was patent, here in the fort, that she had made an immediate and deep impression upon the De Graeffs.

"Lady Helen has been telling us how kind you were to her, captain."

"And you must know that we both are pained to hear of the death of the gallant Captain Hart," the Governor added.

Alert, Ezra caught at that "Lady Helen." Was that, then, the right way to speak of her? Lady de Graeff was the sort of person who would know—who would have known anyway, in any walk of life, and even if her official duties did not call for such knowledge—how an English titled person should be addressed.

Lady de Graeff was large, if not out-and-out fat. She hardly could be called gracious, though she was infallibly polite. Ezra had the feeling that she was bored with life on this barren rock where men talked of nothing but prices.

The Governor, on the other hand, bubbled with good humor. He enjoyed life. A man of florid face, he might have had dark hair: even in this climate he doggedly wore a wig, so that Ezra could not tell. His blue eyes twittered. He liked Yankees, and did not mind saying so. He looked like a man who was just about to propose a drink.

"We'll have some sort of investigation, of course, captain, because I'll be called upon for a report. But I wouldn't worry too much, if I was you."

"I'm not worrying," Ezra told him.

By the side of the Governor's lady the English newcomer indubitably did look a mite peaked, a bit frayed at the edges. This was no more than natural. She had been wearing the same dress, a furbelowed rose-and-yellow silk polonaise, for almost a week; and she had access to no cosmetics or powder. Ezra sensed that she had arrived only a little earlier, being carried up the Bay Path in a chair, he assumed, while he himself was dallying with that *marchande de spasmes* at the Mariners' Rest. He winced a bit, inwardly, at the association of ideas. It was not right that he should think of two such things at the same time. He must guard against this.

Something of the sort, about clothes, must have been in the mind of Lady Helen Ashley, for she sighed as she gazed out over the parapet.

"I don't suppose that I could buy anything really useful down there? I mean, like pomade and plaster clippers and poma-

62

tum and rosettes and perfume and enough brocaded silk to have a gown made out of?"

The Governor's lady motioned, somewhat imperiously, with her fan.

"You can get it all down there, and more besides," she said. "You can get anything you want. But why do that?"

"Eh?"

"Why go down there? What's the good of being a guest of the Governor, my dear, if you can't order tradesmen around as if they were slave boys?"

"Oh."

"La, of course. I've already sent for my seamstress and my hairdresser. They should be here any moment now, and meanwhile I'll send for some drapers."

"Who'll certainly run tick for you," Ezra said.

"He means credit, my dear. Well, once again, what's a governorship for?"

"You're too kind. . . . These others: are they Negro?"

"The seamstress's a *quarteron* and the hairdresser's a *métis*. But you needn't be afeared," she hastened to add. "I trained 'em both myself, and they don't stink."

Ezra smiled appreciatively. He feared that he had a slight advantage in appearance over the English girl, what with his sword at his side, the tricorne under his left arm. He understood how she felt, he believed. Even the women of Saybrook, though so much frumpier than this slip of a thing, put great stock in clothes and would study themselves for long minutes together in their glasses, if they were convinced that nobody was watching. Parson Henderson frequently berated them for that very practice.

The Governor, Ezra was sure, was seeking some excuse for the retelling of the story of how he had recognized the new American republic by being the first foreign official formally to salute its flag. He loved to tell that story.

63

Sure enough, it came out in a wee while, though somewhat circuitously.

"I must remember to give you a letter to Christer Greathead, the Governor of St. Kitts," the Governor of St. Eustatius said to Lady Ashley. "He can be of great help to you."

"Why, thanks."

"Not that he'll amuse you much. He's as peppery as an East Indian soup. My favorite writer of vitriolic letters."

He chuckled.

"Captain," he said to Ezra, "did I ever tell you about the time I saluted your country's flag, the first time that had happened anywhere, and it raised such a hubbub as went back and forth across the sea?"

"Why, no," lied Ezra.

Lady de Graeff did not go so far as to raise her fan to her mouth making to hide a yawn, but it was plain from the stiffening of her features that she had heard the story many times. She smiled at her husband with the brave, fond, loyal smile of a martyr.

Lady Helen Ashley, on the other hand, fairly beamed. That she was soon to pick out material for a gown, and to consult a hairdresser, had rendered her radiant. Her great green eyes glittered as she looked up to Governor de Graeff, a tall man who did not resent such glances.

"La, do tell us, sir," she begged.

He cleared his throat.

"Only time I have ever created an international incident," he said with another chuckle. "This was three-four years ago, right after the English colonies on the mainland had started to revolt in earnest and were avowing themselves to be a new republic and so forth. What is it you called that, captain?"

"The Declaration of Independence, sir."

"Ah, yes. Well, I applauded it. I think we all did, down here.

64

I hope that you'll forgive me for taking such a stand, Lady Helen?"

"La, sir, I know nothing of politics and care less."

"Hm-m-m. . . . Well, one morning a brig put in down there. She was a war vessel all right, must have carried sixteen or eighteen guns, and there was a flag at her masthead that nobody up here had even seen before. It had us baffled. A lot of red and white horizontal stripes it mostly was, as best I could make it out through my glass. Well, we knew by her rig that she was a Yankee—no missing *that*—and so we jumped to the conclusion that this was the flag of that brand-new nation. And when she gave us a regular formal navy salute down there our military commander didn't know what to do about it. Colonel Ravené. He came scurrying to me. If we answered the salute, he pointed out, that might be construed to be a recognition of the new republic, mightn't it? and wouldn't that be an act offensive to Great Britain?

"I said, what of it? I told him to go right ahead, just as he would with any other naval vessel. That was simple politeness, wasn't it?"

"I suppose so," murmured Lady Helen Ashley, who was probably thinking of that gown.

"Well, Christer Greathead over on St. Kitts—that really is his name—he didn't take it that way. My word! You'd've thought we had spit on the Union Jack or pelted King George's portrait with mud, the way he carried on. In just a few days I got a letter from him that fairly burned the paper it was written on."

"What did you do about it?"

"Answered it, after a month or so. I didn't make any promises and I certainly did not even hint of any apology. What for, in God's name?"

"Derrick!"

"Forgive. Well anyway, that did not satisfy Greathead of the great head, who sent me another scorcher. This one I simply

65

ignored. But he went further. Six months afterward I was ordered back to The Hague for explanations, by my government."

"You went?"

"After a while, yes. Lady de Graeff here wanted to see our children again and I had some personal business that called for my attention, so we went."

"And what did the Dutch government do?"

"Nothing. But it did that in a pleasant way. It talked a little while, very vaguely, and then it sent me back here. I haven't the slightest doubt that the whole recall was simply for show purposes. But they do say that the foreign office in London is still simmering."

He turned to Ezra.

"That foreign office in London will be exceedingly interested in getting from the foreign office in The Hague my report on what happened when your vessel and the late *Dundas* tangled last week on the high seas. Shall we retire over a pitcher of wine and discuss this, captain?"

Ezra was in no hurry. He was enjoying himself.

"Might it not be better, sir, if you'll excuse the suggestion, maybe we'd ought to wait until the other side appears here to give its version of what happened?"

"Well now, I suppose that perhaps that *would* be better."

"You won't have to wait long," interposed Lady Helen Ashley. "Listen to that racket at the gate."

It came clearly to them, the low halting voice of the lieutenant, the shrill shouting in English.

"Damn it, man, I tell you I don't *have* to have any credentials! Why, God damn it, I'm a Royal Navy officer and I insist upon seeing the Governor this very minute!"

"Yes, that's Yale all right," said Ezra Bond.

Chapter

12

The lieutenant was insufferable. He roared. He snorted. He shook his fists. He was the British lion gone beserk, the epitome of all that was worst about militarism. By his boorishness and bad manners, by the vehemence with which he insisted that the *Forbearance* and all her crew and officers be turned over as prisoners to the British Navy, as well as by his assumption of prejudice on the part of the Governor, he lost his case before ever he had fairly stated it.

He was not even wearing a sword.

The presence of ladies meant nothing to him, and he was mouthing his ridiculous incriminations as he crossed the court, before he had arrived at the group by the rampart. He was so noisy, indeed, that Ezra deduced that he was afraid.

The Governor, who had been all amiability a moment before, interrupted in icy accents.

"Please show your papers, and after that I may or may not give you permission to submit your plea. Unless you'd rather have me throw you out?"

It did something to sober the man, who remained truculent but no longer loud.

The seamstress and the hairdresser had been at his heels, and the ladies gladly seized this chance to make their departure. Ezra and the Governor bowed them away. Yale simply went on scowling.

A few minutes later the three men were in an office-like room in the residence, which adjoined the fort. The Governor sat down, but he did not offer chairs to his guests, nor was anything further said about that pitcher of wine. Understandably, for his dignity had been ruffled, his rank flouted, De Graeff was angry. He was proper, stern, implacably cold.

"If you gentlemen have a quarrel you must take it elsewhere. This is no tavern for brawling. Now, I'll take your statements informally, and if I think such action is called for I'll later get you to sign affidavits and to support these with the attestations of members of your respective crews. But it's not likely that we'll need to go that far. You understand anyway, both of you, that I can take no official action here. I can only pass on to my superiors at The Hague what you two tell me. Anything further must come from them. And in the meanwhile you two are both free to come and go as you please. Unless," he added grimly, "there should happen to be another explosion of disrespect."

Seated behind a carved mahogany desk, upright, attentive, never smiling, he heard them out, first Yale, then Ezra Bond. He asked no questions, and though paper and pen were before him he took no notes.

"What happens on the high seas," he reminded them several times, "is none of my business—unless it happens to a Dutch citizen. But go on."

The stories were much the same, the only real difference being as to which side had first fired in anger. Lieutenant Yale's contention was that the pursuit shots were no more than hailers, demands that the other vessel heave to for examination. Ezra insisted that they were aimed at the stern of the *Forbearance*, the plain intent being to cripple the sloop's steering apparatus. Not that it made any difference, as far as he could see. Each vessel had

68

been flying its proper colors, each was acting within its wartime rights. At the Governor's request, he produced the letter of marque granted to the *Forbearance*. It had been issued by the Continental Congress itself, not, as often happened, by a single state. It seemed to satisfy De Graeff, who handed it back.

"I will make out my report later in the day," De Graeff said.

"And what will it say, sir?" asked the chastened Englishman.

"That," said the Governor of St. Eustatius, "is my affair."

He rose.

"You are free to go now, gentlemen. I trust you to keep the peace. If not, you will be treated just like anybody else, whether Dutch or visitor. Good afternoon—and thank you."

Yale, whose mood had changed, actually bowed, though only after he saw Ezra doing so. They went out side by side, not speaking, each uneasily conscious of the other. Ezra would have preferred to linger, in the hope of seeing Lady Helen Ashley again, but he could see the logic in Governor de Graeff's attitude. The Governor must display the strictest impartiality. An invitation to Ezra to remain would be improper in the circumstances.

Outside the door Lieutenant Yale, a different man, sunk now in gloom, sighed prodigiously.

"Well," he said, and his voice was as black and bitter as gall, "so I'll be recalled for court-martial."

"What in the world for? You did everything you could."

"I lost."

"That wasn't your fault."

"You don't understand the British Navy, mister. Second-place it just can't see. If you don't win, no matter what the odds are against you, you're a coward and a traitor and you must be broken. Oh, I'll have a trial! But it'll be simply for form's sake. Nobody'll listen to what I have to say."

"It seems to me a mighty silly way of doing things," Ezra cried.

Yale shrugged.

"That's the bloody Navy for you."

It was stabbing, the sight of this stocky young man face to face with a blasted career as he stood, despondent, in the brilliant West Indian sunshine. Ezra still disliked the lieutenant, but he could not help pitying him.

Ezra glanced back at the residence, where assumedly everything was excitement about the new gown. He wondered which window she was near now. He wished again that he could have lingered.

Yale, hands clasped behind him, shoulders hunched high, had gone on, step after step, down . . . down . . . Ezra hurried to him, took his arm.

"See here: I don't know whether this would be of any help to you, but if you want me to I'll go before a notary here and make out a statement to the effect that you certainly did everything you could for your vessel and your mail and your men, and saying that the fire and explosion were the result of a freak accident. Sure I'll do that. And what's more, I'll get my men to sign it too, all of the ones that can write."

Yale shook a sad head. He went on down the steps . . . down and down. . . .

"It wouldn't do any good," he said. "They're going to break me anyway."

He did not even thank Ezra.

Chapter

13

He bought another coat, apricot silk with silver thread facings, and at the same time he bought a pair of false cuffs made of real Mechlin. Coat and lace alike might well have been loot from some long-since sunken ship, but they were in good condition; and at Statia you didn't ask too many questions.

He had the Moses repainted and the oars varnished so that they would flash in the sunlight. In the sternsheets he fitted a jauntily raked ensign pole, on which, when he went back and forth from ship to shore and from shore to ship, he would mount the Stars and Stripes.

He never did go ashore, these days, without the sword strapped around his middle. It gave him a lift of confidence, that sword, as did too the pleasant sound of being addressed as "captain."

He learned to cock his tricorne far forward in front, almost forward enough to block his view, the way the bucks were doing.

He even thought, albeit fleetingly, of buying a snuffbox; but the good ones were too expensive, and he never had cared much for snuff anyway.

He had running arguments about the advisability of all this fanciness—arguments with his uncle Lemuel Hart, in which Ezra sometimes took the dead man's side, sometimes his own. Likely enough he would do this while being rowed—the *Forbearance* was anchored pretty far out—and he had to be careful, in the circumstances, to refrain from moving his lips, lest the man at the oars think him out of his mind. The hands would not take kindly to a skipper they feared was lunatic. In the Street it would not have mattered, for many a man went about worrying, calculating, figuring, and moving lips and vacant stares there were the rule rather than the exception; but the hands could not be expected to know this.

" 'Vanity of vanities,' " the dead skipper would thunder, soundlessly. " 'All is vanity and vexation of spirit!' "

"Oh, I wouldn't say that, sir," his nephew would reply. "I'm not doing it to look pretty, I'm doing it to get business. 'To him that hath shall be given,' and I want to look as if I have. As for the spirit, why, I take it that a new coat is actually good for that."

"Vanity," the old man repeated. "It is all done to attract the green eyes of that witch from England!"

This was harder to take; but Ezra reflected that his uncle never really had seen Lady Helen Ashley—though unaccountably he did seem to know the color of her eyes—and he bit off a sharp and unmannerly retort, his answer, after a pause, being gentle.

"Matter of fact, I hardly ever get a glimpse of her. She's living up at the Governor's house, and since she can get everything sent up there she doesn't take the trouble to come down into the Street, and you can't rightly blame her for that. When I see her at all," Ezra went on lamely, "it's from a distance. The other day, though, she waved her parasol at me."

This was lamentably true. Oranjestad afforded no manner of gardens or parks or public promenades, no place to meet a lady. Unless Ezra was invited to the Governor's house, as each day he hoped, he could look forward to nothing more than checkered peeps of the English charmer. You could not invite a lady for a walk along that boisterous dusty Street between Gallows Bay and Interloper's Point; there was no coffeehouse; and to take her to the Mariners' Rest was unthinkable. There was, of course, the beach; but what lady would like to walk on sand?

What was worse, very soon, he could not even be vouchsafed a now-and-then view, for Lady Helen Ashley was making arrangements to be transported to nearby St. Kitts. After that, it could be assumed, he would never see her again.

"Parasols! Parasols!" the old man stormed. "What would your aunt Bessie Hart think of such Gomorrahean goings-on?"

This Ezra Bond did not feel called upon to counteract, for they had reached the sloop.

Not all of the colloquies ended so indecisively. Most of them Ezra won.

It was on his next trip ashore that he learned that the lady was gone, having with several other St. Kitts residents chartered an interisland schooner that already stood far out to sea.

That hurt. It was true that he had no claim on her, and that she was under no obligation to him, and that he had known anyway, known all along, that her ultimate destination was the neighboring island of St. Kitts. It was true too that she had thanked him, and handsomely, for what little he was able to do for her. All the same, she might at least have left him some word of farewell, perhaps a note. Maybe she thought that this uncouth pirate couldn't read?

Ezra's reaction was entirely normal. Given such a situation, almost any man would do one of two things—either get drunk or go back furiously, frantically to work. Ezra Bond never had been much of a lad for overdrinking. He sought out, once again, the office of Abraham van Bibber, agent for the sovereign state of Maryland as well as for sundry private shipowners, those of the *Forbearance* included.

Van Bibber was short, stodgy of manner, with a venous nose and small vulpine eyes. He looked stupid, but he wasn't. Ezra

73

found him, this morning, elbows-on-counter, talking with a tall grave gray man who had eyes like the blue milk in a pitcher that's just been jogged, and also a slow southern accent.

"Sorry, captain, still no word from Atkins," Van Bibber said. "Maybe the letter went astray. You know how these interisland boats are. I'll write him another."

It was the same story every morning. Ezra had disposed of the staves and the miscellaneous items readily enough, and at a good price, but the bulk of the cargo, dried eels, remained on his hands. This was not for lack of bidders. The merchants of St. Eustatius would bid on anything, for they were sure that they could sell it again, no matter what the nature of the merchandise; but the offers, in this case, had not been anywhere near high enough. Van Bibber had a solution for that. There was a plantation-owner named Atkins who came over from St. Kitts every now and then in search of bargains, and he, as Van Bibber well knew, desperately needed food supplies for his slaves, supplies that he could buy only from the outside. Atkins would jump at the chance to buy those eels, even at Ezra's price. Van Bibber was sure of it. Moreover, Atkins, as Van Bibber knew—for it was an agent's business to know things like this—was not, like so many planters, deeply in debt, and in fact he had on hand a rather large supply of cash in the form of florins. So Van Bibber had written to Atkins; and there was nothing for Ezra to do but wait.

"Captain, I want you to meet Mr. Samuel Curzon."

The milk in the milk jug wobbled, and the two men bowed.

"Your servant."

"Your servant, sir."

They shook hands.

"Mr. Curzon's the new agent for the Continental Congress," Van Bibber explained.

"Oh? Just landed, eh?"

"Yes."

"That's quite a job you boys are doing in Philadelphia."

"Well, we try to. Look, captain: You're the very man I wanted to meet. When you do get rid of those salted eels you brought down, what d'ye plan to stock up with for the return trip?"

That this newcomer should be aware of the eels was not extraordinary. He had been on the island for only a few hours, but everybody at Statia knew everything about everybody else, Abraham van Bibber most of all. The place was one vast whispering gallery.

"Why, molasses, most likely," Ezra answered. "I'll run over to Fort Royal for it. The French are all but giving the stuff away."

"Fort Royal's not the safest place for a Yankee vessel ever since France got into the fight, captain. The British Navy's watching that port like a cat watches a mousehole."

"There's other places," Ezra offered.

Curzon took another tack. He was exceedingly earnest.

"Look, captain: Has it occurred to you to carry back gunpowder?"

Ezra habitually refused to hurry when a deal was involved. Now he rubbered out his lips, and he rolled his eyes.

"Well, I try to think of everything, and there's certainly plenty of gunpowder lying around just begging to be picked up. But in my experience, mister, the men that handle it want too big a profit for their trouble. They get it at forty, maybe forty-five florins a hundredweight in Holland and expect to be paid two hundred and fifty here. So? So what's that leave for me?"

"General Washington'll pay almost anything for whatever gunpowder he can get. Six shillings a pound. Even six-and-six."

"Yes, and he'll pay with Continental paper, which isn't worth wiping your ass with. But *I'll* have to pay with coin to get the stuff."

"No. Gold. The Continental Congress has created a special

fund for this, captain. That's one of the pieces of of news I am bringing. And remember—your country needs it. Our country."

"Hm-m . . ."

"Don't you want to clinch independence, captain?"

"Why, sure I do. I'm as patriotic as the next man."

"Then help out your country when your country most needs it. Listen, captain: Time and again it would have been a different story—at Bunker Hill, at Germantown, at Princeton—if the Continentals had had enough gunpowder. I mean that, sir."

"I don't doubt you do. But you've got to remember that I'm not my own master here," Ezra Bond lied. "I've got my owners to think of. I took over command on the high seas after the unexpected death of the skipper, and I can use my own judgment only just so far."

"And there's another thing," he broke in as Curzon started to speak again, "and that's the element of danger. The hands wouldn't like it one bit, and I can't say as I would myself. Do you suppose I could get them to battle when they know that the whole vessel's crammed full of gunpowder and a lucky hit might get them all blown sky-high any second? No."

"In wartime we must all run risks."

"Sure, but there's still some of us would like to *pick* those risks before we take 'em."

"Yet you will think it over, won't you, captain?"

"Oh, sure. Sure, I'll think it over all right."

In the event, Ezra was not given a chance to forget it. Samuel Curzon, a very persistent man, got after him every time he came ashore. Whether it was in or before Van Bibber's shop, or in the Street, or at the Mariners' Rest, no longer than ten minutes after putting foot on land Ezra was sure to encounter the Congressional agent, who would proclaim almost tearfully the terrible need of gunpowder in the suffering young republic. Ezra Bond could not avoid him.

76

". . . easy to stow, captain . . . and when you get there you can always find a buyer before anybody. . . ."

In this way a week passed, and still there was no word from St. Kitts. Ezra chafed. There was no social life for a man of his station on St. Eustatius, except what was offered at the Mariners' Rest, and you could get too much of that. Ezra did not even have to make arrangements for sleeping ashore. That necessity would arise only when they coppered the *Forbearance*'s bottom.

He had ordered the bottoming job done as soon as, delighted, he learned that it was possible. It would greatly increase the sloop's speed, and to a privateer speed was everything. Copper was rare in the New World: the British shipyard men wanted to keep work like that to themselves. Ezra doubted that he could have had a bottoming done in Boston or New York or Philadelphia; but enterprising Statia had the metal and the men. Ezra winced at the price, but he agreed; and he got into line. For it would take time. There was only one beach on the island suitable for careening a craft like the *Forbearance*. Ezra must wait his turn, for there were other skippers ahead of him. It would be three to four weeks, he was told. Meanwhile the sloop had been emptied, the dried eels stored in Van Bibber's warehouse, and Ezra could not take on a fresh cargo, for that the vessel had to be light when she was careened. There was simply no work for him to do, which, of course, was the hardest work of all.

"This plantation this man Atkins owns," he said carelessly one morning. "Is it anywhere near Lady Helen's?"

Though Van Bibber quite possibly never had visited the other island, Ezra assumed that he would know the answer. And he did.

"Right in front of it. The Ashley place is higher up. The place Captain Atkins has borders on the beach. Why?"

Ezra resettled his hat under his left arm.

"Thought I might drop over there, call on him."

"Huh?"

77

"Well, if the mountain won't come to Mohammed I reckon Mohammed will have to go to the mountain, as the old saw has it."

"But—but St. Kitts is British, and our country happens to be at war with Great Britain."

"Sure. I had forgotten it. I'll go careful, at night."

Chapter

14

The trade winds being as reliable as they were, a run between two islands as close together as St. Eustatius and St. Kitts, where there was no tricky current or race, in good weather was as predictable as a coach ride to any boatman who really knew his boat. And Peter van Braam, a gigantic, impassive mulatto, most emphatically did know his boat. With nothing else to do, Ezra found it fascinating to watch the man, who singlehanded the catboat as casually but as accurately as any oarsman in a scull on a lake.

They had planned it to arrive in a little cove at the end of the valley of the Basseterre, near the capital, which was similarly named, shortly after sundown; and so it came about. This cove, which Peter knew well, was actually on the plantation of which Captain Atkins was manager.

They were never chased, they were not even hailed, and if anybody saw the small white craft approaching the southwest shore of St. Kitts while the setting sun scattered its gilt, what of that? It could have been a fishing boat; and indeed, Peter van Braam sometimes did fish from it, when no more lucrative pastime offered itself. Peter was a free man, and he carried proof of his freedom with him at all times. Peter had nothing to fear. On the other hand, Ezra Bond might have some explanations to make in the unlikely event that he was nabbed.

He was not afraid. If he did not have any papers, neither did he wear his sword or carry any sort of weapon, but he did have on the new apricot and silver coat, which he calculated would impress almost anyone. Since he was not associated with the Continental Army or with the new Continental Navy he could not be accused of spying, even if taken behind the enemy lines. But —what lines? If it was information about St. Kitts that Ezra hoped to get, why, he could get more of that in two hours at St. Eustatius than he could pick up in two days on the British island itself. Besides, St. Kitts was hardly a military objective. The garrison would be trifling, if there was any garrison at all. The militia no doubt was the usual ludicrous West Indian one, hopelessly inefficient, designed not so much to fight off foreign invaders— after all, this island once had been French and the French might try to take it back, if only as a pawn for the peace table—as to be on hand in case of that West Indian planters' bugaboo, a slave uprising. The militia would not be concerned with interrogating a well-dressed wanderer.

There would be no moon before midnight, and when they slid into the shadows of the cove it was like dropping down a well: only an oval of watery starshine gleamed above their heads, while immediately around them everything was harshly dark. Peter van Braam never hesitated. The darkness did not dismay him, for he knew this little indentation of the shore as well as he knew the path to his own privy, if he had a privy. He struck, and they floated. They moved at so slow a glide that there was no sense of motion at all, and when at last the keel grated on stones it was a startling sound: it was like a hiss in the darkness, a low warning whisper. Peter van Braam, who had been expecting that very rasp, put the tiller over hard. He got up and came to Ezra, and he took Ezra's arm, causing Ezra to jump a bit. Peter van Braam pointed. Ezra could not *see* the pointing arm, but rather he *felt* it. He nodded. He took off his shoes and stockings and tied these around his neck; and he lowered himself over the side.

There were only a few inches of freeboard, the catboat was that low, a skimmer, but the water was somewhat deeper than he had been led to expect. It came up to his thighs, making the bottom of his breeches wet. All the same, he waded for an unseen shore. The bottom was stony, but the stones were not sharp.

A branch brushed the left side of his face. It was wet, or seemed so. It was like wet cold fingers caressing him. He shivered; but he pressed on; and soon he climbed to a shore. He never did see Peter van Braam take his departure.

Indeed, he did not see anything. He might have been blind. He turned his back to where the water was, and with arms outstretched he stumbled ahead, frankly frightened, fearful that any instant he might step into a hole and fall on his face.

Fortunately the walk was not a long one. The branches, the hanging moss, fell away, cleared from before him, and he found himself at the edge of a cane field on what in the wan starlight he took to be a sort of wagon track.

Sugar cane is not much to look at. When you've seen one field of it you have seen them all; and Ezra Bond had seen many. He wasted no time staring at this one, but as soon as he had put shoes and stockings on turned to the left, in accordance with Van Braam's directions.

Even there in the open the going was not easy, and he stepped with care. It seemed to him that he walked a long, long way. He had no watch. The track was undeviating, and there was no outstanding object in the dimness on either side of him or before him to mark his progress by.

He had a nightmarish feeling of leaden legs, leaden feet that were an agony to lift. He began to think that he would never get anywhere, that he would toddle clear around the damn' island this way.

There was not the slightest sound, either from near or from far

81

off. It was eerie. It was also, what with his wet breeches, chilly. He shivered, plugging on.

Abruptly a large low building loomed on his right, gray, ghostly, yet for all of this somehow reassuring as proof at least that he was straying upon this very earth itself, not on the moon or across the bottom of the sea.

The building might have been a warehouse or a toolhouse. No light came from it and no sound, but from beyond it, back of it, for the first time there reached his ears a low, even, susurrant sound, as of many men breathing, a sound punctuated now and then by a mumble as somebody strove to talk in his sleep. That, Ezra reckoned, would be the slave quarters. They worked the slaves hard, from dawn to sundown six days a week, and even more at harvesttime, and the slaves therefore would be sleeping well.

Ezra did not fear assault in the event of discovery, for the axes, machetes, and other cutting implements would be collected, counted, and carefully locked up after the completion of a day's work; but any alarm at this stage of the game could be embarrassing, so he gave the slave quarters a wide berth.

The usual rule at plantations—though there could be exceptions—was for the residence or big house, the owner's establishment, to be some distance from the slave dormitories, these latter being not the most fragrant spots in the group, and, if possible, on a somewhat higher site, to catch every stray bit of breeze, so that the owner was physically as well as socially and economically above his laborers. And sure enough, Ezra soon found himself climbing a slight slope.

Suddenly, just ahead, there was a barking of dogs. This was something that Ezra had not anticipated, and he froze.

Could they be guarding against escape by turning hounds loose in the plantation grounds at night? It did not seem likely, for an escaped slave on St. Kitts would have nowhere to go except

82

another plantation or the almost bare interior, where he could easily be recaptured: it was not like Jamaica, for example, an island the interior of which was filled with wild, roving bands of maroons, or escaped slaves, naked jungle men, savage men, killers.

All the same, Ezra found himself wishing that he had brought his sword and perhaps even a pistol or two.

There must have been at least two dogs, and they made much noise. The barking did not come nearer, but neither did it diminish.

Then there was a light ahead, a little higher than where he stood. It was a torch, spluttering, coming closer, as did now the barking of the dogs. Ezra could not see the upper part of the man who held this torch, only the legs, which were swished by a nightshirt, but he could see the musket that the man held. The dogs, two mastiffs, tugged on ahead of this man, and Ezra was comforted to note that they were collared and were held back by leads.

The man stopped. The dogs, growling, would have gone on.

"Who the Devil's there?"

Ezra Bond bowed, though he was not sure that the man could see him doing this. He kept his voice light and amiable.

"A trader from Saybrook, Connecticut, Captain Atkins, and I've got a cargo of dried eels that I hear tell you might like to buy."

"Oh? Who sent you here?"

"Van Bibber. He's my agent at Statia. I came over with Peter van Braam in his cat."

"Bibber, eh? Well, he's right. I *am* interested, if we can agree on a fair price."

"I think we'll be able to do that all right," Ezra said, moving a little closer, though very slowly.

The musket was lowered, the dogs were shushed.

83

"Well, come in, mister. We'll talk right now, and you can stay here the night, unless Van Braam's waiting for you?"

Ezra shook his head.

"Braam'll be there tomorrow night. He's been paid."

"Good. Come in, come in, man. I'll get some brandy. Dried eels, eh? That's capital."

Chapter

15

It might have been a model of the way that business deals ought to be made. In twenty minutes and two drinks they had all the details settled. Atkins had wished to buy, Ezra Bond had wished to sell, and it was as simple as that. At a distance it might have been another matter; but when these two men met face to face, and measured one another, everything went with the smoothness of syrup. The planter would not come up to Ezra's starting price, but he did go a heap higher than any of those who had bid on St. Eustatius, and Ezra could cry an early "Sold!"

Captain Atkins was what Ezra supposed the English would call a gentleman—Ezra never did rightly understand that term—yet it was clear that he was not rich, and he flaunted no airs of superiority. He was slight, he was wan, and somewhat stooped, though very little older than Ezra, and he squinted a mite as though soon he would be needing to mount spectacles on that accipitrine nose. He wore no nightcap, and Ezra saw that his hair was wispy and thin, not just cut short for wig purposes, but sparse. Yet he was wiry; he was alert.

When Atkins went to fetch the bottle, Ezra, seated, looked lazily around. This plantation house, like so many others, was a rambling one-story affair, and he sat in the main hall or parlor, with verandas opening off two sides, a butler's pantry, closets, and the entrance to the kitchen kiosk path in the back, and on the fourth side some bedrooms. One of the bedroom doors was ajar, as the proprietor had left it when he seized his gun at the barking of the dogs, and Ezra could make out there, by the light of a very low night lamp, a huge four-poster bed. It was the only pretentious article of furniture in sight, that bed, and undoubtedly it had been brought over from England. It looked oddly out of place in this jerry-built, sun-scorched house, where the rugs were matting and in the large windows no drapes were hung. As Ezra stared at it he thought that he heard something stir there, something diaphanous and slight, and there was the sound of a soft moan. Mrs. Atkins? Then the host returned with brandy, closed the bedroom door, and poured a couple of drinks; and they plunged into their discussion.

Many a planter in those parts assumed a standoffishness when dealing with Yankees, as Ezra knew from experience. This was in part due to the fact that the planters, though lonesome, always hungry for the company of their kind, considered men from New England to be uncouth, granitic of countenance, adamantine of heart, traders who spoke through their noses and drove too hard a bargain: and it was in part due, too, to the fact that the planters were accustomed to giving orders to large bodies of obsequious men, whereas the Yankees were not, as a rule, obsequious. Captain Atkins was quite different. There was nothing circuitous about him. He dove right into the subject.

Another thing that characterized most West Indian planters or their representatives in the field was chronic indebtedness. It was difficult for Ezra Bond to realize how they could endure this, but undeniably it was an accepted, full-time condition. By habit they owed more than they owned. They never did get off tick, and one of their biggest single expenses must have been interest. In consequence, when they bought anything they hoped to pay either in kind or with some long-range note; and if in kind, then you had no choice of your return cargo; whereas if they paid with a long-term note you could cash it only in St. Eustatius, or exchange it there for goods of your own selection, at a considerable discount. This was standard practice in the islands, especially among the English, whose plantations for the most part were mortgaged to the hilt, and not infrequently beyond.

This did not apply to Captain Atkins. The reason was something that Ezra did not ask. It was enough for him that Atkins had a treasure in coin—not in florins (Van Bibber had been misinformed on this one point) but in Surinam guilders, which for Ezra's purposes were just as good—and that it would not even be required to ship this silver to St. Eustatius, since it was already there. Atkins knew and trusted Abraham van Bibber, and he had known and trusted Lemuel Hart, so he trusted Ezra Bond. All that was called for, once the price had been agreed upon, was for Ezra to give him a letter to Van Bibber instructing that agent, in whose warehouse the eels were stored, to transfer these to Atkins' agent, Farquarson & Son. In return, Atkins would write to Farquarson & Son instructing them to receive the eels and to pay Abraham van Bibber thus-and-so for same. Each agent, of course, would take his commission, but this wasn't excessive.

The business completed, then, Atkins, in ordinary circumstances anything but a chatty man, wished to sit the night out with gossip. Ezra had foreseen this, a characteristic of the class. It was prompted not by graciousness but by a thirst for news, a desire to enjoy to the full a break in the monotony, for visitors from Outside seldom showed themselves. The planters capitalized the word in their speech, Outside, just as Statians capitalized the Street, and just as Englishmen abroad capitalized Home, meaning England. Ezra did not represent Home, but he was from the Outside, even nearby St. Eustatius being in that class, and Atkins, who had not heard directly from Statia for more than a month— he had not received either of Van Bibber's letters—pumped his visitor vigorously.

87

First he wanted to know all about the sea fight, then all about his new neighbor, Lady Helen Ashley, whom as yet he had scarcely met. These details Ezra supplied willingly enough; but when Atkins sought information on such trivialities as the working force at the Mariners' Rest, Ezra cut him short. Ezra had been up since dawn, had spent all day in the sun, had walked five or six miles, and even now sat in wet breeches. He pointed this out. He was blunt about it.

Atkins took it well, and was profuse in his apologies. He showed Ezra to the necessary, then to a bedroom, which adjoined his own. As they passed the door of Atkins' bedroom Ezra heard again the low, half-stifled moan of a sleeping woman; but the host made no mention of this.

Ezra Bond might have been a corpse that night. He did not even hear the five o'clock cannon shot that signaled the start of work, but slept right through until almost seven. Long before that time, surely, Captain Atkins was out in the fields or at the crushing mill, supervising the labor.

Atkins had not forgotten his guest's wish to visit Lady Helen Ashley. A lugubrious but efficient Negro, who said that her name was Sara and who brought Ezra his breakfast of chocolate, melons, an omelet with shrimps, bacon, pineapple tarts, claret, and a hock negus, told him at the same time that Captain Atkins had left word that Captain Bond should have any horse in the stables saddled for the trip. One of Lady Helen's boys could ride the nag back, she added.

It was a beautiful morning, all blue and silver, a day to invite loafing. The house was strangely quiet, with no note of the usual morning clatter. Atkins, Ezra reflected, must live a simple, hard-driving life. The groveling house servants that so many planters thought they must maintain for the sake of appearances would only get in the way of a man like that. Aside from Sara the only person Ezra saw—and he saw her as he was crossing a veranda on his way to the stables—was a lithe, languid, long-legged young woman taking her ease in a deep wicker chair, pillows behind her, her feet on a footstool. Her hair was down her back, and she wore a salmon-colored silk boudoir robe and purple silk slippers with bright yellow pompoms on them. Her complexion—and there was plenty of skin to judge it by—was a very light *café au lait:* she might have been an octoroon, twelve and one-half per-cent Negro. She looked at Ezra with large, very lovely eyes the color of watered-down molasses, and her mouth was formed into an "o" of astonishment, but she made no move to rise.

So that's the way it was? Well, we all have our weaknesses, and here, indubitably, was one of Captain Atkins'. Ezra passed on.

He found the stables readily enough, and an intelligent Negro boy there, a boy who like Sara had his orders, soon saddled him a quiet mare. Ezra habitually picked quiet horses. He did not like to ride—he was a sailor, not an equestrian, and it made him nervous to be mounted—but there were times when it was the only thing to do.

He thought briefly of riding around the plantation seeking out Atkins to thank him for his hospitality, but it was a big place, as he saw at a glance, and he might spend half the morning finding the proprietor. He had not the slightest doubt that Atkins would live up to his business obligations anyway.

So he got the boy to point out the direction of the Ashley plantation, and he rode off that way. He was wondering about her, wondering what she would look like.

Chapter

16

The confrontation knocked the breath out of him, so that he gasped, swaying in saddle.

He had paused to watch a gang of slaves, thirty-odd of them, husky lads, "holing" on the slope of a hill. This was a laborious process. The workers—they were all heavy-set men, no doubt the "big" gang, as distinguished from the "second" gang, which would consist of women and weaker men, and the "small" gang, made up of pickaninnies brought out to the field not so much because of what work they might do as to keep them from making trouble back in the living quarters while their elders were away— were armed with hoes. The ground upon which they worked was part of a cane field that had lately been cut and then the stumps burned. What they were doing was preparing this burned-over ground for a fresh plantage, painfully hacking out parallel trenches about two and a half feet wide and two and a half feet deep, the trenches only a few feet from one another. This was the custom. Why a plow was not used Ezra Bond never had been able to learn. The answer he got when he asked about it was that beasts of burden, such as horses, oxen, mules, were expensive to bring to the islands and even more expensive to maintain. They died easily, and they ate too much. Yet the same planters complained that the slaves themselves also cost too much to import and to feed.

Ezra did not ask this question today, being more concerned with learning where the mistress of the plantation might be found —for something told him that she would be out in the fields rather than up at the mansion—and with this in mind he called over a couple of Negro "drivers" or slave bosses. There was no white overseer in sight, which he thought odd. Lady Helen Ashley might be highly capable; but it was always as well to have a white man around.

These drivers were supposed to be among the more intelligent slaves, often being the only ones to whom the managers or even the overseers would try to talk, passing on their orders. These two were good-natured enough, and eager to please, but Ezra did not believe that they really understood what he said and he was tarnation certain that he couldn't understand any part of what appeared to be on the whole a set of answers. The drivers rolled their eyes and flashed their teeth and swung their arms, pointing, but even the gestures, to Ezra, seemed contradictory.

He thanked them gravely, and rode on, continuing much the way he had been riding before—that is, slightly uphill. After all, if he found the big house he could rest in the shade. It was getting on toward noon, and sooner or later, no matter where she was, Lady Helen Ashley would be riding back for dinner.

He pondered the thought of her, the feeling. Here was a woman of fashion, an aristocrat, out in a place like this, and what did she know about raising sugar? How much could her manager already have cheated her?

The house, when at last he did raise it, proved to be a large and ramshackle affair, once white but now badly in need of paint. It needed, too, repair. Tiles were missing from the roof, which sagged. Several storm shutters swung ajar, and one of the pillars of the porch had been tilted, perhaps by a windstorm, and never straightened again. What had once been a rose garden, he be-

91

lieved, was choked with weeds. A boxwood hedge—and such work it must have been to ship all that boxwood from England!—was so seriously neglected as to be almost unrecognizable. There was a small low white fence, as lacking in paint as the house, with several palings missing, while the gate swung back and forth on hinges that had been without oil for a long while. The whole place, indeed, as he saw when he got closer, had about it an atmosphere of desolation and decay. It was falling apart. It was not even a picturesque ruin, but simply sloppy.

It was all so different from anything he had associated with Lady Helen Ashley that for a moment he thought he must have come upon the wrong residence, and when he turned at the sound of hoofbeats behind him it was with this in mind.

She must have seen him from afar, not identifying the new coat, and she had come fast, probably with questions cocked and ready to shoot. She too would enjoy meeting somebody from Outside.

She was glorious. Except from a distance he had not before this time seen her in anything but the yellow and red polonaise she had worn when she went aboard the *Forbearance,* a handsome gown in truth, and brave with ribbons and ruchings and bright furbelows, but a shade slovenly after the first five days. Here she wore a dashing brown linen riding habit turned over with green that made her eyes gleam even brighter. There was a clump of Valenciennes at her throat, and on her head was a broad tall-crowned felt wideawake, held in place by ribbons. Despite the severity of the habit, there was nothing masculine about her. She was every inch the woman, and dainty forsooth.

Her own hair, fluffed out but not curled, showed no trace of pomatum. A superb horsewoman, she seemed much more secure with both legs over on the same side of the steed she besat than was Ezra Bond, who rode astride.

In her hand, the tip properly pointed to the back of the mount's left ear, was a silver-tipped teakwood riding rod.

"Captain Bond!"

Unmistakable gladness was in her face at first, a spontaneous and happy welcome, and then, instantly afterward, a touch of alarm, which she tried to hide. Did she fear that he was betraying his country? And would it have made any difference to her if he did? Covering her confusion, she whipped a green silk riding glove from her right hand and held that hand out to Ezra.

He did not kiss it. He had never kissed a woman's hand and he did not seek to start now, perched as he was high on the back of a borrowed horse; but he did give it a hearty shake; and he took off his hat and held this over his heart.

"Just thought I'd drop over and see how you were getting along," he said.

Chapter

17

It was like a feast, like an outing, though it was not a frivolous waste of time, for they got a heap of work done. In this, it reminded Ezra of a house-raising back home, when all the neighbors would wallop the applejack and the blackstrap, at the same time putting up the structure. House-raisings, as he recollected them, usually ended in fist fights. It was not so with him and Lady Ashley.

"Hello, captain. Still sailing close to the edge of piracy?"

Immediately after that it began to seem as if in fact she had been expecting him. Certainly she needed somebody to talk to. Shocked by the run-down state of the plantation, on her very first day she had dismissed the manager and the two white overseers. Now she was on her own, in a strange land; but she remained unabashed.

"He marked up repair and expenses he never had anything to do with," she told Ezra at dinner. She was referring to the discharged manager, Callahan. "He let everything go to pot. I've started suit for damages, and I have mountains of evidence, but I don't suppose I'll get anywhere. He's a lawyer himself."

"They usually are."

"Of course he never expected me to come down here by myself and find out what was the matter."

"Of course not. The owners don't, as a rule. Your neighbor Atkins is an exception. All most owners are interested in is profits. They buy themselves seats in Parliament, and then they sit back and try to do everything by mail."

"I couldn't do that," she said. "I couldn't *afford* it. They say seats cost as much as three thousand guineas these days."

They laughed at the thought of a woman in Parliament.

She made no pretense of conventional entertaining, but at the end of the meal she asked him if he would like to look over the plantation, the implication being that she would ride out anyway, with him or without.

"Why, I'd admire very much to do that," he said.

Getting back on a horse made him wince, for he was somewhat saddlesore already and he never had been much of a hand for riding, but the sight of the fields and of the crushing mill made him forget this.

"I'm a sailing man, not a farmer," he told her time after time; but the truth was that he did not lack knowingness of establishments such as this. His own father, whom he did not remember well, like Uncle Lemuel Hart, like so many others along the Connecticut shore, had been "amphibious," a man with a fishing boat and a small farm, which he worked alternately; and before Ezra went to sea he had spent many an arduous hour in the fields back of Saybrook. He told Helen this.

To be sure, he added, swatting a potato bug did not qualify anybody as an agricultural expert, and pitching hay had nothing to do with raising cane—sugar cane. Still, he had supplemented his basic knowledge of farming by visits to Danish plantations on St. Croix and French plantations on Guadeloupe and Martinique. The French and the Danes, he pointed out, did their own work: they didn't try to supervise the operation of a farm from five thousand miles away.

"Neither do I. That's why I'm here."

For an amateur, Ezra had God's plenty of ideas. He expostu-

95

lated, among other things, on the folly of wasting all that labor and time by "holing" burnt-over fields instead of using a plow. There was nothing new about a plow, he asserted. Didn't the Good Book mention it, and more than once?

" 'The sluggard will not plow by reason of the cold; therefore shall he beg in harvest, and have nothing.' 'Judah shall plow, and Jacob shall break.' Isn't that right?"

"It would seem so."

" 'Doth the plowman plow all day to sow?' That's Isaiah, I think."

"I'm sure it is."

"Plows would be cheaper here, and faster too."

"Um-m . . . There must be some reason. I'll look into it."

A moment later she cried: "But pulling a plow would mean horses or mules, and they're murderously expensive now—now that you mainland colonists have started a war."

"What's the matter with the ones you have?"

"They're needed at the crusher. How else could we get any power?"

"Where I come from it's mostly provided by the streams."

"There isn't a decent stream in the whole plantation—not one that you can count on."

"You can count on the wind," Ezra said. "I don't reckon that there's any other place in the world where the trades are as dependable as they are right here. And yet there isn't a single windmill on this island."

"I hadn't thought of that. But how could I get one built? *I* certainly can't do it, myself. And I don't suppose that there's anybody on the island who can."

Ezra nodded in the direction of St. Eustatius, the peak of which, the Quill, was fuzzy on a fuzzy blue horizon.

"Statia's Dutch, and did you ever hear of a Dutchman that didn't know all about windmills? What's more, Holland's pretty nearly the only country left in Europe that England isn't at war with, so it would be all right for any Statian to come over here and do the job any time he wanted. I'll send you one, when I get back."

It was the first mention of his return, and it caused them to be quiet for a little while. At dinner she had invited him to stay the night, an invitation he gravely accepted. He did not worry about failing to make the rendezvous with Peter, who had been paid anyway. Ezra could easily walk to Basseterre and arrange for a return trip with some boatman there.

The two Negro drivers had been amiable enough when he hailed them in the morning, but he did not like the way they looked at their mistress.

"This is no place for a woman alone," he fumed.

"I knew you were going to say that, sooner or later."

"Well, it happens to be true. At least I hope you have a pistol?"

"I have a pistol."

Not until the huge yellow gong at slave quarters spoke the second of sunset did they turn back toward the mansion and supper. The sound of the gong was persistent, if languid, chasing up slopes and across the tops of hillocks, ringing down the narrow small valleys, even seeming to sob, as though it were loath to die. It would speak again at sunrise, Helen said.

Ezra nodded.

"They usually shoot a cannon."

"I can't find a cannon here anywhere. Maybe Lawyer Callahan sold it? But he was charging me for powder all the time. And for ball."

"You don't need ball to shoot a signal cannon. You just use wadding."

"That's one thing more I'll put into the bill of complaints."

St. Kitts is only technically in the tropics, and sunsets there are not as abrupt as they would be farther down near the Line. There was some trace of dusk, enough at least to hang as it were

97

a shimmering gauze before the house as they neared it, blurring the edges, which was a mercy.

The house was as dingy as it appeared from the outside, Helen having known scant time as yet to furnish it; but they could see little of this slovenliness. They lit no candle, for they were fearful of insects, but bathed instead in semidarkness.

In this part of the world, as Ezra knew, it was the custom to take a bath almost every night, less for cleansing purposes than for refreshment. The water felt good. It was tepid, and up to his calves as he stood in the center of a wooden tub, sponging himself.

It occurred to him—he could not have avoided the thought even if he wished to—that her ladyship, with all those provocative curves, was doing the same thing only a few feet away in another tub. When he paused in his own swabbing he could hear her splash in there, a thin wall away.

He remembered those nights aboard the *Forbearance* when he would lie in misery, aching all over, trying to sleep but unable to keep from thinking about the woman a few feet off. He wondered if she slept naked, as he had been told that many women did. He would himself sleep that way tonight, of necessity.

On the veranda it was still light enough to see the food before them, and again they lit no candle. She was a dim figure, diaphanous, in white or maybe a very light yellow, paper-thin stuff that slithered when she stirred. It was clear that she was uncorseted. They didn't talk much.

Afterward she showed him to his bedroom, which was next to her own.

"Good night, captain."

He could hardly see her there, just a misty lightness, but he could smell her plainly enough, as he had done at the table. Gardenia, he guessed. It made him a mite dizzy.

"Anything you want, captain, just shout. Moses'll be sure to hear you. He's a very light sleeper."

They breakfasted at dawn, and then rode out into the fields. Ezra's butt still was sore, and there were times when he gritted his teeth from the pain, but Helen Ashley rode with a fine abandon, never pausing. Their conversation, as it had been the previous day, and as it had been aboard the *Forbearance,* was easy and free, a delight to both. This was curious. They came from different worlds, yet they nattered on without inhibition, charmed with one another's company. They discussed all sorts of things— almost everything, indeed, except what they were really thinking of. At least, *he* was thinking of it. He couldn't answer for her.

It was hardest in the tub, when he knew that she was so close to him, and without any clothes on.

He stayed another day, and then another, but on the fourth day he determined to make for Basseterre the following morning. He was not troubled about his command, which would not be careened yet. Nor was he troubled about leaving Helen alone. He had been wrong about her, at first. She was perfectly capable of running this or any other plantation all by herself. She didn't need a man—at least, not as manager. What Ezra *was* troubled about was that if he stayed any longer he might do something that he shouldn't do.

He had told her of his intention to leave, and they were both quiet that night when they had supper on the veranda. Afterward, she stood close to him.

"Good night . . . Ezra."

He believed that he could have kissed her then. He didn't do so; but when he went into his own bedroom the backs of his hands were wet and his throat was so tight that he could scarcely swallow.

He undressed slowly, folding his clothes onto a bench. He stood a moment, feet apart, head cocked. He could not hear a thing in there. The whole house, indeed, was silent, as was the night outside. He started to tremble.

He went out to the main room and stood a moment before her

99

door. There was no sound, no movement. He crossed the room to the kitchen corridor, where he found Moses, a very old man, too feeble for work in the fields, emphatically asleep. Ezra had almost hoped that Moses would be awake.

He went back to Helen's door. Still no sound. He could not even tease himself into a belief that he heard her breathing.

Suddenly he opened the door and went in. He was trembling even worse now, and it was hard for him to breathe.

There was a rustle of bedclothes on his left. He gasped.

"Over—here," she whispered.

Chapter

18

The gong bonged out its message of another session of labor, and Ezra, at the breakfast table, wondered what was holding up his hostess. It was already full day.

He was more nervous than he had ever been before in his life, and he was bound and determined that he wouldn't let this nervousness show.

When she came at last it was a jolt to see that she had put rouge on her face. There was not much of it, but undeniably some was there. Why? In the life she had lived before coming down to these parts, the high life, it could be that rouge and other face daubments were taken for granted, as much a part of her daily costume as her shoes; but cosmetics scarcely seemed to be called for when a female planter was about to ride around her fields soon after dawn.

He made out that he did not notice it, and she helped this by keeping her head averted, her eyes cast down on her food, after having given him the briefest and most formal of smiles. Was she sore about something? Or had she painted her face because, like him, she was nervous and because she feared that she might be caught in an untimely blush. It was a mite hard to imagine Lady Helen Ashley blushing, but it could happen, Ezra knew: almost any woman, in the right circumstances, might blush. No doubt even whores could, on occasion. Not that he thought of Lady Helen Ashley as a whore or anything like that.

He made up his mind not to beat about the bush but rather to leap into the business right away. He cleared his throat, frowning at the fervent attention that his companion gave to her plate.

"I'll go back to Statia tonight."

"Yes."

There was nothing new here, nothing to startle her. They had agreed upon this the previous afternoon. They had agreed that it might be better all around if Ezra planned his second visit with more care, making sure, for one thing, that he was equipped with some manner of let-pass or letter that would make him look like something other than a Yankee.

"I'll come right back, as soon as I can fix things."

"But if—"

"I think I'll be Danish. I'll run over to St. Thomas and get myself a set of what they call burgher papers. It makes you a citizen, and it won't cost much. Nobody'll believe it, but they'll generally respect it. Being Danish is easy."

"Oh."

"Now, to get down to business, what church do you go to?"

"Well, none here yet, why?"

"Well, I mean what church do you *belong* to?"

"Why, The Church, of course."

"Meaning the Church of England?"

"Why, what else would I mean?"

"Well, there are a lot of churches, you know."

"You didn't suppose that I was a Catholic, now did you?"

Ezra frankly was shocked. He feared that *he* might be blushing a bit. Urgently he shook his head.

"No, no! That's the one that's pretty much the same, though, isn't it? I mean, they have bishops and all that?"

"We certainly have bishops, yes. But it certainly is not the same. Will you tell me, please, what all this is about? I always took it that my religion was my personal affair."

"Of course, of course! But I just wanted to be sure . . . I want for us to know that when we get married it's going to be all perfectly legal. I think you'd feel the same way, wouldn't you?"

"When we—"

She had looked up, and now she was staring at him with those huge green eyes as though she could not believe what she heard.

"When we—La, sir, is this a proposal?"

"Well, I guess so. What did you expect? We've got to get married, don't we?"

She swallowed, still glaring as though she didn't know whether to laugh or to cry.

"*Got* to?"

"Sure. If we don't get married, then what we did last night would be a sin."

"Oh . . . It would be a sin, eh?"

"Why, sure."

She decided to laugh, but it was a hollow laugh; it sounded as if she did it with her head stuck into an empty barrel.

"La, sir, and have you never sinned before, captain?"

"Well, it's different when you—"

"Because for a virgin I must say you showed a great deal of skill."

Now he *was* blushing. He looked aside. Luckily a slave came in just then with more food, and they both made a play of addressing their plates, though neither in fact was munching.

Later he said, soberly: "I don't think that you ought to make jokes about a thing like this."

"A thing like what, pray? D'ye think that we are the only persons in the world who have ever done that, captain—that, what we did last night?"

"Oh, no, I don't. That's why children—"

"And do you think that just because I was tired and bored last night and allowed you to take a few liberties with me—"

"A few lib—"

"—that that means that you have any right to expect me to *marry* you, by God!"

"Now, see here—"

"It *is* a fine plantation, isn't it, captain? It should make a lot of money some day—for somebody. Now that you've had a look at it you think you'd like to own it, don't you, with the mistress of the place thrown in extra?"

He blazed.

"I'm not after your damn' plantation, ma'am! I wouldn't live here even if the war was to end today, right now! What's more, it's probably plastered all over with mortgages, up to the chin!"

"It is that, yes."

There was a pause, and it was as though they were both panting. Then she looked right at him and said:

"And so you think that what happened last night gives you a right to annex me—make an honest woman of me, eh? La, captain, you didn't really think, did you, that you're the first man I ever slept with?"

She had meant it to hurt, and it did. He sat stunned, and he only stumbled to his feet when he saw that she had done so. She was laughing now, a cracked laugh, high. She put a wrist to her mouth, her head back, and she made for her bedroom door, which she closed after her—and Ezra could hear a latch thrown.

He went to that door, and listened a little. The sound that he heard was not the sound of laughter. It was sobs.

He waited a long while, doing nothing, but she did not reappear, and at last he got his hat and started to walk in the direction of Basseterre.

Chapter

19

He had been walking for a long while, most of the morning—in a fashion not aimless for assuredly not direct or rushed either —when he came to a stop, he didn't know why. He looked around.

Ezra Bond, as Lady Helen Ashley had surmised, was no newcomer to the delights of the flesh, but never before had he known anything that remotely resembled the previous night. It had been a different experience entirely from any he knew. It must prove to mark the beginning of a new life, a veritable Garden of Eden, not to be accepted lightly. He had no thought of turning aside at this point, but his rejection by the lady called for a whole new line of action. He had something to get. This needed pondering, and he had been paying little mind to his surroundings as he wandered in the direction of Basseterre.

What had halted him now?

He stood, vexed, scowling.

There were no roads, only lanes that drifted nowhere—what the British themselves called "drift lanes"—and an occasional cart track. Ezra found himself standing in a pasture, a tilted field; he faced the sea and, below him, the capital town of Basseterre. There was nothing notable about that. Ezra never before had been in Bassetere, but he had seen and visited many a town like it—a sun-baked huddle of white houses, a church steeple, a square two-storied government house. This in itself would not have tugged at his attention, yanking him back to earth.

He looked beyond the town, and he saw the frigate *Thisbe*.

The town was little, the frigate was big. Though she was more than a mile out, she loomed enormous with her bluff bows, her heavy spars and tall sticks, her fat, clumsy tumbledown. She might have been slow, and assuredly she was not graceful, but she was incalculably strong. Anything she caught she could smash.

She rode high in the water, so that the top of her copper sheathing showed, like a badly placed garter. Above this was a broad stripe of yellow, a gay yellow, the color of lemons, and the rest of the sides was painted a very dark blue, almost black, excepting that there was another broad lemon-yellow band to mark each of the gun decks. The gunports, checkering these bands, were rimmed blue-black. The masts and most of the upper works were painted mustard-yellow, but a band of scarlet edged with gold ran around the forecastle and continued down the beak to the figurehead, a polychromatic rampageous lion, while the stern-works were brave with glazed windows, a walk, a balcony, and elaborate carvings of lions, cherubs, drums, cornucopias, wreaths, stalactites, whatnot, fairly aflame in the light of high noon. Skippers of frigates and of ships of the line in the British Navy, Ezra had heard, were permitted to paint, gild, and otherwise decorate their vessels to suit their personal taste. This one, he reckoned, must be a man of much imagination, not to say flamboyance.

That was a bird of ill omen, that frigate. She spread only jibs and a foretopgallant, just enough canvas to keep aweigh. Why? If she wasn't going anywhere she would stand out to sea. It was not likely that she was there to take on wood and water, for in that case the stretch between ship and shore would be speckled with barges, plying back and forth like busy tropical ants. It was much more likely that she was in search of deserters, which boded no good for Ezra Bond, who did not carry papers and who was in truth an enemy.

From what he knew about the press methods of the British Navy—admittedly it was not much—Ezra believed that night-time would be the logical time for gangs to operate in cities, their natural habitat. They would not have to range inland. Your mariner never went far from the sea, *his* natural habitat: and in-deed, so outlandish was the lingo in which he expressed himself that he would have needed an interpreter at all times if he was to venture more than a few miles from the waterfront. The pressers, surely, knew that. They would raid an ordinary or a grog shop just before closing time, when the customers were drunk. Later they might sweep down on a brothel or two, or on some small inn, or they might pick a few recumbent figures from out of the street itself.

Basseterre posed a different problem. So far from being a city, it was not even a big town. It had a vast hinterland, the inhabi-tants of which would be acquainted with the curious way in which seamen expressed themselves; and those inhabitants, too, might be expected to sympathize with deserters. If I was put in charge of a press gang, which God forbid, Ezra thought to him-self, what would I do—here? He concluded that he would go ashore early in the day and scour the surrounding countryside, poking especially into all manner of buildings, even slave quar-ters, where fugitives might be hidden, but ignoring the cane fields themselves as being too widespread. Toward sunset, he thought, he would return to Basseterre itself and go through that town with a fine-tooth comb. Then he'd call it a day.

He looked around. He had met nobody in his walk from the Ashley mansion, though he must have been seen from a distance by many slaves and perhaps certain overseers and planters. He didn't know. The truth was, he had been absorbed in his thoughts of the woman of the night before, and had been unaware of much that might have taken place around him. Except for that sixth sense or whatever it was that had warned him a moment ago, and had brought him to a full stop right where he now stood, he might have walked into the capital in this dazed condition—and into the arms of a press gang.

A twinge of panic touched him, but it was swiftly suppressed. For an instant he did think of hastening back to Lady Helen Ashley, but this thought too he suppressed. She was upset, and there was no telling what she might do—or refuse to do. Ezra didn't know much about women, but he knew enough to let them alone when they were bawling.

After a long thought he did the simplest and he believed the most sensible thing. He went to the nearest cane field—you were never far from sugar cane on that island—and having made sure that he was not watched, entered it. He walked or squirmed his way for about fifty feet, and then sat down on the soft dry earth to wait for the sun to set. It was uncomfortable, but it was safe. The pressers would not even dream of searching all the cane fields near Basseterre. They'd need an army for that.

He had plenty of time, then, to think about Helen Ashley. He had no need to plot his own future course with her. He would come back, time after time, until he won her. He just wouldn't take No for an answer.

After the first shock, he had fairly well got over the revulsion he felt when she threw her past into his face. For one thing, he did not entirely believe her. Oh, she certainly knew how it was done, and she might have flirted a little too far with one or two men before this, which Ezra supposed was no more than to be looked for in a woman of the English aristocracy, but he was sure that there never had been the horde she hinted at. She was no slut. Why had she said that she was, then?

Or—had she?

Things had happened mighty fast. This he was not used to. Back to home, when you sparked a woman you took your time about it—years maybe. Yet Ezra did not think that they had overstrained themselves. It had all come about most naturally. The magic of those hours in the saddle, when everything between them twinkled with pure joy, had been the equivalent of many months of more gradual courting. All barriers had fallen away. What followed in bed was no more than a climax, as Ezra saw it, and conceivably even an anticlimax. Not that he was likely to *forget* what had happened in bed.

He could not have explained it to any third person, male or female, old or young, but he was tarnation sure of his own feelings and he meant to keep after her until he got her.

The long walk, the sun, and the wait in the cane field left him a mite stiff, and his legs pained a little, but otherwise he was feeling fit as he made his way down to Basseterre. He noted that the *Thisbe* was no farther away, nor yet any nearer: she seemed not to have moved at all. She would not stay so close to shore when night fell unless she was expecting a boat back. It stood to reason.

Folks in the West Indies go to bed early. Had he waited a little longer he would have found a slumbering capital. As it was, few things stirred in the sleepy streets and he slipped in.

There would be no shore parties from the frigate. Had the skipper been that foolish, every man-jack of them would have scampered away. The best Ezra could hope to find was some small rum shop or ordinary that catered to the fisherman trade, where he would perhaps make a deal with the owner of a small boat.

Still wary, despite the seeming somnolence of Basseterre, he half-circled the town before he entered it. There were few lights and almost no sounds at all—no music, no voices. Ezra could even hear the love-tapping of wavelets against the sides of fishing craft anchored off the beach. Yet for all this, there must have been many persons in the town. Ezra could almost *feel* them breathing, snoring, behind their battered jalousies.

He avoided the main street and went by back alleys to the waterfront. This consisted of a long, ramshackle ropewalk and a dozen small houses or shops, equally dim. It might have been a deserted village, blear in the moonlight, save for one building— a lighted groggery.

There could be no doubt of its identity. A sign hung before it, and clear on the face of the sign was the likeness of a jack of ale. Otherwise the place might have been taken for a fishmonger's or a chandler's. No roisterers were there. No songs rose from it. There was only the eerie creak of the sign as it swung in a weak sea breeze.

Ezra sidled into the shadow of a clump of palmetto, from where he could look through the open front door. Motionless, he stared for some time.

There was only one man in the place, a hulking dark fellow whose blue apron proclaimed him to be the proprietor. He was leaning on the counter and gazing with no expression at the opposite wall. He did not appear to be waiting for anybody; rather, he looked as though he might be thinking of closing shop.

Ezra drew a deep breath. He crossed the intervening space and went through the doorway.

The big man's eye brightened. He liked the look of Ezra's coat.

Ezra wasted no time. He ordered ale and a piece of bread and cheese. A stranger in a small town like this would draw attention at any time, and the sooner he got out the better.

"I want to go over to Statia."

The man did not seem astonished.

"Cost you something," he warned, still eyeing Ezra's coat.

"How much?"

"Well, two pounds six is the usual."

"That's too much," Ezra said briskly. It *was* too much, yet he would gladly have paid it if he had not feared that such readiness would in itself give rise to suspicion.

The proprietor shrugged. He waddled to the door.

"You can argue that out with Ellison. He's your man, and it's what he usually gets for the run. I'll fetch him. He lives right next door."

He went out into the street, and Ezra was left alone.

Ezra did not like it. It smelled wrong. He got up and went to the door and opened this a crack. The street was deserted. The proprietor could hardly have gone more than a few yards.

Ezra went back to his cheese and ale, but he still didn't like the situation.

He rose suddenly, leaving the food unfinished, though he was still hungry. He clapped on his hat and started for the street door once again.

This time the street was not deserted. Coming down it, walking well apart, were four large thick-thewed mariners, men with tattooing on the backs of their hands. They carried cudgels.

They must indeed have been right next door. They must have been waiting for just such a summons.

Joseph had been sold into servitude for the sake of his coat of many colors, was Ezra's thought as he swung back into the ordinary, but it'll happen to me for one of apricot and silver.

He did not pause. There must be a jakes in the rear of this establishment . . . Yes, here was a door, behind the counter. He sped through it.

It was unexpectedly dark out there, darker even than the street. He found himself between two stone walls, in a sort of narrow alley, and he reckoned that there must be a roof of boards or vines to account for the darkness. He ran with one arm stretched before him, the other brushing the wall on his right. He had gone only about forty feet when he came to the jakes, a single-seater, unoccupied now. There was no way to get past it. Was this a cul-de-sac?

He ran back toward the ordinary, this time brushing the opposite wall, and about halfway there he found a door. He flung this open—to find himself face to face with yet another British Navy presser. They knew their business, those boys.

"All right, matey, let's have a peek at your identification."

Ezra kicked him in the belly, hoping to get past him that way, but the man emitting a loud "*oof!*" only was slammed against some manner of trellis, which squeaked but did not give way.

Ezra ran back to the ordinary. He hoped to burst through it and reach the comparative safety of the street before the main body of pressers knew what was going on. But they must have heard him coming. They had their cudgels raised. He never had a chance to run the gantlet or to retreat. He simply had to take it. They started hitting immediately.

It did not last long. Ezra held his arms over his head, but he lost all feeling in them from the first blows, and he found himself on his knees.

He could see nothing, and there was a harsh roaring in his ears. He might have toppled to the floor. He was not sure. He did feel somebody take his purse, as he might have expected, and he felt somebody peeling his coat off. He even felt them pick him up, arms and legs, starting toward the street. And that was all he knew, that night.

Chapter

20

In the morning he would be flogged. It was not enough that they beat him in private, giving him no chance to defend himself, to explain himself; now they must beat him more formally, and of course legally, in public, making him the central figure in a grisly, gory nautical circus, the excuse for yet one more Roman holiday.

There had been no pretense of a trial or hearing. Still only half-conscious, Ezra had been hauled before a sleepy, surly midshipman, a lad in his teens who had sour eyes and a discontented mouth that might have been filled with lime juice instead of spit.

"Deserter, eh? Ought to hang you, but we're short-handed. All right, two dozen of the best, day after tomorrow at the gangway."

"Just a minute," put in Ezra. "Don't I have the right to see the captain in person?"

The midshipman had stared at him in silence for a while, miffed, withdrawn, acting almost as though he had been threatened with assault. The pressers with their cudgels had moved a little closer.

"You have, in theory, if you insist upon it," the midshipman said at last. "But I wouldn't advise you to do that. The captain is impatient with things like this. He'd be so annoyed that he would give you *four* dozen."

"But what if I can prove that I've never even been in the British Navy?"

"Can you?"

"Can *you* prove that I *have?*"

"We don't need to. You're a seaman, you're a mariner, you know your way around on a vessel like this. Look here, my man: you don't deny that?"

"No, but—"

"And you're found skulking in one of His Majesty's colonies, with no identification—and no coat."

"They took my coat!"

"Did you, corporal?"

"No, sir."

"Therefore you are a deserter from the Royal Navy. That's all the proof we need. I have my orders."

"But if I could only summon some friends here on St. Kitts—"

"That you might be permitted to do if we happen to come back here next year or the year after. Right now we're making full sail for Jamaica, where we're overdue. After that—Well, we were only waiting for these fellows to come back tonight. And I must say," he added, addressing the pressers, "that you didn't bring much."

"Sorry, sir," one of them muttered.

The ship, truly, was in motion. It shivered. It began to roll, ever so slightly, and its timbers creaked, a sound, however, that was all but swamped by the multitude of other small and large sounds—the patter of feet on deck, shouts, whistles, the whoom of canvas followed by a rattle of reef points. Battered though he was, and groggy, Ezra Bond was impressed by all this. He had never before been on a vessel as large as the *Thisbe,* and it sounded to him as though there were hundreds of men up there.

"Put him in the bilboes," said the midshipman.

The bilboes turned out to be an iron rail two or three inches above the main deck, to which it was fastened by small clamps, a rail that encircled the mainmast. To it were hooked a dozen or more sets of irons, wrist and ankle alike, though only the ankle irons were fastened to Ezra Bond, who thus was permitted either to sit or to stand—or he could kneel, for that matter—and who was provided with a pail. Thereafter, for a long while, he was, it would seem, forgotten, or at least ignored.

The ship was never still. Besides the steady creak of timbers there were calls from the crosstrees to the quarterdeck and back again, from the forecastle lookout to the quarterdeck and back again, orders to the helmsman, while a bosun's mate at any given time might be seen and heard as he made his rounds, poking and peering into the spaces between the guns, evidently in search of possible gamblers or drinkers. The bosun's mate never glanced at Ezra. Nobody glanced at Ezra. Whether this was because of a rule against fraternizing or even recognizing the existence of a prisoner or whether it was because the sight of a stranger in the bilboes was so common as to cause no comment, he was never to learn.

The night went on and on. Ezra felt himself an exceedingly small part of an extremely large organization, a part that might have been overlooked. His bruises and cuts throbbed, which was bad enough, and when the blood on them dried and he had nothing with which to wash it off—the pail was not for drinking purposes—they began to itch, which was worse. He slept only fitfully.

A little before eight bells bosun's mates and ship's corporals began to appear from everywhere, looming out of the predawn darkness like gigantic ghosts, each with a rope club three inches thick swinging from his wrist. A few went aft to politely summon the officers of the morning watch, but most of them posted themselves by the fore and main hatchways and set up an earsplitting blast of their whistles. Then they began to yell. "All hands! All hands! Hey, all you down there! Show a leg!"

The seamen came tumbling topside, all yawns and gum-eyedness, their hammocks in their arms. They folded the hammocks and tucked them into the nettings. This they did briskly, perforce, for they were conscious of the presence of the ship's peace-keepers just behind them and knew that any lagging, any fumbling, would mean a vicious slap across the rump. The bosun's mates and ship's corporals kept telling them that, blasphemously.

This was a Sunday, which was the reason why Ezra's "punishment" would be put off for twenty-four hours, an added torture, "No lashing on the Lord's Day" apparently being a motto of that skipper with a fondness for bright paint. Hence the men were not obliged to sand and swab the deck, which already, in Ezra's practiced eyes, was as clean as a deck could possibly be. They only dry-holystoned and then swept it. However, there was a great deal of cleaning going on elsewhere. The cooks scoured and polished their pots. The gun crews traversed their guns in order to clean the plank covered by the carriages and remove any mess that might have been put there by careless sweeping. The coppers examined their casks, the armorers their weapons. Suddenly all this was stopped, and the corporals and bosun's mates herded the men—*herded* them indeed, like so many sheep—below for breakfast. One of the corporals came up soon afterward with a wooden dish of some sticky material, which he handed to Ezra. He was the first person who had paid any heed to Ezra, and he did not loiter but directly went below again.

So this was Sunday morning breakfast in the British navy—burgo, which was oatmeal steeped in foul ship's water. It was a nauseous mess. Ezra ate it—he had to use his fingers since he had been given no spoon—because he was hungry; but he kept his eyes closed as he did so, and he would have been happy to close his nose as well. Afterward he had a hard time keeping it down.

When the hands came swarming topside again it was, once more, like sheep, like cattle. The drivers never hesitated to use their rope clubs—"starters" they were called, as Ezra was to learn—on an arm, a leg, a bum, even a head. Once a seaman near

Ezra backed into a midshipman and stepped on one of his glittering boots. It was the sheerest of accidents, and a trifle in any event, but the midshipman—he was not the same one who had sentenced Ezra but he might have been—was furious. "Start that man!" he cried to the nearest bosun's mate, who promptly began to belabor the seaman with his club. The poor wretch put his arms above his head and fell to his knees, but he did not cry out. "All right," the midshipman said, after perhaps six or seven slashing blows had been delivered; and the bosun's mate desisted. The seaman, whimpering a little, trotted off for a lower deck where he might find something with which to clean himself in time for inspection. Nobody but Ezra and the principals had even noticed this incident. Some of the blood had splashed Ezra's sleeve.

"I don't think I'm going to enjoy this voyage," he said to himself.

After that there was a great deal of fussing. Men shaved themselves and one another, and inspected their shirts and—those who had them—their shoes. The old-timers were the only ones with anything that might suggest a uniform, namely queues or pigtails, which now they retarred and reshaped, helping one another.

Then the captain appeared, accompanied by a tall man who must have been the first lieutenant. Ezra took a good long look at the captain, and after he had done so he elected against his previous plan of throwing himself on this man's mercy. For the captain had no mercy in him: this was clear to see. The midshipman had been right. Here was the sort of tyrant who would have doubled the sentence out of pure willfulness. He looked as if he had no blood in him, only acid. His head was a death's head, his eyes the sockets of a skull. Nothing good could come out of such a creature.

Now and then he made some remarks to the first lieutenant, but he spoke to nobody else, nor did he nod, as he walked past the serried men. Whether or not he approved of what he saw it was impossible to tell. He was a man to be avoided.

The captain wore white gloves, and every now and then he would touch some article with the tip of a finger and then scrutinize that fingertip.

Inspection over, it was time for divine services on the quarter-deck, and once again the men were driven, the bosun's mates cursing them. Ezra Bond was not invited to attend divine services, nor was he near enough to hear the chaplain's sermon. Instead he read from his own Book, about the only thing that they had left him, for even his hat was gone.

The absence of that hat threatened to be serious as the day wore on, for even here in the trade wind the sun was hot, and Ezra, because of the clamps that held the bilboes in place, could not keep shifting his seat or his stance in order to stay in the shade of the mast. When the surgeon came to examine him he complained about this.

Though it was not yet noon the surgeon was drunk. His eyes were glassy. He hiccupped. He was not interested in Ezra's complaint and did not even wash Ezra's arm and head wounds. All he wished to do—and he made no bones about it—was test Ezra's heart to see whether he was strong enough to take twenty-four well-laid-on lashes first thing the next morning.

"You'll do," he decided.

"Doctor, this sun is cooking my brains out."

"You can't have any, or you wouldn't have deserted."

"Do you want to have a gibbering idiot on your hands?"

"Might be happier for you that way. I'll send you my assistant."

The assistant was a glad surprise, being decent. He was a young man, fresh out, and appalled by the misery he saw around him. He treated Ezra's cuts and bruises with solicitous care, and he fetched a hat made of screw-pine fronds from the dispensary. More than this he could not do, he explained. He was not allowed to talk to prisoners except in the line of treatment. He went away.

Dinner was at four bells of the afternoon watch. The afternoon was a long one. The night, Ezra knew, would be even longer. It was. Only one episode enlivened it,

Ezra slept off and on, never for long, but he was sleeping when he heard the hiss. As far as he could make out, afterward, it must have been close to midnight.

The hiss came from near at hand, at his very elbow. There was a moon, but this side of the mast was enshadowed, and Ezra could barely make out the small, wizened, bony man who crouched by his side. He looked like something out of a badly translated Bavarian fairy story, a gnome lately emerged from a subterranean grotto. He thrust something leathern into Ezra's hands.

"Here, mate. Some of us below, we know what it's going to be like, so we chipped in our rations. Not much, but it might help. But for Gawd's sake, don't let them see you drinking it."

Ezra felt a catch at his throat. He had heard of how much the tiny rum ration meant to seamen of the Royal Navy. They were giving him what they treasured most in this world, in the hope that it might make his ordeal a little easier—him, a man they didn't even know. He was touched.

"Now, see here, I can't take—"

"Sh-sh! Good luck, mate."

He was gone, scuttling across the waist like a spider. From the aft end of that waist a large and ominous figure, a bosun's mate, stepped out from under a ladder that led to the poop. He acted like a man who might have heard something. Actually, his head was cocked, as though he listened. The gnome, who had frozen at sight of him, soundlessly nipped into the shadows between two guns.

The bosun's mate approached that spot, swinging his club.

Ezra called suddenly, in a loud voice: "Say, don't I even get a drink of water? They want to lash a *corpse*, do they?"

The bosun's mate looked over at him. He put his arms akimbo.

Slowly, as if trying to make up his mind what to do, he walked across to the bilboes. In that moment, Ezra saw that the gnome had taken advantage of this trick to slip out of the space between the guns and disappear without a sound down the main hatch.

The bosun's mate studied Ezra.

"I'll get you a drink," he said at last. "It ain't my job, but I'll do it."

Ezra then had to drink some of the water he brought, and it was the worst he had ever tasted. But the bosun's mate never did see the jack of rum, which Ezra had hidden in his shirt. From the sniff of it, Ezra deduced that it was straight rum too, not the watered concoction they called grog. There was perhaps a pint of it. At first Ezra fully intended to leave it behind him, untouched; but with the coming of dawn his courage failed him and he began to sip the stuff. After the morning watch had been piped up and the deck sanded and swabbed and holystoned and swept, this sipping was difficult to do unseen; and very early he swallowed too much of the stuff, and coughed, and spit it up, and then he was sick, vomiting into the pail.

Nobody offered him breakfast, and he wouldn't have touched it if anybody had.

Afterward the "All hands" was piped again, and the whole crew began to assemble at the gangway.

Two burly bosun's mates lolled over to Ezra.

"All right, Yankee. Now let's see how much you can take."

Chapter

21

There are many kinds of fear, even many kinds of *physical* fear, and when Ezra Bond was led to the place of punishment he was gripped by a most unexpected fear, one for which he did not even know the name. A playactor would have called it stage fright.

Every man on the ship must have been there, looking, looking. You could not see an empty space. Not only were they lining the gunnels and standing on the longboat and the various gigs and sitting astride the cannons, they were also in the rigging, the larboard and starboard ratlines being black with them.

The officers—many more of them than Ezra had thought to exist—were on the poop, each wearing sword, sash, and a hat that was decorated with gold braid. The captain himself, gaudiest of all, was in the middle of them, but he took no part in the proceedings and showed no expression of any sort at any time. The tall first lieutenant gave the commands in the name of the captain. He did it as though he had done it many times before.

Behind these personages there was drawn up a whole company of polished, pipeclayed marines, very stiff at attention, their bayonets glinting in the sun.

The midshipmen and civilians and warrant officers were in

the waist just under the break of the poop, among them the assistant surgeon, already green of face with the dread of what he was forced by regulations to watch, his lips trembling, his temples agleam with sweat.

At the forward end of the waist were ranged the petty officers— bosun and bosun's mates, armorers, master-at-arms, master gunner, the cooper, and the rest.

These were the nearest to Ezra, but it was not the presence of them that so disconcerted him. It was rather the great anonymous crowd of common sailors above and beyond them, the beaten, the driven, who stared at Ezra stony-faced. There was no note of the festive in that crowd. This wasn't a Roman holiday atmosphere after all. A few of the men might have been pleased to get out of the labor they would customarily be put to at this hour, but most of them, it would seem, just did not care. They had been brutalized beyond repatchment. They would never be human again.

Yet somewhere in that vast mass of men were five or six or more who last night had contributed their precious tots of rum to a prisoner they did not know, in the hope that it would make his beating a little less terrible to endure. Kind men!

Before the officers Ezra could feel only a slow deep rage. Before the men he was amazed to find himself feeling humble.

The first lieutenant said, tonelessly: "Strip him."

They did not go that far, for which Ezra was grateful, even though there were no women present. They took off only his shirt. He did not even see the man behind him who did this, though whoever he was, he was gentle and the shirt was not torn.

The first lieutenant made a slight bow in the direction of the captain, and then whipped off his hat and began to read from an opened, leather-bound book. Everybody else who had a hat took it off, even the captain himself, that expressionless god, that pharaoh. The marines ported arms. It was quite a display.

As near as Ezra could understand it, the lieutenant was reading that particular section of the Articles of War that pertained to desertion. Nobody really listened. The removal of hats assumedly was out of respect for King George, or something.

Ezra wished that they would get on with it. He hoped that he was making a decent appearance, even though he had to stand there half-naked.

The lieutenant finished reading and put on his hat, and all the other hats went back on. The marines grounded arms.

"Seize him up," said the lieutenant.

Two men took Ezra from behind. He made no resistance when they walked him to the gratings, and the men, if firm, were not unnecessarily rough. The gratings were two wooden grills that in better circumstances would serve as hatch covers. One was on the deck, flat, and the other was upright and made fast to the poop railings. Ezra stood on the one, facing the other, while the unseen men expertly and silently spread-eagled his limbs and made fast with twine his wrists and ankles, so that he must stay in that position. Then the men stepped back. He never saw them.

"Seized up, sir."

He never saw the brute who lashed him either, or the cat-o'-nine-tails itself. He did hear a steadying shuffle of feet behind him and a tentative swish. He caught up his breath.

"Do your duty," said the lieutenant.

Ezra was slammed against the grating so hard that it might have blackened his eyes or smashed his nose. It was not at all like being beaten with, say, a horsewhip. It was more like being hit, and hit hard, by a whole set of clubs. At first it did not so much hurt him as stun him. It knocked the breath out of him.

Then came another . . . and another . . .

Ezra's chest ached abominably. His throat was flooded with something—blood?—and he truly feared that he might be about to choke to death.

Another . . . and another . . . and another . . .

The world went wild, swaying. His back flamed all the way

123

to the tips of his fingers, all the way to the tips of his toes. He hoped above all that he was not screaming. He couldn't know. He wished that he could breathe again. He would surely die, suffocated.

Another . . . and another . . .

Sometimes it burned from the right shoulder to the left buttock, sometimes from the left shoulder to the right buttock. Were there two men back there, with two whips, and did they cross-strike? He still could not catch up his breath. Panic filled him. He wanted to cry out that he was being choked to death.

Another . . . and another . . .

He could no longer count and did not know when the flogging was finished, but he was conscious enough to be aware of it when they cut him down. He still did not believe that he was breathing, and he marveled that he was alive, if he was. He thought that his eyes were open—they stung hideously—yet he could not see anything.

He could even smell the surgeon's breath and feel the tap of the stethoscope against his chest.

"He'll live," he heard the surgeon say. "Take him down to the dispensary."

But Ezra could not remember them carrying him away.

Chapter

22

Except that it was overcrowded, like every other part of the frigate, and that it smelled of sulphur and vinegar, the sick bay was surely one of the least obnoxious parts of the *Thisbe*.

The vinegar and sulphur were used for fumigation purposes, and from time to time in clear weather were burned elsewhere on the ship as well; but they were kept smoldering all day and all night in the sick bay, giving off an acrid, choky odor, and plenty of eye-stinging smoke as well. For the first few days Ezra was conscious of it only fitfully, and there were moments when he really did believe that he had died and was in Hell, as the air suggested. But after all, he was a seaman and used to stinks.

There was another pungent unpleasant odor during those first few days, and Ezra got the worst of this, since it emanated from him. His impression while under the lash that something was being smashed inside him—he had supposed that that was blood in his throat—was not entirely without warrant. The small steel balls that tipped the ends of the cat had bitten savagely into the flesh between his shoulders, battering his ribs, but certain of them had slashed somewhat lower. His kidneys on either side, organs of which he had never before been aware, must have been badly bruised. At any rate, for several days as he lay on his belly in the sick bay, and without wanting to or meaning to, he urinated almost continuously. It was only a dribble, but it was a steady dribble. How could anything be more humiliating than to be changed like a baby again and again? And it did not make him popular with the loblollies.

These loblolly boys, as they were called, were more likely to be old men, or at least physically weak men, men unfit for the rough labor of the decks, the guns, the tops. They were, most of them, waisters, and as such looked down upon as the lowest of the low—excepting always the marines, who were hated by everybody. Yet Ezra found them a comforting crew, less given to grumbling than most, and sometimes even exhibiting a mite of those rarities in the Royal Navy—kindness and understanding. The loblolly boys were not trained nurses. They were only men lent by the deck to the sick bay or dispensary at the request of the surgeon, under whom they worked. They were, naturally, the ones that the deck could easiest afford. Their principal duties were keeping the place clean, feeding the fumigation braziers, and bringing in the food. They were denied a rum ration, but they were permitted to sleep in the sick bay when there was room for them, and without too much trouble they could feed themselves from the trays they carried.

Both the food and the sleeping accommodations in the sick bay on the *Thisbe* were superior. There were horsehair mattresses. There were even linen sheets, something that Ezra had not had as captain of the *Forbearance*. As for the food, basically it was the same as the hands got, but there were extras, tidbits. Whenever any fresh fruits or vegetables were brought aboard, whether from bumboats or by means of a shore party, or when any fish were caught over the side, these went first to the officers' mess; but almost invariably that mess sent a sizable portion of them to the sick bay, along with, likely as not, a few bottles of wine. So even though the loblollies had to give up their beloved tots they were pleased with their posts, and they worked hard.

For the saturnine, ungiving, laconic surgeon himself Ezra had some respect. Here was a man who would never be ingratiating, but he knew his job. He was disagreeable, but he was thorough. For his young assistant, who was aghast to find himself in such a place, Ezra could feel only pity.

He saw little of the work that these two did. The actual passing out of pills, the treatment of minor sores and of ulcers—the biggest complaint of all, ulcers—was done on deck. The patients in the sick bay came and went, but there were about twenty of them when Ezra was there, and all, without exception, were suffering from scurvy. They were a sunken-eyed, choppy-breathed, aching, moaning, dejected lot, scarcely good company. The surgeon saw to it that each one ate two raw potatoes a day. He stood there and watched them do it. Ezra did not have to do that.

Ezra was told that the malady most widespread aboard the *Thisbe* was jail fever, that unaccountable but pernicious ailment of the underworld, the reason being that so much of the Royal Navy "recruiting" was done in noisome prisons, but that the surgeon would not admit these patients to the sick bay, it being his belief that sunlight and hard work were the best cures.

It was disconcerting—the third day in sick bay, when the pain had subsided a little, allowing him at least to turn over—to discover that his head had been shaved. This threw him into a rage so hot that he had to sink back on the bunk, gasping at the pain. He berated the assistant surgeon the next time he saw him.

"Are you a damn' Iroquois, that you want to scalp me?"

"I'm sorry, but—"

"Taking advantage of a man when he didn't know what was happening!"

"But it's regulations, really. Conscious or unconscious, it has to be done. And we've been boiling your clothes too."

"How thoughtful of you."

"You'll get them back when you're discharged from here."

They did issue nightcaps to the patients, to Ezra's amazement.

In this southern climate that seemed unnecessary, but Ezra did not refuse to accept his. After all, he had never before been bald, and if he was to escape he had to think of his health.

The sick bay was located in the forecastle, on the starboard side, and despite the braziers the air, thanks to a wind funnel the assistant surgeon had rigged from the deck above, was comparatively fresh. There were no regular visting hours, but anybody working nearby who had a messmate among the scurvy victims might pop in, furtively, for a gam. The surgeon forbade this, but they didn't do it while he was there: the surgeon spent most of his time drinking anyway, in the civilian officers' mess. The assistant surgeon knew that he was supposed to forbid it, but he had not the heart to do so.

As a result, even before he became an active working member of the crew of the *Thisbe*, Ezra Bond out of hearsay began to learn a lot about that vessel. He kept his mouth shut and his ears open. The atmosphere in the sick bay was relaxed, not strained, as it would have been outside.

One thing that Ezra did learn, and he was startled to hear it, was that he himself already was something of a hero belowdecks. This was because of the way he had taken his flogging. Those men who had stared so impassively at him from the gunnels and from the standing rigging had made bets, many of them, as to how soon he would start to scream. This, Ezra gathered, was normal procedure. British tars would bet on anything. They did not bet money—there was precious little of that aboard the *Thisbe*, for pay habitually was withheld out of fear that it would be used to bribe a way to freedom—but smaller items that were, however, at least as precious. They would bet, for example, a pair of stockings, or a kerchief, or a pinch of tobacco; but their favored currency, and the one that all of the others were based on, was their rations of rum for so-and-so-many days or even weeks.

In the case of the latest lashing all of these bets had to be called off, so at least nobody lost. It was extraordinary. There were those who averred that they had *heard* of men so tough that they could take two dozen without screaming, but they never had actually *met* such a man.

"If I didn't scream it was only because I couldn't," Ezra said to himself, but not out loud.

He was not displeased. Ordinarily he would not be proud of prestige among such riffraff, and such jail-sweepings, but prestige might come in handy when he made arrangements for his escape.

For he had no thought but to get out of this floating hell as soon as ever he was able to do so. His mind was occupied with this problem when on the eighth day after the flogging he stepped out of the sick bay, wobbling a bit as he did so, in order to take his place on deck.

Chapter

23

The men among whom he was thrown called him "Yank" or "Yankee," as did the petty officers who ordered him around, but none of them was interested in his wail about unjust impressment. Most had themselves been impressed, and they took the system for granted. They cursed their luck; but that's just what they considered it—luck.

"But you yourself call me 'Yankee.' You admit it."

"Why not? That's just like saying that you come from Cornwall or Cumberland or something."

"Not a bit. There's three thousand miles of ocean between them."

"Take more ocean than that to wash the English blood out of you. Once an Englishman always an Englishman. Everybody knows that."

"I'm not English! I'm American!"

"Well, it's the same thing, now ain't it?"

The first thing that he must do, Ezra decided, was learn where they were and whither they were bound.

This proved to be difficult. The officers would know, but it was not for the likes of him to be questioning officers, howsoever respectfully. Ezra had been assigned to a mess, and he went to work early on his five messmates, but not one of them had the faintest idea where the *Thisbe* was, except that it was in a warm place, for which they were grateful. As he widened his inquiries he learned that these companions were not different from the others in this ignorance. Nobody he asked knew even which way the frigate was heading, and nobody seemed to care. This was their home, this was their life, this vessel. Many must have been secretly plotting to desert; but perhaps "plotting" was too definite a word; perhaps they only hoped for a chance to jump ship, no matter where the ship was. Such men, of course, would not confess their hopes, for the gun decks were stippled with informers who surreptitiously reported to the bosun or to the master-at-arms, and who were known—Ezra never did learn why—as white mice.

He met too with many who had frankly given up and were resigned to spending the rest of their lives aboard this or some other British vessel of war. Some of these had not set foot on land for three years or more.

Anyway he got nowhere with his inquiry.

The sun told him that the frigate was headed in a generally western direction, and this was some comfort. At the same time, she was in miserable condition—the rigging rotten, the sails over-patched, the sticks unsteady, the hold awash with bilge in which dead rats and garbage floated—and it was logical to conclude that she should soon be going back to English for a much-needed overhaul. There were no facilities for such an overhaul in the West Indies, as Ezra knew. The midshipman had mentioned Jamaica, which lay west of St. Kitts, and had said something too about the frigate being overdue. It was at Jamaica, in the broad bay between Port Royal and Kingston, that merchant vessels from all over the British West Indies gathered a couple of times a year—so Ezra had been told—to meet up with a few war vessels that would escort them to England, frowning off the pesky French and Continental privateers. Was the *Thisbe* on such duty? It seemed probable.

Anything you turned your back to down on the orlop deck, where Ezra was hammocked, was rather more than likely to be stolen; the pandanus hat had disappeared early. However, he never had any occasion to go up on the quarterdeck. His work kept him in the waist, when he wasn't below, and it called, usually, for an averted head.

For Ezra was a waister now, and low even as that looked-down-upon class went. He was a "prayer-booker."

He did not mind. The humbler the position the better he liked it. But it made up one more example of the stupidity of the Royal Navy, to Ezra's way of thinking. They howled that they needed men so badly that they felt justified in getting men from jails or simply hitting them on the head and dragging them in. The material obtained in this fashion was admittedly low-grade; and it most assuredly was not professional. The great majority of the men who slept on the orlop, including all five of Ezra's messmates, had never been on any other vessel save the *Thisbe*. They knew nothing about seamanship, as they cared nothing.

So when the Navy nabbed a prize like Ezra Bond, a veteran mariner, brought up in the tradition, a skipper of his own vessel, who could do anything aboard any ship, even navigate, did they examine him to determine his talents, if any? No. Did they use him to their own best advantage? They did not. Instead they beat him so savagely that for more than a week he could not do any work at all, and even when he could work at last he was obliged to make several trips a day to the sick bay for treatment and from time to time the pain in his back was so severe and made him so dizzy that he had to stop work for a little while to recover—a condition that the petty officers understood, pampering him. And the Navy made that man a prayer-booker.

Every morning except Sunday, before breakfast, the day watch's first assignment was the cleaning of the main deck. Holystones for this purpose came in two widely differing sizes. Most of the work was done with large square holystones, on opposite sides of which rings were fastened. These were pulled back and forth by means of ropes reeved through the rings, two men to a holystone. The other kind, from their shape and size, were called prayer books. These were held in the hand and were used to get at out-of-the-way places, such as under bitts, under carronade slides, back of guns. It was nasty work, and the prayer-booker had to be down on his knees while the deck was awash with dirty water—and all this fourteen hours since his last meal. Ezra Bond did not complain.

On the fourth morning after he had joined the orlop-deck mess he trotted topside—the *Thisbe* was a "smart" vessel, which meant that everything had to be done on the double—with the consciousness that something was different. The usual squealing of timbers was very light, almost as if they were standing still, and when he got up on deck he could hear the frigate "speaking" at the bows, but that sound too was less than usual. Even in the darkness he could see that the main and fore courses and topsails had been struck and that the frigate was drifting along under only jibs and topgallants. This meant that they were approaching land —or at least that the skipper believed they were approaching land. Ezra could see no land ahead, and no lights, as he took up his prayer book and fell to his knees.

(It was the only prayer book he ever *had* held while on his knees, for he had been raised to believe that such articles should be classed with candles and censers and so forth as shamelessly Romish, an abomination.)

After breakfast they could see the land. It was none that Ezra Bond ever had seen before, and he asked an old-time seaman, one Al Spence.

"That's Port Royal, that is. I've been there many a time."

"That's in Jamaica, isn't it?"

"Aye."

So far, thought Ezra, so good.

133

Chapter

24

Ezra was not the only one who was thinking in terms of escape. Many a seaman's heart must have sunk and many an officer nodded in grim approval when, still ten or twelve miles from shore, the total complement of marines was put on duty and special parties of bosun's mates were set about checking all gunports.

There were thirty-odd marines, and customarily they kept to themselves, being berthed and messed apart from the seamen. They had their own officer, a lieutenant, and their own sergeant and corporal. They were subject to the same discipline as the sailors, but seldom was a marine punished, perhaps because they had little chance of wrongdoing, being a close-knit organization. With the daily routine they had little to do, standing as guards at the captain's cabin door and before the entrance to the magazine. They were ornamental, colorful, but not notably useful. To the crewmen it seemed that they spent most of their time brushing their scarlet tunics and their black felt hats or pipe-claying their precious crossbelts or polishing their cartouche boxes and their high black-leather boots. They were trim, they were immaculate at all times. "Don't do nothing to get dirty, so it's no wonder," was the disgusted verdict of the tarrybreeks.

Now the marines were posted along the gunnels, at every hatch-way, and in the waist, and undoubtedly when the hook was dropped there would be one stationed at the top of any ladder that was let over the side. They were very trig, very proper, and bright. Their muskets were loaded, their bayonets in place. And they meant business.

At the same time there was a stir among the white mice. It was not that the master-at-arms and the bosun had instructed their informers to display special vigilance; it was rather that the common tars with something on their consciences had anticipated such a command in their own way. The white mice were known. It was believed belowdecks that the best way to treat them was to work on them before they could squeal, giving them some notion of what they might expect if they *did* squeal; and indeed there was a great deal of suppressed scuffling and screeching down on the dark orlop deck all through that day as they neared and entered Kingston harbor, and afterward there were many black eyes and puffed lips to be seen, so that everybody would know who the white mice were—or were believed to be. It was an effective system. The officers undoubtedly knew what was happening, but they would not dare to go belowdecks where they were so cordially hated, and they pretended not to hear, not to see.

Any entrance into any port raised all sorts of hopes for release.

Ezra studied the situation, even while he worked his prayer book, and he decided that unless there was some dramatic change in it, unless there was some unexpected and unaccountable "break," he would not try to escape here in Port Royal. He was perfectly willing to risk his life in order to get free, and indeed he would in all sobriety rather be dead than be aboard the *Thisbe*; but he did seek something like an even chance; and emphatically he did not want to risk being caught on the way out and flogged again.

Others did not feel the same way, being perhaps overeager.

The *Thisbe* was five days at Port Royal, taking on routine supplies, but at no time was the vigilance of the marines, the officers, and the bosun and his mates relaxed by so much as a minute. The only crewmen ever allowed ashore were the members of the various press gangs, trusted petty officers who after combing Port Royal, Kingston, and Spanish Town, as well as the intervening countryside, came in with three miserable old men, each of them insensible whether from drink or from a beating, and each duly pronounced to be a deserter. They were all flogged. Meanwhile, three men, healthy hands, really did try to slip over the side. Each was caught in the act, and each, like Ezra, was warned that he might have been hanged and *would* have been hanged if the frigate was not so short-handed—and then was sentenced, as Ezra had been, to two dozen "of the best."

The *Thisbe* was not a "cat ship," Ezra was informed by the old-timers, all of whom had known much worse. There were vessels, he was told, on which every morning, except Sunday, you would be forced to watch at least one back-bloodying at the gangway, sometimes two or three. There was nothing to prevent the captain from ordering as many as he wished, and for any reason or for none. Many of them were much longer than his own comparatively brief slashing, he was told. A hundred was not rare. When such a sentence was carried out a fresh bosun's mate took over after every twenty strokes, to ensure strength and freshness. There were skippers who boasted that they had left-handed bosun's mates so that the back design could be criss-crossed, or ambidextrous ones, like the man who had laid it on Ezra. Early in these sessions the cat would be clobbered with blood and with shreds of flesh, which the bosun's mate would carefully wipe off after each stroke, so that the knobs would not stick together and perhaps somewhat soften the blow. Not only were there more strokes but these sessions were longer also because from time to time the victim would faint and the punishment would be stopped until he could be revived by dashing seawater over him, since it would be against the whole spirit of the thing to lash an unconscious man.

Nobody ever really survived one of those hundred-of-the-best bouts, Ezra was told. The poor beggar either died under it or died soon afterward from its effects, or if he did indeed survive he was no longer a real man but a toddling, gibbering idiot, as broken in mind as in body, good for nothing whatever.

No, the *Thisbe* skipper was relatively humane, they said, for all that he did look like someone who had recently risen from the grave.

Ezra listened to this with pursed lips, and he thanked his stars that the *Thisbe* was not a "cat ship," for those five days in Kingston harbor so sickened him that he feared he couldn't take any more but would go stark raving mad. Watching it, he thought, was even worse than taking it; and he *had* to watch it, for they were given no option. There were times, as he listened to that fiendishly regular wet smack, when he feared that he might keel over in a faint, like any woman. He would stand rigid, his face expressionless. He did not think that any of the men enjoyed the spectacle—they seldom discussed flogging at the mess or at work —but it could be that most of them had passed a sort of callous point beyond which they could be shaken or shocked no further. As for Ezra, he was more horrified each time. He would grit his teeth and tell himself, inwardly, what he was going to do if he ever got back to civilization. He had hated the Royal Navy even before he fell into its clutches, but he hated it with a burning zeal now, and everything that it stood for.

If he ever got back . . . The chance seemed a remote one. The bay was filled with vessels of all sorts, with more coming every day, and there could be no doubt that the *Thisbe*, together with a couple of sloops of war already on hand, had been told off to act as the guardian of this pack, the shepherd, the chaperon.

The vessels were of all sorts, all sizes, and each was low in the water. They were charged, he reckoned, with coffee and cochineal, with salt and indigo and molasses, but most of all with sugar cane. Was some of Lady Helen Ashley's cane there? Had one of these merchantmen touched at St. Kitts?

On the fifth day a fourth hand tried to get off the ship, and was caught. This one, a second offender, they hanged. Was the captain getting panicky?

As was the custom, the execution was public as all get-out. The entire crew was mustered and made to face in the direction of the foremast yardarm, from which the wretch was "turned off." It didn't take long. Hundreds who lined the shore also witnessed this hanging, for the *Thisbe* was anchored only a few hundred feet out.

They left the body hanging there for several hours, turning languidly in the breeze. They would have left it for several *days*, esteeming it a deterrent, had not the buzzards found it and started vigorously to work on it, which was too much even for old Death's Head.

This deed was jeered and catcalled from the shore, where the onlookers disapproved of such summary justice, which was rather odd, inasmuch as the Port Royalists were scarcely a cow-hearted crowd: the place until a few years ago had been a notorious pirates' hangout. It could not have been this discouragement, however, that caused the *Thisbe* to spread sail and depart from the harbor that very afternoon; for the Royal Navy, whatever its faults, was not prone to back away before taunts. There must have been something else.

It was sundown by the time that Ezra was able to get Al Spence aside, for as captain of the foretop Al was a busy man that afternoon. By that time they were standing well out to sea, making a more or less easterly course—they had to tack almost dead against the prevailing winds—but keeping the south coast of Jamaica within sight.

"If you ask me, the Old Man's ascared of losing a big chunk of his crew and he wants to get to some place where there won't be any rum or any whores or—well, anything. Some place along the coast where we can wait for the rest of them to catch up with us. Negril Point I'd say, if you asked me. That's the very east end of the island, and they often use it to rendezvous there. Good anchorage."

"And why wouldn't some of the men try to desert there? Just because there aren't any women or any drinks?"

"Because of what there *is*. Swamps there. So thick you'd sink into it like molasses, and you'd drown. Poisonous snakes there too. And then the Maroons. The hills back of those swamps are just thick with Maroons. You know, they're escaped slaves. They go around stark naked, and they'd eat you as soon as look at you. Oh, no! there won't be anybody slipping over the side off Negril Point."

"That's what *you* think," said Ezra Bond; but he did not say it out loud.

Chapter

25

It was a dark shore, a low shore, and looked poisonous indeed, miasmic, treacherous. Ezra estimated the distance at about a mile and a half. He wished he had his glass.

How far the swampland stretched it was impossible to tell, for it was flat. Behind it rose hills that might have been another part of the earth, so startling was the contrast. The hills were mostly bare, and looked rocky, though there were patches of wood. Here and there—he counted four—were what might have been man-made structures, perhaps palm-frond huts: they looked for all the world like hayricks back home. Nothing moved on that bleak landscape, and no smoke stood against the sky.

This was Friday, the day of their arrival between North Negril Point and South Negril Point, and just after they had let go the hook. Sunday, at seven bells of the graveyard watch, was the time he had selected for his escape.

He was not afraid that this would be waiting too long. Even if the vessels from Kingston harbor were to start coming in the very next morning, it would take at least two days for the stragglers to arrive and for the convoy to be put in order.

Seven bells of the graveyard watch was half-past three in the morning, before even the first streakings of dawn. It was the time, folks said, when sleepers slept the most soundly, when all human senses were at their lowest point. The Indians believed that. They used to attack just before dawn.

Ezra had another and more specific reason for selecting this hour. Sundays aboard the *Thisbe* were comparatively easy, weather permitting. It was not necessary to swab the decks, this having been done late Saturday afternoon, but only to sand and sweep them. In consequence, the bosun's mates and ship's corporals did not pipe their "All hands" directly on the dot of eight bells; and to those already on watch topside a little more leniency would be allowed in the matter of sleep. It was unofficial, this leniency, but it was real, an accepted tradition. Technically, sleeping on duty in wartime was an offense punishable by death. Actually, on the *Thisbe* at least, it usually brought the sleeper no more than a mild clubbing. On Sunday morning it brought him nothing at all; and anybody on watch topside, provided he was not actually on lookout duty, could "take a caulk"—a nap on deck. This, then, was the time when the *Thisbe* was least alert.

A spell of dirty weather would spoil this, for the tradition did not apply in dirty weather, when all hands would be called up and put to work. There was not likely to be a real storm at this time of the year off Jamaica, but even a rainstorm, which *was* a possibility, would mean the piping of an "All hands," in order to capture all the fresh water that could be captured. Fresh water always was needed on a ship. That the tanks had just been topped at Port Royal would make no difference. The "All hands" would be blown anyway. It was a risk that Ezra had to take.

He had given the matter much thought. There were three ways of getting off the *Thisbe* undetected. One was to dive over the gunnel and into the sea, but even if this was done from the waist it would cause too loud a splash. Another was to lower a line and hand-under-hand it down, entering the water quietly. Without an accomplice—and he was determined to do this thing alone, trusting nobody—that would mean leaving the line there, a giveaway.

Also, it might be very hard for a man in Ezra Bond's position, a man without a knife, to get such a length of rope. True, he might purchase a knife. Almost everything conceivable was on sale down below, and Ezra had saved his last four rum rations, which would buy a good knife. But buying a knife in itself would be a suspicious action. After some pondering he vetoed this.

The third method would be to slip out of one of the lower gun-ports.

The orlop, where Ezra swung his hammock, was about at the water level: it might even be a bit below that. So it had no ports. It was lighted by a few horn lamps, "purser's glims," fastened to the bulkhead, very dim, only suggesting the way to the head, the way to the hatchway ladders. For all practical purposes, night and day, men found their way around down there by feel.

There were sometimes sentries stationed at the several hatchways at the head of the ladders leading from the gun deck, where most of the men slept, up to a main deck topside, and there would certainly be such sentries when the frigate was within sight of land; but no sentries were stationed at the ladders leading from the orlop up to the gun deck, there being no evident need for such. The hammock and mess quarters on the gun deck were even more crowded than those on the orlop, since it was a more desirable location. The guns were large ones, 32-pounders, as distinguished from the 24-pounders and the carronades topside, and the ports were about four feet square, made of heavy timber, since they formed part of the side of the vessel. In fine weather these could all be left open, and even in moderately rough seas some of those on the lee side could be opened a little, thus giving all the men—for the orlop benefited indirectly—some much-needed fresh air. These ports at Port Royal had been ordered closed and fastened, and the order still stood here in Negril Bay. This was a disappointment to Ezra, but he was prepared for it: he had anticipated it. Prowling at night—the only time he had a chance—he had examined the device that held the ports shut.

This was a simple iron bar that slipped through several iron eye-holes. It was like an oversized door latch. It would not be hard to slip one of those bars out. The trick would be to do this without making any noise. After that the port could be pushed a little way open, up and out, by means of the tackle that ran through a hole just above it. *That* would be hard; but it would not be necessary to open the heavy port all the way, only a few inches, enough to permit Ezra to slip through; and he had a stick of wood, a sort of peg, to hold it open while he did so.

He had selected his port with care. The *Thisbe* was anchored only at the bow; and with the prevailing winds the way they were —and there was no reason at this season to think that they would shift—this meant that her stern was pointed at the land. Therefore, the farther astern he could drop out, the better. Working his way along the side of the vessel would be a ticklish business at best.

There was another consideration. It was important that he work quietly and alone; for though few seamen would do anything to prevent a fellow prisoner from deserting, if he was overheard he might be mistaken for a thief and badly beaten on the spot without being given a chance to explain himself. That happened almost every night. There was a great deal of thievery belowdecks, and the men defended themselves as best they could. When a thief was caught he could be turned over to the master-at-arms for formal punishment. Theft was a flogging offense. However, the men of the orlop and gun decks generally preferred to treat thieves in their own fashion, which was not gentle.

With this in mind, and because it would not be possible ever to get far from a hammock in the densely overcrowded gun deck, Ezra picked a port that was not only far astern but also was near some noisy sleepers, mighty snorers. He had soaped the lock-bar and the eyeholes of this port, and had tested the tackle. He was satisfied that he could open it a little when the time came, and with no sound.

There was yet another matter, and a mighty important one, that need tending to. He must get a float.

He had estimated the distance at a mile and a half, but his eye was not infallible, and it might be farther than that. There could be currents that he did not know about. Also, he might be forced to take an oblique course or to zigzag in order to throw off pursuit.

He knew that many sailors, probably most sailors, never had learned to swim. Ezra Bond himself, brought up on the shores of Long Island Sound, could not remember learning to swim: he had always taken swimming for granted. A mile and a half, in ordinary circumstances, would not faze him, though it might tire him a mite. But the circumstances were not ordinary. He had always taken his strength, like his swimming, for granted; but he could no longer do so; a dozen times a day he was reminded, by unexpected weariness, that the flogging had taken even more out of him than he had supposed. That his back still hurt, that it was difficult for him to get into a comfortable position in his hammock, and that his kidneys went on aching: this much he might have expected. That his muscles would no longer respond as a little earlier they would unhesitatingly have done: this was wholly *un*expected. But it was true; and he had to take it into consideration.

A boat was not what he sought. A mere plank would do, some slight assistance in the swim, something that would allow him to rest his arms from time to time.

Well, he had his plank; or, at any rate, he had it loosened and ready. He had looked a long while for it, and found it at last in a board partition between the main part of the orlop deck and the forward portion chambered off for the marines. This was a flimsy, temporary partition: they could hear the marines talking over there. The orlop head was located right against it—a coyly curtained-off row of tubs—and this fact was much commented upon by the men who used the head and who frequently and indeed almost invariably expressed the wish that they could piss right clear through it onto those bloody lobsterbacks.

The board was loose, and it was low. It was about four feet long, eighteen inches across, three-quarters of an inch thick. It would not support him like a real raft, but it would help. It could easily be carried from the head to the gun-deck port Ezra had picked out. It might immediately be missed by the next man to use the head, but it was not likely that such a man, at such an hour, would report this. For all he'd know, one of the marines might have taken it from the other side.

Getting the board out was another matter. His fingernails were not strong enough. After many tries, he went shopping for a cold chisel, offering in exchange his four saved-up tots of rum. He found such a chisel with gratifying promptitude. He explained to the man he bought it from that he wanted to take it into his hammock with him nights in order to slash down at sneak thieves below that hammock, a common practice. Some men used a knife for the purpose, though possession of a knife by other than petty officers was against regulations. Possession of a cold chisel might be an even more grave offense, if he were caught with it. Almost certainly this one had been stolen from the carpenter's shop, and hence it was His Majesty's Property—and as such sacred.

With the aid of this instrument, then, he had worked out the loose board, which he promptly replaced. *Now* his fingernails would be sufficient. He kept the cold chisel anyway, he didn't know why. It and his Book, wrapped in a piece of oiled silk, and the holder-opener for the part, were the only things in his pockets.

So it was that he felt confident when he climbed into his hammock that Saturday night, the second night in Negril Bay. All he had to do now was stay awake until seven bells of the graveyard watch.

145

Chapter

26

A petty officer was allowed two whole feet of space in which to sling his hammock, but for the common seaman the allowance was only fourteen inches, and that did not leave him much room in which to twist. So read the regulations. In Ezra Bond's experience it did not work out as bad as that. For one thing, the *Thisbe* was short-handed; for another, not all of the men slept below at the same time. Still, it was uncomfortable enough down there, and made him feel, nights, like a pickle in a pickle jar. It was a major operation when anybody got out of his hammock to go to the head, an operation that involved all manner of grunts, bumps, and muffled curses. The head itself, though pungent enough in all faith, was almost fragrant in comparison with most of the sleepers.

It was a long night. The work had been hard that day, and Ezra's muscles ached. Moreover, he could not keep himself awake by the conventional method of shifting position; for every time he shifted, the stripes on his back would sting anew, admonishing him to be still. He lay as quiet as he could, listening to the sounds.

The sounds were small, but they were multitudinous. Immediately surrounding him, and also drifting down from the gun deck, were hundreds of mumblings, mutterings, heavy breathings, and out-and-out snorings. Some men talked in their sleep. Some men whispered back and forth, while others shushed those who did so. Some would get up now and then for a trip to the head or a simple stroll up and down the aisle that separated the starboard from the larboard watches, an aisle dimly lit at both ends, so that their figures wavered, ghostlike.

Twice, astonishingly, the master-at-arms mate responsible for order on the orlop, a shaggy scowling brute called Lester, came down from above, walked the length of the aisle, and then went up again to the gun deck, where he was entitled to quarters. Why? Ezra could not see him well, but he thought that he detected a certain determination in Lester's way of walking. Was he looking for something? What? There had been no disturbance, nothing to call him down. As nights on the orlop went, this was an exceptionally quiet one—so far. Had some white mouse slipped a secret to Lester? Had the loose board been spotted, and was a trap being laid? The thought at least did serve to keep Ezra awake. It did not shudder his spirit. He was going through with his plan, no matter what happened.

There seemed to be no thieves prowling the orlop tonight, which was unusual. Most nights you could hear them softly scampering around underneath now this hammock, and now that one, seeking anything that might be loose, scurrying when alarmed like so many rats, as, in a manner of speaking, they were. Many a man, hearing one, would lunge down under his hammock with a knife kept for that purpose. Sometimes there would be a squeal, even a scream; but the thieves, through long practice, had become artful at dodging.

There were sounds from topside as well, muted sounds, the "All's well" called to the quarterdeck by lookouts eager to assure the officer there that they had not fallen asleep, and the half-hourly ringing of the bell. Twice Ezra counted the seconds between the ringings of the bell, thirty times sixty, thirty times sixty. It did not come out right. He cut a second too short.

When at last seven bells of the early-morning watch did ring, Ezra was so stiff that he could scarcely climb out of his hammock. A fall would have created a racket. He made it, but only just.

He was fully dressed except for his shoes, which were tied around his neck. There was nothing unusual about that, in case anybody was watching. You never left anything behind you when you went to the head. Nor did he need to simulate the stumbling of a sleep-groggy man. He *was* groggy.

There was nobody in the head, and he went directly to the loose board. He was glad, now, that he had retained the chisel. His fingernails, it was proved, would not have been enough to work the board out—at least not without a great deal more time than he could have spared. With the persuasion of the chisel it came easily. He slipped the chisel back into his pocket and lifted the board in both hands.

"So you're the one?"

He wheeled—and found himself face to face with Master-at-Arms Mate Lester.

Ezra charged, holding the board like a pike, and he drove one end of it into Lester's midriff.

The man went *"oof!"* and fell right over backward into one of the tubs, after which he did not move. The breath had been knocked out of him. There had been very little stir, a mere scuffling. Even so, there were mutterings from some of the ham-mocked men, and when he slipped out of the head Ezra was care-ful to part the curtain as little as possible, so that nobody would see the recumbent Lester.

He had meant to go right along the aisle to the ladder, board and all. It was only about a hundred and fifty feet, and nobody was likely to have an eye open at that hour. The knocking-down of Lester made it different. In the aisle, even if he ran, Ezra

148

could have been grabbed and held from either side by some curious or suspicious man who had just been awakened.

He dived instead under a row of hammocks, and, crouching low, clutching the board to his bosom, he ran under rump after rump. He might at any moment be slashed. But he wasn't. He made the ladder.

There was not a sound from the head.

Up on the gun deck he dropped all precautions and went straight to the gunport that he had selected. Even in the dark he had no trouble drawing out the soaped and therefore slippery bar; but the port itself was another matter, much heavier than he had estimated. He tugged with all his might at the tackle, but the thing did not budge. Three men of a gun crew did this task at drills, as he knew, but he had counted on desperation to lend him strength.

He dropped to his knees and started pushing at the bottom of the port with his right shoulder.

It gave abruptly—so abruptly, indeed, that he was all but precipitated into the sea without his board.

He wedged the peg into place, holding the port open. He grasped the board to his bosom again, using his left arm. He slithered over the sill and hung for a heavy instant with his right hand alone. He swung himself out a little, away from the ship. He let go.

Chapter

27

It was not far. He had expected a shock, but the water was warm. How much of a splash he had made he couldn't tell.

This was on the larboard side. There was no moon, as he had known even without his tables. He wasted no time, for at any instant, he was sure, Lester might awaken—with a bellow. Trailing the board behind him with his right hand, he began to make his way toward the stern by catching with his left hand along the just-exposed top of the copper sheathing. This, he reckoned, would save him a trifle of strength.

When he reached the rudder he paused a moment, one hand on it, and slipped the board under his body, his chin hooking one end of it, his feet and lower legs protruding out over the other. Before he started, he turned his head for a fish's-eye view of the aftercastle.

Even unlighted, it was magnificent, a polychromatic mass of cupids, flowers, cornucopias, lions, and the like, all painted and varnished. There was a gilded balcony, for the use, no doubt, of the captain. There was an enormous gilt lantern raised high above the whole structure.

Ezra had not counted on a stern lantern. The only times he had been topside after dark were the two nights he spent in the bilboes, but from there, the waist, the stern was not visible. He did not know, then, whether this old-fashioned but undeniably lordly lantern was practicable or purely an ornament. If it was practicable it would be lighted when the alarm was sounded, and it might shine a long distance.

He had no time to ponder this, but pushed off, stroking with his lower arms on either side of the board.

His back had started to burn again at the first touch of salt water, and the exertion with his arms and shoulders made this even worse, so that it felt almost as bad as it had felt when he was getting those stripes. He slowed his stroke a little, for he was fearful that he might faint from pain.

Some of the welts extended clear up to the back of his neck, and these too burned whenever he lifted his head to see where he was going. Most of the time he kept his head down. The shore, when he did glimpse it, was no more than a thick dark shadow; and it was impossible, now, even to guess how far away it was. He made as straight a line for it as he could.

After a little while he heard bells behind him; a shrill whistling; then shouts.

"*Ahoy the crosstrees!*"

"*Ahoy the deck!*"

"*D'ye see anybody in the water astern, swimming?*"

"*Swimming, sir?*"

"*That's what I said, wasn't it?*"

There followed an anxious period during which Ezra, head down, paddled slowly, being careful not to splash. At last:

"*I don't see anything, sir.*"

"*Well, keep your eyes peeled.*"

"*Aye, aye, sir.*"

Ezra broke his straight course and began to oblique to the left. It would mean more swimming, but it was safer. For he was sure that they would send a boat. He himself meant little, a miserable waister who would not be missed, but the principle of the thing, in the eyes of the British Navy, was of stupendous importance. One successful desertion might inspire a whole series of tries. Oh, there'd be a boat! He swam harder, though his muscles shrieked at him, and he was less fussy about splashing.

Suddenly the water all around him was red, so that for a fleet moment he feared he was in delirium; but when he turned his head he saw that the light came from that high rococo stern lantern, in which a torch burned brightly. It seemed to Ezra Bond he must be exposed to all the lookouts, lying there full-length as he was, without, momentarily, the strength to take another stroke—and the shore still far away. Yet nobody hailed the quarterdeck; and when a little later a longboat was launched from the waist it took a course directly for the shore, as Ezra himself at first had done.

There were six oarsmen in that longboat, besides four marines, a tillerman, and in the bow, holding high a spluttering pine-knot torch, a hulking, bent-forward figure who might have been Master-at-Arms Mate Lester himself. Ezra could see them all clearly; but it was equally clear that they could not see him. They were moving very fast.

He started to paddle again. He did not change his course. He reckoned now that he had an even chance, all he asked. When the boat touched shore and the men in it saw no sign of the fugitive, they would turn either to the right or to the left, seeking disturbed foliage. If they went left he might run spang into them, or come so close that he would be seen and easily captured. If they turned right he was safe, at least for a few hours. That is, unless another boat was sent ashore from the frigate. He did not dare turn his head to see.

The redness around him waned. But the sky was getting light. He had known that there would be no beach, no surf, however

152

gentle, for he had been able to see as much from the *Thisbe;* but he was not prepared for the way the sea almost imperceptibly slid into the swamp. It was as though the shore had taken pity on the paddler, and had reached out to enclose and pull him in. He had no sensation of *landing.* He simply found himself surrounded by vegetation. The board bumped what might have been a stump. Something brushed the back of Ezra's head. Spanish moss? Something slyly slapped his face. Yet when he put a leg over he could feel no bottom, not even ooze.

The water around him, once the red had faded, had begun to glitter with the first touch of dawn; but now he was in utter darkness, the darkness of a tomb.

Either his estimate of the distance had been wrong, or else—and this possibility frightened him—he had paddled himself smack into a floating island of foliage broken off from the swamp and was even now being carried out to sea.

As blind as a burrowing mole, he pulled himself from one unseen branch or root or vine to another, pursuing, he fervently hoped, an inland course. All of the things he grasped were slimy. When the board grounded he was not at first aware of it, simply supposing that his strength had failed. He tugged harder at the thing that he was holding, making no more than a sad wet rattle. Then he put a leg over and learned that he was in mud covered by scarcely more than a film of water. Sobbing, he got off the board. Arms held before him, he started to stumble away.

But he turned back, and with wet hands that trembled he sought out the board again. After all, he had no notion of how near he might be to the open bay. He might have been going in circles. With the coming of full daylight there would be more than one boatload of men from the *Thisbe* poking watchfully along the shore. The board, the plank, if they espied it, would be a most excellent starting-point for a penetrating search.

Clasping it to him, like a mother her babe, he staggered on a

153

little farther, his stockinged feet making sucking sounds, his legs like strings of beads.

When at last he came to a place that his feet told him was at least solid, though not actually dry, he gave up. He just let himself go. He was not even conscious of landing on the ground.

Chapter

28

It could scarcely be called bright, there under the mangroves, yet what light there was hurt his eyes, so that he squinched them shut. Almost immediately afterward he popped them open again. Had he really seen something, or was he having a nightmare?

Two enormous Negroes were looking down at him. Because of his prone position and because of his great weariness—he might even have had a touch of fever as he lay there—it could be that he exaggerated their height and breadth as he looked up at them; but they were huge by any definition, giants.

If these were Maroons, as he promptly conjectured, then Al Spence, the topman, was right on at least one point: they were stark naked.

Ezra Bond was embarrassed; but he was not terrified. These big blacks showed wild, certainly, but not ferocious. Indeed, when they rolled their eyes at one another and then looked down at him again, Ezra distinctly got the feeling that they were sorry for him. Perhaps, like any other hunted animal, he exuded an odor that only their jungle-trained noses could detect, and perhaps in truth this was why they had found him, smelled their way to him. He wondered. He wondered, too, what, if anything, they were about to do. He had no inclination to speak to them. He doubted that they knew any civilized language.

To be sure, when the voice came—and this *was* in a civilized language—the giants jumped a bit, but Ezra sensed that this was because of the nearness of the voice rather than the nature of the words, which must have been unintelligible to them.

"If that bloody bastard of a Yank has to go over the side, then why the fucking 'ell does he have to pick out a place like this for?"

Ezra too jumped a bit. The voice seemed to come from no more than a few yards away, though in this thick swamp, he would have assumed, sound traveled sluggishly and not far.

They could hear other sounds then: the squidge and squodge of feet in muck, heavy breathing, a clank of sidearms. These did not come any nearer, but neither did they seem to be going away.

The giants appeared to understand each other, without so much as an agreeing grunt; they appeared to divine each other's thoughts. They stooped, one to a side, and lifted Ezra Bond off the ground. They carried him away.

What with the flogging, the hard work, and the revolting rations aboard the *Thisbe*, Ezra might have been down to a hundred and seventy pounds, but there was still a lot of bone and muscle to him; yet they carried him as though he was a baby.

They did not go far, and when they stopped, and had solicitously lowered Ezra to a bed of ferns, he saw that he was in a sort of grotto or leafy den that must have been at least in part manmade. It was presently serving as a storeroom, being piled with fresh fish that had been stacked with ferns separating them, and with roundish yellow-brown melons that somewhat resembled the Injun squashes back in Connecticut. The melons too were neatly stacked.

It did not need a wizard to deduce that these two were village hunters or tribal hunters visiting the swamp solely for the purpose of gathering a supply of fresh food, unobtainable elsewhere, to take back to the others. Ezra did not see any manner of implement, and in particular he noted the absence of any fishing tackle. Did they catch them with their bare hands? He wouldn't have been amazed to learn that they did. He wouldn't be amazed by anything any more, he reflected.

He was not uneasy. Whether his hosts were men or overgrown monkeys, they were creatures of good will; they were well disposed toward him, as they proved by offering him a melon and a raw fish. They spoke no word to him or to each other.

He declined the fish as politely as he knew how, but he broke open the melon and wolfed it down. It did not *taste* like an Injun squash, being much more sweet. It was the first food that he had had since supper the previous afternoon aboard the *Thisbe*, a good twenty hours ago.

They could no longer hear the search gang, and Ezra gathered that this grotto was deep in the swamp, perhaps at its very center. The seachers would not penetrate this far.

A majority of the *Thisbe* mariners, Ezra knew, were landsmen, but this was only because the press gangs had found the pickings so slim that they had been obliged to take whatever they could get. The petty officers, the captains of the tops, the chief gunners, the corporals, the bosun's mates, everybody with any shadow of authority—and this went for the marines as well—were career seamen, full-time professionals. It was from the ranks of such as these that the landing parties would be made up, for they were the only ones who could be counted on not to seize the chance to desert. And such men would not get any farther from the sea than they had to. It made them nervous.

As soon as he had finished the melon Ezra fell asleep. When he awoke it was to a consciousness that the light was slanted differently—what light broke through into this remote, dim place—and his seaman's instinct told him that it was early morning again. He must have slept all afternoon and all night. Well, he'd needed it.

The two Maroons were waiting for him. Squatting on their haunches, still naked, they did not frown but regarded him gravely; and when they saw that he was awake they rose. Each had before him a huge basket or net made of some sort of vine, one being filled with melons, the other with fish. These looked much too heavy for any one man to hoist, but the Maroons shouldered them stoically and seemingly without effort.

Still no word was spoken, no sign was made, but Ezra Bond, after he had put on his shoes—they'd been hanging around his neck all this time—took it that he was expected to fall in; so he stepped behind one, before the other. Immediately they started along a trail Ezra could not even see.

He assumed that the Maroons could see that trail or path, for they never faltered or hesitated in any way. They must be, he reckoned, so wild that they had the jungle instincts of a tiger, say, or a lion. They could hear sounds that no ordinary person could hear, and smell things that no ordinary person could smell. The old Indians were supposed to have been like that, from what men said; though as far as Ezra was concerned, the Indians he had sometimes seen around Saybrook didn't look as if they had sense enough to come in out of the rain.

The swamp remained dim, but Ezra could see sunlight ahead. Evidently they were approaching an open space.

The first Maroon stopped suddenly, causing Ezra to collide with him. The second laid a gentle hand on Ezra's shoulder, to hold him back. Except when they carried him, it was the first time either of them had touched him.

The first Maroon moved ahead a little, then quickly returned and squatted on his haunches. The other also squatted. So Ezra did this too.

For some time nothing happened; and then Ezra began to hear the search party approach. It would come very close, to judge from the jingle it made. The men must have been tired, since they didn't talk.

Ezra glanced at his companions, one after the other, but neither stirred or changed expression in any way. They might have been asleep.

The party passed within twenty-five feet of where these three squatted. They could see it plainly. There were four seamen armed with cudgels and two marines with muskets. They looked unhappy.

A sneeze, a hiccup, at that time—and it would have been all over. But Ezra remained as still as his companions.

He wondered afterward what the Maroons would have done if somebody *had* coughed. Would they fight and be killed? Would they flee, and if they fled would they carry him with them? He was never to learn.

The Maroons were in no hurry. They squatted there all day, the strangest day that Ezra Bond had ever spent. They might have been statues, stone figures mounted on a gateway. Much of the time their eyes were closed, though Ezra was convinced that they could have sprung to life like a couple of cats if anything occurred to alarm them. Now and then one would rise to make water —that was all. One ate a fish, raw, sucking the bones; and later the other ate a fish; and they offered one to Ezra, but he declined, though he was very hungry.

It was too much for Ezra. Grateful though he was, and anxious to fall in with the ways of these, his saviors, he had to get up from time to time and walk about a bit. He reckoned that, when you stopped to think of it, millions of persons esteemed it perfectly natural and even comfortable to squat like that for hours on end. These two, for instance, no doubt had never even seen a chair and wouldn't know what to do with one if they had it. He remembered hearing somewhere that though we take eating utensils for granted, actually only about one third of the total population of the earth eats with knife, fork, and spoon, while another third uses chopsticks, and the third third eats with its fingers. That rocks you, to think about. And he supposed that

159

maybe not more than one third of the persons on earth ever sat down on a stool or chair or bench.

At last, at dusk, they rose. They shouldered their baskets and took off for the open space, Ezra between them again, only this time they did not walk single file but spread out. They left the swamp.

As Ezra had observed from the *Thisbe*, the line was sharp. At one moment they were slipping past wet hanks of Spanish moss, trees darkly agleam with mist around them, and at the next they were climbing a treeless rocky hillside, the ground under their feet being solid, dry.

Were these curious friends of his afraid of the British, or had they waited all day only for his, Ezra's, sake? He must thank them, somehow.

He could remember little of that walk afterward, how long it was. It was all uphill, though the slope wasn't steep: he knew that much. His legs were very stiff, and the scars on his back had begun again to burn.

At last they came to what must have been one of those structures the waister on the *Thisbe* had thought resembled a hayrick on some Connecticut farm. It was indeed, as he had surmised, a thatched hut. He surmised too that he was meant to occupy it. They gave him another melon, another fish.

He thought of giving them, in return, his most valued possession, his Book; but they would not know how to read, and they would desecrate it, if unwittingly. He thought too of giving them the cold chisel; but what would they know of even so simple a tool, they who probably had never before seen iron?

Impulsively he took one of the Maroons by the right hand, which he wrung. The man looked startled at first, then puzzled. The other was calmer when Ezra repeated this performance, but he too seemed puzzled.

They did not bow or smile or anything. They simply disappeared. It was as though they had evaporated. Ezra did not even know in which direction they had gone.

He entered the hut. He felt around. The floor was bare, the walls were bare. The only thing that the hut contained was a bed or couch made of dry ferns. Ezra Bond stretched out on this.

It wasn't any palace, but oh! how much better than the British Navy!

Chapter

29

He stayed five days in that aerie, with nothing to do but loll and recover his strength and enjoy the view of North Negril Point, South Negril Point, and the vast brilliant bay between, where, the second day, the fleet from Kingston began to assemble. When that fleet was organized and had started for England, he decided, then and not until then he himself would move away— in the opposite direction. Where he would go and what he would do when he got there he did not yet know. He would worry about that later. Just now he was so happy to find himself alive that he could not care.

Lazy-eyed, smiling a mite, he watched the vessels take up their anchorages. He had counted forty-one at the end of the second day, and they were still coming. They were of all kinds and sizes, though most were small, and except for the *Thisbe* and a couple of sloops-of-war they were all, clearly, merchantmen loaded to the last cubic foot of capacity, lumbering vessels, exceedingly slow.

Old Death's Head was not giving Ezra up until necessity so demanded. Every morning, right after dawn, at least one longboat-load of marines and bosun's mates came ashore, to split into small searching parties. Conceivably they had found the board where he'd left it in the swamp, and this had given them a modicum of hope, though the real reason for such efforts, Ezra believed, was show—to prove to the ratings—that the British Navy didn't give up easily and that desertion was the worst of all possible crimes.

As they had probably done when Ezra was still down there, the searchers each day poked along the juncture of the swamp and sea, the whole longboat disappearing under the overhanging foliage from time to time for short intervals, and then they broke into smaller parties to encircle the swamp from the land side, darting into it only occasionally when they thought they saw something, but never remaining in it for long. How they hoped to catch anybody that way he could not understand. Maybe they didn't? Maybe they were just going through the motions for the benefit of some officer with a glass?

The nearest they ever came to Ezra's high hut was when they skirted the swamp at approximately the point where he must have left it with his two Maroon companions. They went past this point many times, but they never did seem interested in the hillside and what might lie beyond it. As far as he could make out— he prudently kept inside the hut when they were down there —they did not even look up in his direction. There was a chance, to be sure, that he would be seen by glass from one of the vessels in the bay, and the *Thisbe* captain notified, so that a party would be sent up the hill. He moved about as little as possible, and never with any swift or sudden motion that might catch the eye, and he never did have a fire. He was ready for them if they did come, nevertheless. He would have had a good head-start, and *he* wouldn't care how far *he* got from sea and ship.

So engrossed was he by the maritime spectacle to be viewed in, as it were, his own front yard, that he scarcely noticed his more immediate surroundings. He saw no other man near at hand, and no smoke other than that which came from the vessels in the bay. He heard nothing save the distant tinkling of those vessels' bells. Yet he was assured that the friendly Maroons were not far away, perhaps just over a fold in the hills, for every

163

morning he awoke to find two melons in his hut. They had learned that he didn't like raw fish.

He never heard those melons left there; and if he had, he would have done nothing about tracking a donor who wished to be anonymous. They were excellent. They did make up a somewhat monotonous diet, but every sailor is inured to monotony. There was a spring beside the hut, the beginnings of a brook. Who could ask for anything more?

From a pile of bones behind the hut, and from dried droppings in the vicinity, he deduced that wild pigs and wild cattle sometimes roamed this hillside, where they must have been hard put to it to find anything to eat; and it was safe to deduce as well, he reckoned, that this hut had been built by and for the occasional hunters, whether white or Maroon. It could be a skinning-out post as well as a place to sleep for a few nights. The spot had been selected, no doubt, because of the spring. The other huts that he had seen from the *Thisbe* he could not see here, but it was likely that they served the same purpose.

He often read from his Book. Some moisture had got to it, despite the sheet of oiled silk in which he kept it wrapped, so that a few of the pages were blurred, but in general Ezra knew the words so well that this made little difference. He did not pray much, only each night.

Not infrequently, as he gazed down over the assembling convoy, his thoughts slid back to Lady Helen Ashley, and he never ceased to be amazed at the difference between the woman he had met on the plantation and the woman he had first met on the *Forbearance*. It was more than a matter of paint, powder, and patches, more than a matter of pomade. On St. Kitts she had seemed straighter. Her whole manner had changed. For one thing, she seemed to have given over that irritating habit of starting every other remark with a fashionable "la," a verbal fan-flipping. "La" might be all right for French women and doxies of the court, but it would scarcely become a plantation manager. She was past the "la" stage, he hoped.

He wondered often about her, how he would renew his suit, which he had no thought of dropping. If this tarnation war ever ground to a stop . . . There had been a condition of war in the colonies, in the new United States of America, for virtually all of Ezra Bond's adult life, and it was going to be a wrench to adjust himself to a world in which there was peace, a world in which men could go from place to place as they wished, minding their business, selling their goods. He had sometimes cursed the war, sometimes been pleased by it when it gave him a chance to make money. Now his whole thought was to help end it; and this impulse came as much from his love of Lady Helen Ashley as from his hatred of the British Navy. Well, he'd have to get back to Statia first.

He did not question his own ability to do this. As soon as the fleet had left—and he was feeling more fit every day—he would start on foot for Kingston. That would be a long walk, more than a hundred miles, he reckoned, and he would stay away from the sea, proceeding from plantation to plantation inland. He wouldn't beg; he wouldn't have to. There was always ample hospitality for any well-spoken white man in the West Indies, especially back in the more remote plantations, where they longed for the sight of a fresh face, the sound of a new voice. The story he might tell at his stops could depend on the circumstances. Shipwreck would serve, but he could also plead a simple love of adventure, or he could even confess frankly that like a fool he had allowed himself to be impressed into the British Navy, from which he had now deserted. There was little love of the Navy in those parts, where Yankees in general were respected. What if somebody did try to turn him in? He could run; and it was hardly likely that they'd call out the militia for one wayfarer. He believed that he could easily reach Kingston intact, and indeed in better shape than he had left Port Royal right across the bay a little over a week ago.

There it would be a different matter. No press gangs would be roaming in a city a little while ago overrun with them. At one time, he had heard, R.N. skippers sometimes left a small gang behind in a place like Kingston, figuring that once the convoy had departed the deserters with inland friends would start coming down out of the hills—and be recaptured. He did not believe that they could have afforded to leave even a single corporal behind, the situation being what it was. He'd be safe enough from such. However, there were always officious officials in a seaport, men who were forever looking for a bribe, or a smile from their superiors, or just the chance to show their power; and he must walk with care, for his clothes were ragged and his pockets empty. What he would seek out was an interisland skipper who was shorthanded and who would welcome with open arms an able-bodied seaman who was willing to work his way to St. Eustatius on a no-questions-asked basis—and without pay. There must be many such.

Late on the afternoon of the fourth day he saw that the convoy was making ready to leave. Gigs scuttled back and forth in more profusion than ever. The *Thisbe* hung up a whole string of signal flags. There were whistlings and horn-blowings and bell-ringings galore.

At dawn, sure enough, they started out. It was a glorious sight, and Ezra stood all morning watching it.

Then he put on the pandanus hat he himself had woven—for his hair still was short, and Jamaica was hotter than St. Eustatius or St. Kitts—and he ate his last melon. After that he started west. He wondered if the Maroons were watching him go.

Three weeks later, to the day, he stepped off a ratty little schooner on the quay at Oranjestad.

The *Forbearance* still was there, as he had seen coming in. She was at a far-out anchorage, but even at that distance he could see that the Gallows Bay careening job had been done, for the sun shone on the top of her copper sheathing, riding light and unladen as she was. No longer would Ezra need to worry about the ravages of the teredo, that pesky pale pulpy critter that could worm through the stoutest oak as though it was cheese. But he'd have to clear for the north mighty soon, for the hurricane season was almost upon them.

> "June too soon,
> July stand by,
> August come it must,
> September remember,
> October all over."

All coatless, swordless, and unshaven though he was, the first thing he did when he landed was call for writing materials and get off a letter to Lady Helen. He did not go into details—those could wait; but he pointedly repeated that he considered her betrothed to him, and he expressed eagerness to see her again.

Then he strode to the office of Abraham van Bibber, whose cries of astonishment he cut short by curtly addressing a visitor, Samuel Curzon, representative of the Continental Congress.

"All right, where's that gunpowder you talked about? I'll carry as much as I can pack aboard, as soon as I can clear."

"But, captain," Curzon cried, "what made you change your mind?"

"Yes, Ezra," said Van Bibber, "what are your reasons for this?"

Ezra Bond took off his shirt. He turned his back.

"There are my reasons, gentlemen! All twenty-four of them!"

Chapter

30

Men said—some with a salacious leer, others proudly—that you could get *anything* in St. Eustatius. They were mistaken, as Ezra learned.

Getting the copper bottom had been expensive and had taken a much longer time than expected—fortunately, or the sloop might have sailed without him—but the job had been duly and well done.

Getting a new outfit of clothes and another sword was easy. He had no money—no *personal* money, as distinguished from ship's money—but his credit was good.

Getting the gunpowder was almost too easy. Gunpowder—called "grain" locally, for no reason that Ezra could divine—had been overused as a product of speculation. The mysterious firm of Rodrique Hortalez et Cie., which despite that Spanish-sounding name was located in Paris and secretly backed by the French government, had been shipping many tons of "grain" to St. Eustatius, the plan being that American blockade-runners should pick it up there and finish the voyage, the risky part, to the creeks and inlets of Virginia and the Carolinas. Now that France had openly come into the war on the side of the American colonies, it might be supposed that this trade would cease, to be carried on directly, all the way in French ships. But—the stuff kept coming in. And blockade-runners, now that the British had taken Charleston and had stippled the Carolina coasts with cruisers, were by no means as numerous as once they had been. Oh, there was God's plenty of gunpowder! And because of the fear that the war would end soon the dealers on Statia were offering it at a lower rate than Ezra had dared to hope. It was French powder too, the best in the world, most of it from the royal works at Essones.

Getting a safer stove for the cook and materials for a fireproof magazine presented no difficulties. There was always a demand for such materials at St. Eustatius, and so there was always a supply.

Getting the men to agree to all this—*that* was another matter. It was good to be back aboard the *Forbearance*, to feel her deck under his feet once again, to see the familiar faces. It was even better because his welcome had been unashamedly glad, an outpouring of high spirits and relief. They had been elated to see him back: no doubt of that. The end of uncertainty about their jobs could only in part account for the joy he saw in their faces. They had just lost one beloved skipper, in fair fight on the open seas, as might happen to any man; but it must have been unsettling to have his successor disappear without a trace. Tom Garrettson *sans* Ezra had not known what to do, and characteristically he did nothing. Until Captain Bond's dramatic return, no *Forbearance* hand knew where he stood or what would happen next. The vessel might be sold over their heads, and themselves left to find their own way home as best they might. This had happened before.

There were no black looks; there was no talk of mutiny; but Ezra's preparations and his purchases ashore had made it plain enough that he planned to carry gunpowder, a great deal of it; and a considerable proportion of the men—close to half, Ezra reckoned—openly opined that they had no eagerness to work in a vessel so laden. It was too tarnation dangerous, they declared.

If they were expected to run a risk like that, they ought to be paid more for it. After all, they had seen what happened to the *Dundas* packet.

In other circumstances Ezra might have slapped some of the ringleaders into irons and threatened to starve them unless they did the work that they had contracted to do. But these weren't foreigners. For the most part they were Yankees, many of them friends of Ezra's, some neighbors. He felt personally responsible for them. He understood them too, he believed. They were not city rats to be pushed around. They were independent-minded; and the town-meeting instinct was strong in them. They would talk over everything, talk long and earnestly, before they made up their minds.

Ezra was the skipper. He could enforce his orders. The world everywhere, every port, gave him that authority. In the captain's cabin he now occupied there hung a cat-o'-nine-tails, but he doubted that it ever had been used.

Also, trouble with his hands on this, his first command, might make it hard for him to get another skipper's berth. The seamen along the Connecticut coast were choosy. They would not grab at anything.

Those among the hands who were not Yankees were mostly English, many of them, Ezra believed, deserters from the British Navy. There was no muttering among these men. The habit of obedience was strong in them. They might grumble, but they would do as they were told. There were not enough of them, however, to handle the *Forbearance*, much less to make up a prize crew in case of a capture; and though with the wages he was willing to pay it would have been easy for Ezra to fill out a full crew by pick-ups from the beach, such pick-ups would all be foreigners, and he did not want foreigners.

Every one of the Connecticut men could write, and every one of them had signed on for the return trip, the West Indies and back. Ezra would have been within his legal rights to dump them ashore and sail home without them. But there was more to it than this. To a very large extent, the *Forbearance* was a community project, so many men in and around Saybrook having helped to build her, having sailed aboard her at one time or another, or having bought lays in the present voyage. You don't just treat such persons like ordinary business investors.

So he temporized. He argued. He cajoled. Indignant, he kept his indignation to himself, and he consented to explain, over and over again, the elaborate fire-prevention measures he was taking, and to insist that the *Forbearance* so fitted out would in fact be a safer vessel than the *Forbearance* that had fetched barrel staves and dried eels to this, the Golden Rock. It did no good. They shook their heads. And at last, sighing, he agreed to draw up a whole new contract, granting each and every one of them a twenty-percent raise in wages. Their lays were to remain the same. The voyage thus far had not made a penny. Mr. Atkins, the planter, had paid promptly, as Ezra had been sure that he would do, but all of this money had gone for the sheathing and the gunpowder.

In addition, Ezra had bought a "topper" of molasses, contained in barrels similar to those that contained the gunpowder. This "upper deck," in the event of a stopping, just might be examined no farther. He paid more for the molasses in Statia than he would have paid in nearby Martinique, but he thought that the time saved was worth the difference.

The signing of the new contract—all hands came ashore in relays for this—took place in the presence of Samuel Curzon, who as the representative of the Continental Congress was in effect American consul at St. Eustatius. It occupied all one afternoon. Other skippers, chance-met in offices or at the Mariners' Rest, told Ezra that he was a tarnation fool; but he felt better about it, once the business had been done.

He took on only one new hand, a lank, leathery, prodigiously tall down-easter, Epaphroditus Champion by name. Cham-

171

pion's left ankle had been crushed in an unloading accident several weeks before, and his vessel, a schooner from New Hampshire, had gone off without him. He wanted to get home, naturally; and he came cheap. He still limped, though the cast had been removed, but otherwise he looked as good as ever. Epaphroditus Champion was hardly a jolly companion, but he was efficient, he was effective. He was a man who would stand for no nonsense. Ezra signed him on as first mate.

It had been Ezra's first notion to make the bosun, Jared Brown, second mate, promoting Tom Garrettson to first; but Jared had been one of the stirrers-up in the demand for more pay, and Ezra was reluctant to promote him. As for Tom, he'd never mind. He was in his middle thirties already, and he just wasn't made of first-mate stuff, as he himself realized.

These preparations completed, Captain Bond climbed the Bay Path to the executive mansion. Letters could miscarry, in this casual place. He wanted to learn something about Helen at first hand.

Chapter

31

Seen from on high, the Street, the beach, and the roads glittered like toys on a nursery floor. It was curious to see movement down there, men scurrying back and forth, and on the water gigs and longboats, barges and Moses boats. From the parapet of Fort Oranje they looked like bugs. The warehouses too, though close at hand they could be grim enough, from the fort shone a dazzling uniform white, their roofs red, all drenched in sunshine: they might have been cut out with a mold clamped into the sand of a sandbox.

The fort itself, with its old-fashioned, romantic, and utterly useless towers, its curtains, its crenellated parapet, its brilliantly white flagpole, its blue-and-orange sentries with their polished cartouche boxes, their muskets, and their dutifully rapped-out *Wie gaat daar*'s—the fort, even when you were in it, showed unreal, fantastic, a place never to be taken seriously.

"Do you suppose that those cannons would explode, if anybody ever tried to fire 'em?" asked Ezra Bond, waving toward the row of ancient if well-swabbed twelve-pounders that scowled out across the town, across the roads.

"Well, I would not want to try it," said Captain de Roock. "We don't need to, you understand, because we've got a cohorn for saluting purposes."

173

"But—what would you do if anybody ever attacked this town?"

De Roock hooked fat thumbs into his lower waistcoat pockets, and he teetered back on his heels. He was smiling. He was almost always smiling, this plump, pleasant young captain with the pink cheeks, the yellow hair, the big blue eyes. He spoke English with no more than faint traces of an accent.

"Now, who would want to attack Statia?" he said. "We never hurt anybody. We are friendly. We're at peace with the world."

"In the old days—"

"In the old days, yes, this would be a plum for the pirates. The buccaneers. They would swarm all over it. But back in the times when there still were buccaneers among these islands, I don't need to remind you, mijnheer, we didn't have those warehouses down there. It was just a bare rock then. And now the buccaneers are gone. And they'll never come back. After all, there *is* such a thing as the Netherlands Navy, mijnheer."

"There's such a thing as the British Navy too. My own short experience in it—"

"Ah, a miracle that was, kaptyn! Out of the jaws of death!"

"—did not include many conference with the upper officers, such as captains and commodores and admirals. All the same, I'll give my eyes for it, captain, that *they* hate this rock of yours."

De Roock smiled a slow sleepy smile.

"We have many good friends among the English. We do business with them. And to the English, business is sacred."

"Islanders," pointed out Ezra. "Planters, estate agents. But not Englishmen in England. Not Whitehall."

"Whitehall? That is so far away!"

"It's got a long arm, my friend."

"They did get upset, there in London, when His Excellency ordered a salute to your Yankee flag. Did he tell you about that, mijnheer?"

"He did."

"More than once, I'll warrant? The truth is, he'd had a mite

174

too much of wine at the time, and didn't realize what he was doing."

"Oh?"

"So they didn't like that. But all of their feathers are back in place by this time, mijnheer."

"They didn't like it either when you Dutchmen allowed John Paul Jones to sell his prizes at the Texel. To them Captain Jones is no more and no less than a pirate."

"They'll get over that too," De Roock predicted.

"Um . . ."

"And after all, mijnheer, Great Britain already is at war with France and with Spain—"

"And with the United States of America."

"Of course! Forgive me, mijnheer!"

"And you reckon she wouldn't dream of taking on yet another nation?"

"Ah, that would be unthinkable!"

Ezra pushed forward his head and rubbered out his lips, stroking those lips with a thumb and forefinger.

"From what I've seen of the English," he ventured, "the unthinkable is just the sort of thing that they *might* think of."

De Roock chuckled complacently.

Ezra decided to change the subject.

"I'm sure you'd hate to have your tranquillity disturbed here. You like the life on the islands, don't you, captain?"

De Roock smiled yet again.

"Ah, I love it, mijnheer! The only thing is," and his eyes were misted over, for he was a sentimental young man, "I miss my wife."

"Why not send for her?"

"I haff done so. But it takes a long time. It is not as though she was only over there, in St. Kitts, like your Lady Ashley."

He colored, and he bit his lower lip. That "your" had been ill-advised. It had slipped out. Captain de Roock was instantly prepared to apologize, if Ezra called for an apology.

Ezra had been startled, but at the same time delighted. So far from thinking of a challenge he felt like hugging the genial Dutchman. Ezra already had been informed that Governor de Graeff was on an official inspection trip to the neighboring island of Saba, and that Lady de Graeff was indisposed. Of these two he would not have hesitated to ask for news about Helen. He did not like to ask an underling like De Roock, but he had been about to do so—when De Roock himself most obligingly brought up the subject.

"She's uh, she's been over here lately, has she?" Ezra asked, as carelessly as he could.

"Oh, yes. Only the week before last. Just a few days before you returned from the fond embrace of the British Navy."

"A visit, eh? Shopping?"

"Why, no. Looking for you."

"Oh?"

"That was why she crossed. She was worried about you. Could hardly keep from weeping and wailing. Seems she had been to Basseterre to buy something, and she saw a man wearing your coat. It wasn't you. She'd have remembered you."

"Well, I hope so."

"It was that apricot-colored coat."

"Yes," bitterly.

"She recognized it, of course, and she started to ask questions. How much she learned I do not know, but at least she did learn that there had been a press gang busy in the town just before the *Thisbe* sailed for Jamaica, and she must haff had some reason to think that *you* had been pressed. Anyway, she came here and pleaded with His Excellency to do something about it. I heard this. It is a small place, you understand?"

"It is."

"And I am His Excellency's military aide, you knew that?"

"I hadn't known, no."

"And of course he could not do anything except make inquiries. It was out of his jurisdiction, and he had to tell her so. She was all but hysterical. She wanted to know if he could not arrange for her to go to the island of Jamaica, to Kingston, and find out whatever she could? He said that he could arrange that, yes, but he advised her against it. He knew that the convoy at Kingston was already overdue to start, and he reckoned that it would start as soon as the *Thisbe* got there and took on her supplies, and in that case Lady Ashley would haff made her trip for nothing. She at last agreed. But she was extremely wrought up, I can tell you that, mijnheer."

"Thank you," whispered Ezra. "You've been very helpful."

"I hope that I haff not 'chewed your ear off,' as we say in the Low Countries, kaptyn?"

"You've been very helpful," Ezra said again.

When he went back down the Bay Path his feet scarcely seemed to touch the stones, and he was singing.

> "O, how joyful I shall be
> When I get de mon-ee.
> I will give it all to dee,
> O, my diddling honey!"

His ebullience met with a sharp check, however, twenty minutes later down in the Street, when the small saturnine Van Bibber happened to remark that Lady Helen Ashley and Captain Atkins were seeing a great deal of each other these days over on St. Kitts. How he knew this he didn't say; but the British West Indies, together with sundry Dutch, French, and Danish possessions in those parts, constituted a vast whispering gallery. Atkins and Lady Helen might have been playing in Van Bibber's own front yard.

The agent was no malicious gossip. He had not made the

remark to see how Ezra would react. He was interested only in the possible effect of such a relationship upon his own business.

"Might be that one's planning to buy the other out. That would call for a lot of conferencing, a deal like that."

"Yes-s," said Ezra, who was thinking of that long-legged languid octoroon on the porch of the Atkins plantation house one morning a month or more ago. "Yes, I expect that that's what it is."

But he had ceased to sing.

The *Forbearance* sailed next morning.

Chapter

32

Morning was the worst time—early morning, dawn. If the sky had been clear and the moon out a man could scan the sea pauselessly through the night, and feel safe; but if there had been overhang, rain, an early setting of the moon, or (as they got farther north) patches of fog, then the first streakings of sunrise might reveal something uncomfortably close. Ezra did not doubt the ability of the *Forbearance* to outrun the average war vessel, large or small, except under extraordinary circumstances—pursuit by a heavily sparred square-rigger, say, in a blow so vicious that there was no choice but to run before it—if she was given any sort of start; but what if when the firmament began to lighten you looked around to find yourself right under the guns of a man-of-war? This had happened. It was the chiefest dread of the Yankee privateers.

He took what precautions he could. He kept the deck most of the night himself, sleeping in the daytime, and he stressed to Ep Champion and Tom Garrettson and Jared Brown, and through them to the hands, the need for undiminished vigilance. Dinner was at four, and long before dark the last embers of the galley fire would have been seawatered out. They mounted no running lights, and it was not necessary to warn the crewmen against candles or lamps: these had been prohibited in the carefully spelled out new fire-prevention laws, to which the hands paid much more than perfunctory heed, for as one of them put it, "twenty-one thousand pounds of gunpowder would make a mighty big bang." Ezra kept a man at the masthead all night, two-hour shifts, but he forbade the routine calling from masthead to deck and back again every five or ten minutes in order to prove that the watch had not gone to sleep. There would be no hailing at all, he decreed, except in an emergency.

Nevertheless, it was an eerie thing, and heart-binding, that first cautious, squinting look-around with the coming of dawn.

They were lucky. They did sight a few sails—none of them small enough to pursue—but they were never, as far as they knew, chased.

Ezra was berthed now, as befitted his rank, in the cabin previously occupied by his uncle, Lemuel Hart, while across the corridor Tom Garrettson and Ep Champion shared the cabin Ezra once had used. It was not of his uncle, however, not of the man whose body had made so small a splash, that Ezra would lie thinking through the long hot afternoons when sleep stayed away. Rather it was of Helen Ashley. It could not really be true that the perfume she used and the odor of her body lingered in this narrow place. That was Ezra's imagination. But the smell was just as strong to his nose, imagination or not.

It was in this way that he lay, twisting, about noon of the thirtieth day out of Statia, when they raised Montauk. He heard the cry, which he had been expecting, and he tumbled out of the berth and onto the deck, wearing only his underdrawers.

He fetched a grateful breath. It was warming to be home. For he was as good as home, here. The eastern end of Long Island Sound had been his front yard for as far back as he could remember. He knew it the way he knew the palm of his hand. It had no secrets from him. Once he had poked past Judy he might as well be nosing into the mouth of the Connecticut.

All the same, he shortened sail. Well as he knew the Sound, he had no wish to enter it at a point where his canvas might be seen. The British, he recalled to mind, were rendezvoused behind Gardiners Island. They would be making an occasional sweep of the east end of the Sound, peering around Block Island, just to make it hard for the runners to run. It was not the ironbound blockade that they were able to maintain at the Narrows, the outside entrance to New York Bay. Here near Judy they had a much greater spread of water to cover, and the currents, too, were tricky. All the same, the British did a thorough job. It would be as well to keep out of their way. Ezra would hug the northern coast, skirting Point Judith as closely as he dared, staying as far as possible away from Gardiners Bay.

It was humiliating. It was as though a man came home after a long absence—and had to sneak in by the back door.

There was little breeze, and what there was was failing. The air was spongy and smelled of rain. The sky darkened, lowering. The sea too was dark, and so slick that it might have been filmed over with whale oil. There would be fog soon.

Ordinarily Ezra would not have ventured close to Point Judith on such a night, for the waters there were treacherous even for an old hand like him. Ordinarily he would have stood off-and-on, well outside in the open sea, until the weather was clearer. But that would mean another day, or even two or three days, and naturally as many nights. He decided to run it. His crew was touchy.

The fog came, not in a rush as though late for an appointment, but with characteristic stealth, silently, sinistrously. Almost at once the land to starboard, which had been no more than a blur anyway, was blotted from sight: it was as though somebody had whuffed out a candle.

The bows spoke with a low hiss. There were wobbly ribbons of water on either side of the sloop, and the wake was a scarcely perceptible cuddle of eddies. Soon even this ceased, and the *Forbearance* slid to a stop.

The fog had taken over completely. It was as though the vapor itself had slowed and finally halted the sloop. Sometimes they could not even see the water over the side, and it did them no good when they could.

It was past midnight, and could even have been getting on to sunrise, when they first heard the sounds.

Only the fog was *seen* to move, and its motion was mazy, an agonized writhing that sometimes ceased for minutes together. Conceivably the sloop itself drifted, though there was no feeling of this, nor could any ripples be seen on the surface of the water —when the water was visible—as proof. Or, again, the phenomenon might have been caused by the fog itself, which does strange things to sound, smashing it, baffling it, swallowing it whole, to release it later in reluctant puffs, distorted, disfigured, but once again audible—and unreliable.

It was Tom Garrettson who first heard the sounds. Tom was a stupid man, but he had qualities that made him valuable aboard the *Forbearance*. Without imagination, he was without fear. He was a reliable navigator. He had a keen pair of eyes and the best hearing apparatus that Ezra Bond had ever encountered.

Tom, all unconcerned by the predicament in which he found himself, had been pacing the poop with a measured step, when abruptly he stopped, his chin lifted, his nostrils twitching, for all the world like a hunting dog that had just struck a scent.

"Something going on out there," he said after a while.

Ezra leaned over the taffrail to listen, but he could hear nothing —at first.

"A lot of noises," Tom reported. "A whole passel of them."

Then Ezra began to hear. Only the vapor was visible, but out of that came, intermittently, a jumble of muted sounds—a bell, a splash, the shouts of men, a chopping, a whistle. Again, as the fog took over, all would be silent, so that even Tom Garrettson could not hear anything. Then the sounds would start again.

Ep Champion, another man never touched by worriment, was asleep, but Ezra called Jared Brown up to the poop and also commanded the helmsman to bend his ears. Each reacted as Ezra himself had done, declaring at first that he could hear nothing, and then going slack-jawed and goggle-eyed at the multiplicity of thin, feeble, twisted, but persistent sounds.

"My God, they must be dozens of men out there," cried Jared Brown. "They must be *hundreds!*"

"Sh-sh!"

"It's a ship all right," whispered the helmsman.

"A big one," said Tom Garrettson.

Ezra Bond felt cold, and as wet all over as though soaked in the very fog itself. A big one, yes. Indubitably. Warships carried crews much larger than those of commercial ships—ton for ton, four or five times as large. This was chiefly because of their guns. Warships were noisier, clear around the clock. On a warship, in any weather, at any hour, there were men prowling, snooping, banging things, clanking things, inspecting, shouting. Yes, Ezra knew those sounds. He knew them all too well.

There were, literally, hundreds of men out there, maybe one cable length from the *Forbearance,* certainly well within cannon range.

Somehow, in the night, in the fog, they had drifted close to a frigate or man-of-war. When they were seen—and it would be soon—they could only surrender, or else be blown to Kingdom Come.

It must, of course, be a British warship. In the early days of the rebellion these waters swarmed with small craft fitted up with guns—pinkies, smacks, pilot boats—and equipped with papers to attest that they were units of the Connecticut or New York or Rhode Island or Massachusetts navies or the navy of the Continental Congress. These had long since been chased away. They had all been tiny. Then Congress had authorized the construction of some real, honest-to-God war vessels, frigates, the *George Washington*, the *John Adams*, and others, and one of those too might occasionally be seen in Long Island Sound. But the frigates faced with the congregated might of the British Navy, had perforce retreated up rivers and bays, had been grounded, and had been burned to prevent capture. There was not one left. There was not even one a-building.

"What are you going to do?" asked Tom Garrettson.

Ezra had been asking himself that same question. His first thought had been to put the longboat overside and man it and try to get some way, howsoever snail-like, on the *Forbearance*. But he doubted whether this was possible, since the longboat had room for only ten oarsmen. Anyway, it would make a lot of noise.

Had the sloop been equipped with sweeps he would have used these, perhaps combining them with the longboat and its oars; but there were no sweeps—an omission Ezra determined to remedy if ever he got out of this scrape alive. For a wild moment he did think of making some jury sweeps, perhaps ripping planks out of the deck for this purpose; but it was an idea that he promptly dismissed, for the process would have been the noisiest of all.

He gave strict orders that the bell should not be touched and no voices raised, whatever the provocation. He made sure that the yardarm was so fastened that it would not swing the mainsail broadside-on to the hidden warship. That much whiteness might be glimpsed in a lull. He had the creaky helm lashed. He caused Ep Champion to be awakened, and all the men brought topside. He passed out boarding weapons, once again enjoining silence. He had the stern chaser loaded and shotted.

184

"It's thinning a bit, if you ask me, sir."

It was. No part of the neighboring ship showed, but the sounds came through clearer, and a considerable stretch of water now could be seen. Overhead was an opalesque glow: the moon was striving to break through.

"Well, it would have been too late anyway," said Ezra.

A moment later a dozen voices cried: *"There she is!"*

There indeed she was, the biggest vessel any of them ever had seen. She loomed like a mountain. There were three rows of gunports, all open. The guns had not been run out, but this could have been done in a matter of minutes, and anyway there were plenty of murderers, swivels, and brass chasers on the main deck.

"Allo!"

"That doesn't sound like English to me."

"Some of those Londoners speak a language all their own."

"Quel vaisseau cela?"

"What in Hell *is* he trying to say? He ought to get a new trumpet."

"I think I know," said Ezra Bond, who had not traded at Martinique and Guadeloupe for nothing.

He cupped his hands.

"Est-ce que vous parlez anglais, matelot?"

There was some confusion, and then a slim white-clad officer took the trumpet.

"What vessel is that?" he called.

"So that's what he meant," muttered Tom.

"Sloop *Forbearance*, out of Saybrook, returning from St. Eustatius," Ezra called. "Continental Congress charter."

The slim officer conferred with somebody. Then: "Stand by. I am coming aboard."

"Come ahead!" And Ezra added, under his breath: "Frenchy!"

It took them less than three minutes to get a longboat into the water and man it with six rowers and six brilliantly uniformed

185

marines, each of whom held a musket with bayonet attached. The slim officer sat in the sternsheets.

"There's seamanship for you," Jared Brown remarked.

"Put those boarding weapons away and drop a Jacob's over the starboard quarter," ordered Ezra, as he started for his cabin. "I've got to get my sword on."

He emerged to meet a girlish officer, the one with the speaking trumpet, the one in white. This personage clicked his heels. He waved a lace-fringed kerchief, and there was an odor of jasmine.

"Lieutenant le Comte Desmoulins," he announced.

Ezra nodded.

"Pleased to meet you, Count. Ezra Bond, letter of marque. Would you maybe care for a noggin of rum?"

When full morning had come, and the fog was gone entirely, blown off by a mild-mannered breeze out of the southwest, the girlish lieutenant, satisfied with what he had seen—and drunk—returned to the ship-of-the-line *Conquérant,* which with many other French war vessels was based at Newport, having crossed the sea to help France's new ally.

"This Saybrook," he said as he scrambled down the Jacob's ladder, "it is at the mouth of the big river?"

"Aye. The far side from here."

"We will escort you, in case that you meet some British," the lieutenant promised. "But I think you will not. They have become very hard to find in these waters, you understand, monsieur le capitaine?"

"I understand all right. And—thank you."

The *Conquérant* did not attempt to go up the Connecticut River —it drew too much water to risk that—but it did indeed escort the *Forbearance* all the way to Saybrook Point, where it ran up a gorgeous white silk flag of salute, and slammed away seven times with a stern piece, while its crew lined the gunnels and squandered themselves across the rigging.

"There's that little fellow there, on the quarterdeck," reported

First Mate Champion. "What ever is he doing with his hands?"
"I can't be sure, but—" Ezra raised the glass to his eye, and was silent a moment. "Yes, it's the way I thought," he finished. "He's throwing us kisses."

"Well, I'll be damned," said Epaphroditus Champion.

Chapter

33

Ezra placed the pane of glass before her, very gently, on the table. It was a big pane, fully twenty-four inches square, thick too, and almost without flaw. She still wept a little, but not convulsively, for she was a seaman's wife, all her life accustomed to the thought that each voyage might be the last—and herself a widow, as now she was. She had been well braced against that shock.

This was Aunt Hart—Aunt Bessie Hart, as Ezra called her, to distinguish her from Aunt Emma Hart, who was not really an aunt of his at all, as Aunt Bessie Hart was.

"I know he planned to buy you this. He told me so one time. But of course he never did get to a place where he could. But you can buy *anything* at Statia, and so I got it for you. Figure it's really from Uncle Hart."

"Th-thank you, Ezra. You've been k-kind."

Glass of any sort was extremely hard to come by in New England. Horn or even waxed paper was what was principally used, even in the town like this. A pane such as the one Ezra was giving his aunt would mark any house as the property of a prosperous man, a man with high mercantile connections. It would be stared at, commented upon.

"It'll look right handsome in that window to the right of the door there," he opined.

"Yes."

He rose. He put a lemon on the pane of glass.

"Here's one of these too. I know Uncle Hart would have brought you one."

It had been a good-will policy of the late Lemuel Hart to distribute lemons among friends and business associates in Saybrook at the end of every voyage, and it was a practice that Ezra would not allow to fall into innocuous desuetude. Lemons, cheap in the islands, were almost beyond price in Connecticut. They were good-looking, exotic. They were durable, and traveled well. And they were popularly believed to be a purgative, if ever a body could bring himself to eat one.

"I'll tell Missus Taylor next door," he promised, "and I'll look in on you myself again this afternoon."

"You're not going to stop here with us—with me?"

"I would if I thought I could be of any use, Aunt Hart, but I'd only be a worry for you when you want to be alone. Anyway, it'd hardly be worth the trouble of moving my chest, I'll be staying in port so short a time. I aim to clear out day after tomorrow, if I can."

"Why don't you at least come and have dinner with me then?"

"Now I'd admire very much to do that, and thank you." He took up his cap. "Well . . ."

He stopped at the saltbox house next door. Deliverance Taylor, herself a sea widow of several years' standing, was in no wise astonished.

"Heard you'd been sighted, and when I didn't see him coming up the slope, but I saw you instead, then I was pretty sure what had happened. He was always a great one for hurrying back to Bessie."

"Yes."

She took off her apron.

"Well, you can feed me the details later. I'd better get over there right away."

It was quite a different kind of woman he met when he went down to the center of the village. He had been walking with his head low, and she appeared before him suddenly, as though popping up out of the ground. Abigail Blake. It jolted him.

She put a hand on his forearm.

"Ezra," she said in a low tense whisper, "I'm going to have a baby."

The world spun around him. He staggered. Fleetingly he saw the face of Lady Helen Ashley, and it was fading, ebbing. But common sense asserted itself.

"You can't! How can—Why, it's been almost half a year—"

He stopped when he realized that she was laughing at him.

"It's all right," she said. "No, it's not your child, Ezra. It's Jonathan Simmons'. We're married."

"Oh."

"Not long after you left. I'd have waited for you to come back if you'd only asked me to, but you didn't."

She still had her hand on his arm. She gave it a small squeeze, managing to be sarcastic even in this. She was a great one for sarcasm, was Abigail.

"It's easy to see that your heart is broken," she said.

"Well, this was so—Well, congratulations."

"Thank you." She giggled. "Only I wish somebody else had been here to see that expression on your face."

"And congratulate Jonathan for me too, won't you?"

"Sure."

"Well, I've got to go. Got an appointment with the army purchaser, a Mister Costain. Excuse me."

"Sure."

He made a bow.

"My, aren't we getting fancy," she said.

He hurried away.

His face felt hot, and the palms of his hands were wet, as he had been badly affrighted for an instant there. He was always sure that he had not been the first to tumble Abigail Blake, but he didn't want to be the last either. He wanted to be the last somewhere else, far away. He could remember Helen's laugh, that terrible morning at breakfast. He could remember—he would never forget—the way she had said: "You didn't really think, did you, that you're the first man I ever slept with?" He was beginning to fear that maybe he showed a mite foolish in the presence of women. He quickened his step. Well, at least he knew how to handle *men*.

Henry L. Costain did not pose much of a challenge to any horse-dealer, he was so pathetically eager to get powder for the Continental army. That pitiable body would be expected to cooperate in some manner with the newly arrived 5,500 French soldiers, but for the present it was ragged, undermanned, half-starved, and without sufficient gunpowder to start any manner of offensive. The Continentals were scattered in camps all the way from West Point to Morristown, with the main one at Tappan. Mr. Costain would see that the stuff got to them as soon as possible. He would arrange to have drays right down by the dock, and he would hire men to help Ezra's own hands unload.

Best of all, he paid in gold, as Mr. Curzon, the Congressional agent at Statia, had promised. He had it right there. And the price was right—thirty pounds sterling a hundredweight straight down the line: a man couldn't ask for anything better than that.

Mr. Costain went further. He offered Ezra a pass to the French camp at Newport and a letter of introduction to the commander-in-chief there, Count Rochambeau. Ezra thanked him, but declined.

"You're missing something, I can tell you, captain. Everybody around here who can afford it—and can arrange it—they're all going. You never saw anything like it in your life. They've got four regiments there, and they're lots of them dressed in *white*. Imagine a soldier in *white!*"

"I met one early yesterday, only he was a sailor, an officer. And he was a count."

"They're practically all of them at least counts or chevaliers, the officers. Or viscounts, or marquises. There's even a few dukes, I understand. I tell you, captain, you ought to see that army. The Deux-Ponts, all white. The Saintonges wear white and purple and green. All the time, I mean, not just Sundays! The Bourbonnais have black coats turned over with red and all piped with yellow, and the Soissonais—"

"It all sounds very interesting," cut in Ezra, "but I want to get away again as soon as I can, back to Statia."

He gave Mr. Costain a lemon.

"And will you bring us back some more gunpowder, captain?"

"You're dang right I will! You just keep that gold handy!"

Chapter

34

"Kaptyn Schietpoeder" was what they came to call him, which is to say, in Dutch, "Captain Gunpowder." Sometimes they varied this with "Mijnheer Schietpoeder."

In Saybrook he took the quickest cargo that was offered, except that he drew the line at live horses as being too dirty. It was always food of some sort—hardtack, dried fish, salted beef, rye, Injun. The West Indies never could get enough food. Ezra would dump it into the lap of Van Bibber and he did not ask what happened to it, though he believed that it was purchased by English planters who paid for it with English money. Ezra asked only for credit with which to buy gunpowder, and by the time the Van Bibber deal was completed he would be loaded and well away.

Even in Saybrook he did not loiter, but would take on cargo and be off almost before the hands had had a chance to go ashore and get drunk. He was not safe anywhere on that run, save in Statia road itself, where the neutrality of the Netherlands protected him and his vessel; but he was the least safe off Saybrook, his own home town. The British Navy in America had been substantially increased, and the French fleet that had accompanied the French army to Newport was bottled up there by superior forces that ranged the length of Long Island Sound all the way from Hell Gate—for the British still occupied New York City—to Montauk Point. The war vessels could not get up the Connecticut River, but fast-moving, heavily manned cutters from those vessels could do so—raiders, hit-and-run boats. The Royal Navy was proud of its "cutting out" specialty; and Ezra Bond wanted no further dealings with the Royal Navy. He entered and left the mouth of the Connecticut only after dark. He did not linger there.

Nor did he linger at St. Eustatius. He did not diddle-daddle, asking prices, shopping, arguing, fussing, but simply called for as much gunpowder as the *Forbearance* could be made to carry. He demanded the best, and he got it. He bought cannonballs too, in hundred-lots, storing them far below to act as ballast, gunpowder itself being a relatively light cargo. There was always a market for cannonballs in the Continental army, he had learned, and as in the case of the powder he was paid promptly and in gold—French gold. The poor starving soldiers were obliged to take Continental paper, which wasn't worth anything. Ezra could not help that. *He* was making money.

The only other thing he would take aboard at St. Eustatius was a "cover cargo," usually molasses, which fetched a good price in rum-making Connecticut, though you were never sure when you'd get the money or in what form. This was a layer of barrels placed on top of the gunpowder. It was a shield, a showpiece. Lemuel Hart had taken the precaution of buying—at Statia, where you could buy anything—a forged let-pass purportedly signed by Admiral Howe himself, testifying that the *Forbearance* and her crew were regularly engaged in carrying food supplies to the British Army in New York and should not be molested or detained. In case of a capture at sea or in the Sound this *might* be made to work. A search party *might* be convinced that the entire cargo consisted of molasses, as set forth in a second set of sailing papers—not the proper set, which would be hidden— and such boarders *might* look no farther. It was worth a try.

The "cover cargo" had a secondary advantage in that it helped to reassure a somewhat edgy crew, the members of which —mistakenly—believed that it was an extra protection against fire and explosion.

His men complained that Ezra rushed through Statia, each time, like a man who hurries to catch a stage; but there was one thing that he never forgot to do. Invariably, when the arrangements with Van Bibber were finished, Ezra would sit down and write to Helen. These were not long letters and they were not notably warm ones, for writing came hard to him and he was not gifted with eloquence; but if they were sober letters they were also stubborn. In each he assured her of his love and of his intention, as soon as this pesky war was over, of rejoining her and with her, as he somewhat inelegantly put it, "finishing the affair we started that night." That is, he continued to propose marriage, if not always in so many words. He did not know whether she got all of those letters. He never did receive a reply.

He made two more trips to Saybrook and was in Statia preparing for a fourth when his career as a smuggler came to an abrupt and violent end.

This career had been sensational, but sensational because of its smooth success, not because of any difficulties met or obstacles surmounted. It had been packed with peril, but in itself had been suspiciously silent.

The greatest danger, he sometimes told himself, bitterly, came not from the enemy but from his own seamen. The hands were leary of all that gunpowder on each northern passage. Ezra occasionally wondered whether, if called upon, they would consent to fight. He did not mean to put them to the test. He had ceased to be a privateer—though he still had the warrant—and had become a blockade-runner pure and simple. He was not looking for prizes. He did not seek a gam. He ran from every sail he saw. And he never failed to get away.

He pointed this out, placatingly, to the men. He showed them the forged let-pass. He swore that a fight was the last thing he wanted. Still, they were uneasy.

They were not as numerous as once they had been. A privateer needed a swollen crew, especially at the start of a given cruise. Hands costing what they did, a vessel like the *Forbearance* ordinarily would sail out of any New England port with about forty men and boys. There were cannons to be handled, besides the sails and the helm. A boarding party might be called for while the cannoneers were still slamming it in; and in any event a large group of men on deck, men who looked fierce and who fiercely waved the weapons they held, could do a great deal toward causing a menaced skipper to strike without resistance. Then too there were the prize crews. Three or four prizes at sea and a privateer would have barely enough labor left to limp home with.

On his first visit to Saybrook as a captain, and in pursuit of his new blockade-running policy, Ezra Bond had let fully half of the hands go. Thus, and though he still had to pay the fantastically high wage they had wrung from him at St. Eustatius—for he had been advised that he couldn't squirm out of this—his pay chest nevertheless was lighter than before. Also, he needed to carry less water, firewood, and rations, which made more room for gunpowder.

Always gunpowder. He insisted upon it. He seemed obsessed with it.

On the first return to Saybrook, too, he had sold four of the six carronades, all he could find buyers for in the time he had. If you weren't going to engage, where was the profit in having all those guns? He would sell the others as soon as he could.

He was doing well. Perhaps he was doing *too* well? Something would happen soon, he told himself.

He was right. Something did.

Chapter

35

Kaptyn Schietpoeder. A name like that could be a help in certain circumstances, a lift of prestige, but it could also be a pesky
nuisance, forasmuch as it gave any insolent outsider the right
to address you. Ezra liked most folks well enough, he guessed, but
in a port like St. Eustatius you could not be too careful about
whom you fell into conversation with; and Ezra definitely did *not*
like the macaroni who accosted him in the Mariners' Rest one
morning just before he was ready to start for Connecticut the
fourth time.

Ezra visited the Mariners' Rest for two purposes—one, to discuss a deal, and two, to go upstairs. In the latter case he was always alone. He was alone today, and he had finished. He was
enjoying a tankard of Dutch beer.

"Mate Bond, I believe?"

"Captain Bond," Ezra softly corrected him.

That this man standing next to Ezra's table *was* a macaroni was
evident and indeed would have been just as apparent even at a
distance. He flaunted himself. The cinnamon-colored coat slashed
with silver, the doeskin waistcoat, the quizzing glass through
which he stared down upon Ezra as though upon some repulsive
insect, the Valenciennes jabot, the bicorne cocked so high that

its crown was not visible—all of these attested to the designation. And to these things Ezra had no objection—though he would never himself have gone so far as to carry a quizzing glass —for his own taste in clothes ran rather to the clamorous, as folks in Saybrook had more than once found cause to complain. It was the man's face to which Ezra objected.

The man was tall and very thin. He looked even taller than he was because he stood by Ezra's table, while Ezra raised nothing but his eyes. Ezra had smelled him even before he heard and saw him, for the fellow stank of perfume.

The face too was thin and excessively long, a mite horsey. Though it shone of pomade, it was utterly pale except around the eyes. The taproom at the Mariners' Rest customarily was kept dim, and in that light Ezra could not be sure whether the man had outlined his eyes with antimony, seeking for a sinister effect, or whether the coloration—or discoloration—was natural. Nor did Ezra care. He only knew that here was a character who was determined to inspire fright.

You'd say at first glance that if he might have the manners of a dancing master, he assuredly had the morals of a thug. It was unmistakable.

"*Captain* Bond, then."

He had a high, thin, reedy voice. He continued to regard Ezra through the quizzing glass.

"I don't like your face," he said.

Ezra nodded.

"Lots of men feel that way," he admitted. "Can't say's I'm mad about it myself."

He must avoid brawling. It would be a pleasure to punch this elegant beanpole, but it might result in delay, and Ezra had made all plans to sail inside of two hours.

"My cousin Lieutenant Yale"—he pronounced it *lef*tenant, for he was emphatically English—"told me that I might expect an ugly man. Yes."

Ezra made no reply. He only gulped his beer. He was wondering what the macaroni, with his la-di-da airs, meant in picking on *him*. The mention of Yale might explain it. Some perverted idea of clearing his cousin's name, perhaps?

The stranger took snuff, in a languid manner, having folded away the quizzing glass.

"He also told me that you fired first on his vessel and that when he was *in extremis* you refused to help him."

"When he was what?"

"When he had that fire."

"Oh. Well, if Yale told you that I say he's a liar."

What happened then happened very fast, and it was quiet. A few men lifted their heads, not certain whether they had heard anything. Hendreck came around from behind his counter.

The macaroni's right hand, only inches away to begin with, moved with the speed of a striking snake. And in truth it felt like that against Ezra Bond's cheek—like a snake. It was instantly back in place. This insulter did it well. He had done it before, many times.

The blow was hard, no frivolous tap. It stung.

"My name is Albert Desmond, and I can be reached through the British consul, who will represent me in any negotiations that may be called for," said the macaroni.

He went out.

Rage did not come to Ezra in a rush, as might have been expected. Puzzlement was there first; and indeed it was almost as though that expert slap had been a bludgeon applied to the top of Ezra's head, stunning him. He did not ask himself why this outsider should treat him like a gentleman. He did not warn himself to sit still and to remember that the *Forbearance* was loaded and cleared and ready to make off. He was, momentarily, dazed.

The door had closed behind Albert Desmond before Ezra

snapped into a real awareness of what had happened. He rose, muttering.

"Need any help, captain?" asked Hendreck, who had come halfway across the floor.

"No, I'll handle this myself, thank you," said Ezra; and he went outside.

It was always a shock, emerging from that dim taproom into the blaze of day. No matter how many times you had done it, it stopped you like a hand on the chest; it blinded you for a moment.

Ezra paused, blinking.

Shamelessly tropical blooms were on either side of him, and before him was a rather prim gravel path that led twenty-five or thirty feet to the Street. Albert Desmond was down there, bowing low, "making a leg," his hat over his heart, before a woman he had, seemingly, just encountered.

It was Lady Helen Ashley.

Ezra stepped back inside, closing the door after him. He couldn't have said why he did this. It was instinctive. He had to have a moment alone, in the half-darkness, to get his wits back. The rage was gone, sopped up by the sight of the woman he loved.

He had not seen Lady Helen since that memorable morning on her plantation, a year ago. He thought of her often, and from time to time he would hear snippets of gossip about her, nothing scandalous, though it did seem as though she was seeing a great deal of her neighbor, Captain Atkins. Ezra had no intention of dropping the attack, but he hestitated to make another trip to St. Kitts. What he had really been hoping was that he would run into her here on Statia, and he had been keeping an eye open for her. Yet when he saw her, just now, it gave him such a jolt that he had to back away. He was astounded, he was flummoxed, by the intensity of his own feeling.

What was she doing in the Street anyway, a lady like her?

With her influence at Government House she could readily

remain there and command the merchants to climb the hill to her, as she had done when she first came to these parts.

And why was she chatting with that perfumed pimp, Desmond? She seemed to know him almighty well. Had her being here in Statia today anything to do with *his* being here?

Ezra would go outside again, and confront them. But before he could reach it the door latch turned, the door opened.

"May I come in?" asked Lady Helen.

Chapter

36

It would be a red-letter day in the history of St. Eustatius. A woman at the Mariners' Rest! More than a woman—a lady! Such a thing never had been known before. Even Susette, the Queen of Upstairs, who most certainly was no lady, only visited the taproom in pursuit of her business of making appointments with the customers: she never loitered there, and never sat down. Even the fabled houris themselves, when they were taken out for their exercise walks, did not cross this sanctum sanctorum but were routed through a back door. So far as anybody knew, there was no municipal ordinance *against* female patronage of such an establishment as the Mariners' Rest; but it just never had been done before; it was unthinkable.

There were seven men in the taproom, besides Ezra and Hendreck, and every head was turned toward the door, every pair of eyes popped, each mouth formed an "o." As for Hendreck, who was ordinarily so sure of hand, he dropped and broke a goblet.

None of this fazed the newcomer, who tossed Ezra a toothy smile.

"It's been a long time. La, sir, you've neglected me."

She gave him her hand, knuckles up. He bobbed over it. He did not kiss it.

"Aren't you going to ask me to sit down? Have you lost your manners entirely, captain?"

"Sure. Here. Sit here."

She wore pink silk that rustled as she moved. Her face was made up, but very lightly, and her hair was not powdered. She looked sure of herself; but she was not frivolous, despite the resumed "la"; she was deadly serious.

"What are you doing here?" he demanded.

"Why, I came looking for you."

"How did you know—"

"Your ship's out there, obviously prepared to sail. I'm not such a lubber that I can't see that. And this is a small town as far as gossip is concerned. They tell me it's more or less a custom for a skipper to have a last drink here before sailing, with his agent and maybe one or two traders, to go over last-minute details."

"That's right."

"An anchor drink, they call it."

"Yes. But I've had it already. In another ten minutes I'd've been gone."

"I was lucky, then." She took off her gloves. "And speaking of drinks, do you suppose that I could have a glass of wine? It would give me something to do with my hands. Such an attentive audience makes me nervous."

She didn't look nervous. She smiled at him again. He summoned Hendreck.

"A glass of sherry for the lady."

"Yes, sir."

When she had been served he asked her: "Who was that man I saw you talking to outside?"

"Lord, lord, how possessive we've become!"

"I don't like him."

"I don't know anybody who does. Well, if you must know, his name is Albert Desmond, and I had a nodding acquaintance with

203

him in London. No more than that. He is not," she added slowly, "one of the men I mentioned the last time we were together."

He winced. She put a hand over his on the table, to tell him that she had not meant to be cruel. She was looking hard at him, her eyes, even in that light, as lustrous as ever.

The others in the room no longer were agape and they pretended to resume their several conversations, but Ezra and Helen remained the center of surreptitious attention.

"This Desmond, what's he do?"

"Fights duels. Or threatens to."

"Well, he can't make a living that way."

"Oh, yes he can. Not a very steady living, and certainly not an admirable one. But he makes out. He's a bully-boy. A high-toned bully-boy. He doesn't often have to go to the field. Usually his reputation protects him and the other man backs down. He's paid to *threaten*, mostly. But when he is called out I'm told that he is a crack shot and perfectly cool. He doesn't try to kill. He shoots them in the right kneecap."

"Why the kneecap?"

"When a two-ounce ball hits one of those at ten paces it cripples the man for life. He'll always have something to remember Desmond by—a limp. Besides, it hurts terribly. It's the most painful place a man can get shot."

"What's he doing here?"

"I don't know, but I *suppose* that he doesn't dare stay at Home or in any part of the British Empire, and we're at war with France and Spain and the American colonies, so he comes to a Dutch place to ply his trade. I hope he didn't approach you?"

Ezra told her what had happened. She was grave.

"He's probably just landed, and he wanted to start getting a reputation as a dangerous man right away. That's why he went for you."

"But why *me?*"

"Ezra, I don't think you realize how famous you are in these parts. It started with the blowing up of the *Dundas*, but your name's been getting bigger all the time since then. You're just too busy to notice. If Desmond could frown down Captain Gunpowder himself he'd be off to a good start. I do hope you're not going to challenge? You're not obliged to, you know. The man's a professional, and he's probably not related to Lieutenant Yale at all. Anyway, he is not a gentleman. I'll tell that to everybody I know."

"I never even thought of challenging. He took me by surprise and I let him walk away, but I was going after him when I saw you."

"You were going to fight him?"

"With my fists. The way we do where I come from."

"Oh. Well, I'm glad I was there then."

"So'm I."

There was some silence. She was still unabashedly holding his hand, and now she gave it a squeeze. She was no longer smiling.

"Ezra, I've been brought up to be a flirt, you know that, don't you? It's part of my training as a 'lady,' God help us. It was as natural for me to hurt you, that morning at breakfast, as it would be for me to flip my fan at a ball. I couldn't have helped it. Oh, I wasn't lying! And I did want you to know that. But I was sure that you'd charge on, and when you went away I was sure that you'd come back."

"I would have—except for what happened."

"I know, and it was terrible. As soon as I learned, I did everything I could to get you out. And I bought back your coat—that handsome apricot-colored one. It's up at Government House right now, with your name on it, and you can have it any time you like."

"Thanks," he whispered; and he had a hard time getting even that much out.

"As soon as I heard that you'd escaped I came right over to Statia here, but you'd already taken off with a cargo of gunpowder, and ever since then you've been a hard man to find."

"I—I have kept busy."

Her hand on his was moist now, sweating, but she made no move to lift it. She was looking down.

"I got your letters, Ezra," she said suddenly. "At least I got three of them."

"I sent four."

"I only got three."

"You didn't think to answer them?"

"Yes, I did think to, but I decided against it. What I wanted to say I'd have had a hard time saying in a letter."

"And what was that?"

She still looked down.

"Ezra," she said after a while, "I came over here to Statia each time. And each time I was too late, by a little bit. Today I made it."

"And what was it you wanted to tell me?"

"I—I've sold my plantation."

He frowned a little. He did not wish to change the subject.

"To Captain Atkins," she went on. "He's going to run both places."

"Oh. Well, I don't know. That could have been turned into a pretty good thing."

"Oh, I had it in fine shape, and it would have made money for me."

"Yes."

"But that's not my kind of life, Ezra. Captain Atkins paid a good price, and it's in gold. So I plan to go back to England. That is, unless—"

"Unless what?"

"Unless you still want to marry me."

He sprang to his feet.

"You're damn' right I do!"

He pulled her up and kissed her. The customers at the Mariners' Rest had a notable show that morning.

"Come on, we'll do it right away," cried Ezra. "Governor de Graeff can marry folks here, now can't he?"

"Yes. I asked him, just before I started down the hill."

"Come on!"

He forgot to pay for the drinks. He didn't reel, as she did, when they ran through the doorway and were splashed with sunshine. He was too eager to get them a couple of chairs.

"*Chair!* Here, you, *chair!*"

Chapter

37

It was a gala occasion. The Street below was more than usually abustle, astir, and the anchorage was crowded: there might have been as many as a hundred and fifty vessels down there, all the way from frail interisland skiffs to the ponderous Dutch 38-gun frigate *Mars*. More vessels, large ones, were moving in from the open sea, seemingly a great convoy, as though all West Indian shipping approached for the purpose of congratulating Captain Gunpowder and his bride-to-be. Nobody ever had seen so many vessels at one time.

Government House and the adjacent fort too were crowded and noisy with life. The garrison of fifty-some men had been turned out and was being reviewed by the colonel, Abraham Ravené, and his second-in-command, the Governor's military aide, plump contented Captain de Roock. This had not been done in honor of the bridal couple; it was a routine review; but the effect was the same.

Additionally, the skipper of the *Mars*, Count Frederik van Bylandt, a crony of the Governor's, had seized this occasion, quite by chance, to pay a more or less formal visit. He was accompanied by a large number of officers, all of them in dress uniform.

This caused some confusion; but it did give Ezra Bond something to look at and listen to during the edgy half-hour when he drifted about, waiting for the re-appearance of Lady Helen. Lady de Graeff, the Governor's wife, though clearly she disapproved of the match—she thought that Lady Helen Ashley was marrying beneath her class, especially now that she had all that money— had taken the bride to the house in order to "pretty her up." Disapproving or not, every woman loves a wedding.

The Governor himself, delighted, agog, prayer book in hand, could hardly wait to do his part—and to open the champagne afterward. He now had a double excuse to drink in the middle of the day; though he could scarcely start until the ceremony had been performed.

The view from the parapet of Fort Oranje was celebrated, and several of the *Mars* officers had brought glasses. One of these handed a glass to Ezra as Ezra was about to stroll by, saying something polite in Dutch.

"*Dancke,*" said Ezra, this being one of the few Dutch words he did know; and put the glass to his eye.

Understandably, like a parent, he first sought for and found the sloop *Forbearance.* There she was, as trim and sleek as ever, poised on the water like a bird that might fly off at any instant, at the stamp of a foot. He was proud of her.

He lifted the glass a little, meaning to examine some of the convoy vessels that were grouping outside of the mole.

At first he thought that he must have moved it the wrong way and picked up the *Mars.* But—no. He moved the glass from vessel to vessel. He was right. He had been right the first time.

"Those are warships," he cried.

The Dutchman smiled and called to a fellow officer, who it developed understood English. Ezra repeated his remark to this man.

"Yes, mijnheer. We have just learned that for ourselves."

"Dutch?"

The officer smiled, and shook his head.

"No, mijnheer. There are not that many bottoms in the whole Netherlands Navy. No, it can only be Rodney, up from Grenada."

"But what's he doing here?"

"This is what we were asking ourselves, mijnheer. He couldn't be paying a formal visit without previous notice—and anyway not with a huge fleet like that."

"Has Count Bylandt been notified?"

"A man is on his way to him now. I have no doubt that he will conclude, as we have done, that Rodney's on his way to Martinique or to Guadaloupe, and just paused here for a good long look at the Golden Rock."

"It's no thing of beauty. Why should he want to stare at it?"

"Perhaps the fascination of the hated?"

"Oh?"

"He abominates this place, you know. He calls us a 'nest of vipers.' Could he perhaps not be able to resist the temptation to peer at a nest of vipers?"

Ezra began to chuckle.

"Mijnheer?"

"So I am to be married with half the British Navy looking on, eh? Well now, that's right sassy of them to show up at a time like this."

The officers had not previously known who this casual acquaintance was, and when the English-speaking one had interpreted, Ezra was pummeled with congratulations, his hand vigorously wrung.

In the midst of this scene Lady Helen Ashley appeared on the parade ground, where the marriage was to take place. The Government House might have been too small. And it was a beautiful day.

Ezra went to her, and took both her hands.

"I'm so happy," she whispered.

"Well, I sure am too."

They were joined right then and there. Governor de Graeff

read from the prayer book phrase by phrase, first in Dutch, then his own free translation into English. Even so, the service took only a few minutes.

The Governor whooped, and he kissed the bride with gusto. Wine was opened everywhere. A soldier handed the Governor a letter, but De Graeff, more interested in a drink, shoved this impatiently beneath his tunic. The soldier, clearly troubled, spoke to Colonel Ravené, who in turn spoke low and urgently to the Governor, who frowned, took out the letter, put on his spectacles, and read.

Then it was as though the Governor had been clubbed. He staggered. The letter was not long, no more than a note, as they all could see; but he must have read it three times.

Pain ran across his face, and when he looked up he had forgotten about the champagne.

He motioned listlessly toward the parapet.

"Great Britain has declared war against the Netherlands. That's the British fleet out there. This letter is from Admiral Rodney himself, and I suppose he must have got the news by some fast dispatch boat. He commands me to surrender the whole island and everything on it—immediately."

He had spoken in English, directly to Ezra, possibly the only man whom in his grief he could distinguish; but enough of the others understood English to cause a stir. Count Bylandt, without so much as a word of farewell, started for the gate; and he was followed by all his aides.

Ezra grabbed the Governor's arm.

"*What are you going to do?*"

The Governor shrugged. He was limp, like a broken toy, like a rag doll.

"Do? What can I do, against all that force? They could blow us out of the sea. I'll surrender."

Chapter

38

Pandemonium ensued. Men ran back and forth, shouting. Men stood at the parapet and shook their fists at the British fleet, which they at the same time pelted with curses. Others prayed; and a few wept. But most of the men—and there was always a crowd at Fort Oranje—immediately and most noisily set about gathering together for purposes of concealment their most valuable possessions. Because these for the most part were in the town or in vessels in the roads there was a rush down the Bay Path.

Seemingly the only two sane persons left in that scene of uproar, Ezra Bond and his wife, stood side by side, their hands joined as they had been throughout the ceremony, and in silence for a little while they looked out over the town, the anchorage.

He shook his head. He sighed.

"*You'll* be safe, anyway. A lovely woman in a place like this isn't going to be mauled. You probably have what you call connections anyway?"

"I do have, yes. And they may be powerful enough to get you clear."

"Oh, no," he said quickly. "I don't trust the British Navy. They stand by their mistakes—of which I am one."

"They wouldn't—"

"Oh, yes, they would! They'd trice me right up at the nearest gangway and keep lashing me until I was reduced to a gibbering idiot. What if I could manage to clear my name afterward? What good would that do? No. I'll not be flogged again, Helen. I'd rather be hanged. There's a good chance of that too, of course."

He felt her hand tighten in his. There were tears in her eyes, but she kept them there, refusing to allow them the liberty of her cheeks: she was never a woman to sniffle.

After a while she said, carefully: "What are you going to do, then?"

"Fight—if there is a fight."

"Do you think that there will be?"

"No, I don't. The Governor's already said he's going to give up, and nobody's likely to talk him into changing his mind." Ezra nodded toward the open sea, the British fleet. "They've got maybe five-six thousand marines and soldiers down there. Professionals. And here—well, even if the militia could be assembled in time, which it couldn't, we wouldn't number more than about that many *hundred,* all raw. No, I don't look for any fighting, though if there is I'll want to be in it, naturally," he went on. "But there's just a chance that this is a hit-and-run raid on a large scale. Bringing up a force the size of that one down there to take over an island the size of this one—why, it'd be like using a sledge-hammer to squash a cockroach with. Anyway, a heap of those goods down there, and of that money, is English."

"Admiral Rodney might not know that. Or he might make out that he didn't."

"That's true. And this is a rich prize, a whole heap richer than any Spanish plate fleet in the old days. But it would take a long while to comb the goods and dispose of them, and Rodney is supposed to be hunting out the French fleet and fighting it. That's what he's here for, isn't it?"

"I suppose it is."

213

They stood, soundless, while around them the hubbub increased. Their hands were slippery with sweat now.

"If it isn't just a quick strike, and if they decide to stay a while, whatever'll you do then?" she asked at last.

"My first duty, after you," he said slowly, "is to my men and my owners and for that matter my country."

"Maybe your first duty is to yourself, for my sake? Why couldn't you be just quiet and not do anything, and maybe they wouldn't notice you?"

"No. For a fee or a favor there'd always be somebody to point me out. You find Judases everywhere. Besides, I'm just plumb too famous. You said it yourself, just a little while ago, down there in the—uh—the tavern. Oh, the Royal Navy'd love to get their hands on the notorious Captain Gunpowder! What a wonderful example I'd make, high up on the end of a rope, after they had finished slashing my back to shreds! You wouldn't want a husband like that, now would you?"

"I—I can't believe that they'd be that cruel."

"I can. I've seen it. From their point of view, remember, I'm not a privateer at all. I'm a pirate. And you know what they do with pirates, don't you? No, my dear, if they're going to stay around for a while I must blow up my vessel. It's packed to the gunwales with powder, as usual. It'd make a beautiful sight. But first, and no matter what happens, I must go down there and open up the ship's money chest and pay the men off, ahead of time. That will at least give them something to defend themselves with. But if they want me to lead them into the interior, to camp out for a while until this has blown over—why, I'll do that. It's what I plan for myself anyway. Way I see it, it's the only thing *to* do."

"It—it will be hard on us, Ezra," she whispered.

"Yes."

"On both of us."

"Yes."

"It may be days before we see one another again."

214

"It may be weeks," he said grimly.

"Oh, my darling!"

They turned, crushing against each other, and they kissed for a long while. It was Ezra who broke away at last. He did not speak any word of farewell, for he didn't trust his voice. He simply ran off with the others on the Bay Path.

He did not look back. He did not dare to.

Chapter

39

The Street was a madhouse, Bedlam. From there, virtually sea level, even with a glass it would have been difficult to distinguish the vessels beyond the mole as war vessels, and there might still have been a few skeptics; but if so, they were not many. Fear spreads as it always spreads when there's a crowd, in fast-widening circles, crackling meanwhile like fire. Indeed it reminded Ezra of just that—a forest fire. He could almost smell the smoke.

Some men were engaged in a frantic effort to board up and otherwise fortify their shops and offices, seemingly in the silly belief that this would keep the enemy out. Most were trying to get away from the town, with everything that they could carry.

Two things struck Ezra as curious. One was that nobody seemed for a minute to doubt that the British were about to pounce upon an unprotected island that offered great loot, and this before news of the declaration of war could have reached it. Ezra himself would not have put anything beyond the Royal Navy, but he was amazed to see that such cynicism was widespread. The Dutch traditionally distrusted the English, but there were also many Yankees among the traders on the beach, and indeed more than a few Englishmen.

The other thing was that so few men instinctively turned to

the sea for escape. This would have been as futile as the barricading of buildings along the Street, for the entrance to Statia roads was a narrow one, and the British undoubtedly would block it with a flotilla of many-oared and heavily armed cutters, boats that could easily outspeed any sailing vessel; but the Statians were a sea-oriented people, and Ezra would have thought that in a moment of fright they would turn to the sea, howsoever foolishly. In fact, the few who were doing this were, like Ezra himself, quite clearly skippers or mates who wished to get to their ships while there was yet time, to release the crews, to lift the money chests, to grab personal belongings or articles of value.

The Street was so crowded that any haste along its mile or more was not possible. It was always so; but today progress was further impeded by the many packages that the men toted, whether on their backs, their shoulders, their heads, in a barrow pushed ahead, in a sled dragged behind. These were chests and bundles, boxes of all sorts, household effects, clothing, weapons, and all manner of utensils and produce that ranged from sadirons to mangoes. Ezra saw one man staggering along under the weight of a featherbed, no doubt having reasoned that he might as well sleep comfortably in the jungle, while another, who apparently liked his bread fresh, carried a sack of flour. Almost everybody was weighted down with coins, most of these in canvas bags, though Ezra did see one prominent trader who hugged to his belly a chamberpotful of Surinam guilders.

Van Bibber was literally shoveling coins into a chest—Spanish eight-pieces, Portuguese gold Joes, double-Joes, and half-Joes, Amsterdam guilders, French crowns, British guineas.

"That's a handy thing to have," Ezra commented.

"Kept it here for just such an emergency."

"You're a farseeing man. I never even thought of it. It'll make you popular inside the Quill."

"Not going into that hole. Wouldn't be safe to bury this there. Too spongy. And all those rats."

"You're heading for the rocks at the west end of the island?"

"That's right. Harder to find cover there, sure, but at least my money would be safe for a little while, and if it turns out that this is just a hit-and-run raid I may still be solvent at that."

"It won't."

"I'm afraid you're right, captain. Here, here's what I owe your vessel."

"That's exactly what I came for. Thanks."

Aboard the sloop he lined up the men, and passed out small arms and pay, explaining the situation.

"I've paid you first so's you won't have to worry about making up your mind what to do. We're all quitting the ship, each man to take as much of his stuff as he can carry. You can stay in town if you like, and just wait to be captured. Me, I'm heading for the hole in that big hill up there. I've been there. It's no paradise. It's mighty thick and mighty hot, but you could hide out there for a long, long while.

"Now, first I want to tell you that there's still a faint chance that the Governor might offer resistance. He couldn't hold out any length of time at the very best, because there's just not enough food. He could be starved out without any fighting at all. They've got enough vessels to surround the whole island, bowsprit to sternpost. But there's a French fleet at Fort Royal that's supposed to be headed for Virginia or maybe New York to help General Washington, and Admiral Rodney might not want to take the chance that it could slip away in case this operation takes a long time. That's just a *filmy* chance, y'understand. But if the Governor does elect to fight, I'm going to stay with him. But you can do what you want, and no hard feelings. Right?"

He spread his feet, facing them. He fisted his hips.

"Well, what d'ye say?"

To his astonishment they voted unanimously and without any argument to stay with him whatever he did. It actually stung Ezra's eyes and made a lump come into his throat to hear that. He had not thought that he was notably beloved by the crewmen of the *Forbearance,* who to a man had adored Lemuel Hart. Ezra had to turn away for a moment, swallowing.

"All right," he said gruffly. "Put the longboat over and get your things. Some of you take off the main hatch and fetch a spare topsail. And iron nails. Cook, is your fire going?"

"Yes, sir."

"Keep it that way. Don't let it die."

He made the torch out of tarred rope-ends. It would burn stodgily but persistently—and for a long time.

When they saw him do that and heard him give an order to fold the topsail four times over the open hatch and batten it down at the edges—for there was upwards of twenty thousands pounds of gunpowder down there—a few of them might have felt afraid; but he reassured any such.

"You start ashore right away, all of you. I'll do it alone, at the last minute, if it's got to be done."

As it happened, he did not need to go ashore to learn that De Graeff had formally surrendered. Around the end of the mole swept the first of the Royal Navy advance cutters, clean, smart, fast. It would never move like that if there was a possibility of cannonshots.

It was followed by another, and then another, and more . . . and more . . . Ezra counted sixteen, and they were still coming when he turned aside.

The British were not losing any time, and not taking any chances.

"Shove off," he called to Tom Garrettson, in charge of the longboat.

He took the torch and got it well lighted at the galley stove. It spluttered peevishly. He swung it several times around his head, to be certain. He tossed it onto the stretched topsail, which had been dampened.

For a mad instant he feared that the two men he had left in

219

his gig overside, two of his best men, the ship's money chest at their feet, oars run out, might themselves shove off—in fear. But they were still there when he clambered down the Jacob's ladder.

At the quay he looked back. The British were closer, and coming fast. There must be at least thirty of the cutters now, and each had, besides its rowers on either side, about forty standing redcoats, their bayonets glittering in the sun.

"Well, come on," Ezra said to his men.

They must have been almost halfway up the side of the stubby old volcano when there was the sound of a distant pop behind them. It was no louder than a child's squib, a firecracker from China, yet surely it had been an explosion.

"That couldn't be *Forbearance*," Ezra muttered as he turned to look out over the roads. "She'd make a much bigger bang than that."

It wasn't. It had been a minor accident on one of the quays. The sloop from Saybrook, serene, imperturbable, her hold crammed with gunpowder to the last cubic inch, still floated, far out, intact. Ezra scowled. Evidently the torch had gone out, and he hated to think of all that fine stuff falling into the hands of the British; but it was too late to go back now.

"Come on," he said.

Chapter

40

It was like climbing down into Hell. Once they had crested the lip of the volcano they entered a world different in every way from the world outside.

If some gigantic lamp or candle had been whuffed out, the sun itself expunged, the coming of darkness could not have been more abrupt. It was not as though they walked into a gloomy place, but rather as though gloom had rushed forward to engulf them. The slopes of the Quill had been hot, drenched in sunshine, but with the air in motion—sea breeze all day, a land breeze at night. Here in this hellish hole there was no movement of air whatever. It was hard to breathe, as it was even hard to *walk* through that thick wet atmosphere, like pushing your way across a cloud of steam. It was even hotter than it had been outside, and everything—the ferns underfoot, the branches above, the slimy liana vines that hung everywhere—was wet. It was not a recent wetness, fresh, as though after a shower. It was a permanent condition, a state of affairs. Everything here, you were quickly convinced, had always *been* wet. It stank of rotting vegetation. Outside there had been sounds, if faint ones, growing fainter as the men had climbed the Quill—the breeze, querulous seagulls, the tinkling of ship's bells. Here there were no sounds;

and their own words, when they whispered to one another—for it seemed natural to whisper—were gulped by the soggy air almost before they had left the mouth, and were followed by no echoes.

"I'm afeared of this place," Tom Garrettson said.

"So am I," said Ezra, being careful to keep his voice low. "It's no spot for a sailor."

If they could not see their own feet and knew about the dark-colored lianas only when they collided with them, they could see nothing at all above, no patch, no scrap of sky, though it was early afternoon. They learned of this when after a few minutes, during which time they heard only themselves, there came a screeching above, a hideous sound of pain and fright, followed by squawks and the flapping of many wings. Every head was raised, to no effect.

"Something napped a bird," a man muttered.

"A snake maybe," said another.

"There are no snakes on Statia," Ezra said severely.

"Well, it was *something*, anyway. Scared the others away."

Ezra, the only one who had been there before—though he had not ventured *far* in—knew what it was. It was rats, perhaps even worse than snakes. Rats are very ingenious and adaptable animals. If they could climb the bole of a coconut tree and crack open the green fruit, as Ezra had seen them do, they could easily clamber up a liana or the moss-encrusted trunk of a tree in order to attack birds perched high in its branches. He said nothing of this. The men were twitchy enough already.

They did not go far. Ezra, who did not wish to lose touch with the lip of the crater, and who had only a vague idea of the size of the place, early called a halt. The men sat down or lay down on their possessions, exhausted, covered with sweat that they knew would not dry, and uneasy still about those snakes—or whatever they were. Ezra told off two of the most reliable, appointed Tom Garretson to command the rest, and retraced his steps to the north side of the Quill, the side that faced down on the fort, the town of Oranjestad, the roads.

They did not *literally* retrace their steps, for these were hard to discern, even when they leaned close to the earth; but rather they made their way back mostly by feeling for torn vines, broken twigs, violated bark and moss. This would be an easy place in which to get lost. It would also be an easy place in which to avoid pursuers.

What he expected to see when he poked his head above the edge of the crater and looked down the side of the mountain he could not have said. He was tense, half-prepared to spot a British patrol, perhaps only a few feet away, coming toward him. Or it might be that the slope would be strewn with the figures of frightened men fleeing from the invader. What he did see—on the slope, that is—was nothing.

There was God's plenty of activity in Oranjestad and in the roads, beyond the mole too. More than one skipper had fired his ship before quitting it, so that the air was black with swirling smoke, and from where he crouched Ezra even thought that he could hear the faint crackling of flames, a sound like eggs in a frypan. Others had cut their cables, so that some vessels drifted aimlessly, turning around and around. More redcoats were being landed all the time. Most of these carried bayoneted muskets, but there were a few with short, stumpy battering-rams improvised out of spars. All up and down the Street doors were being smashed, goods were being hauled out and piled on the pavement for appraisal. As far as Ezra could see, nobody was molesting the Mariners' Rest, which probably would be turned into an officers' club, but the Bay Path was crowded with traffic going both ways.

Though there was nobody climbing the Quill—on this side anyway—small groups of fugitives were pouring out of town toward the north and east. They too, like Ezra's men, were laden with everything that they could carry. Assumedly they were head-

223

ing for the five smaller hills in that part of the island, a bare territory, where, however, they might hope to catch a wild goat now and then—goats put there many years ago by pirates. Nobody chased those fugitives or strove to stop them. Perhaps the invaders, who surely were well trained for their job, were glad to get them out of town, out of the way, so as to leave elbow room for the glorious business of plunder.

It could be that the redcoats were contemptuous of those who fled, knowing well that they could be hunted down later, or perhaps forced by hunger to come back to town.

After all, what *would* they eat? What would Ezra and his men eat once they finished the rations they had brought with them, a matter of two or three days? The others, at the upper end of the island, at least could try for those goats, and conceivably at night they might do a little offshore fishing. The crater of the Quill, in Ezra's mind, offered a safer sanctuary, a better chance to hold out against hunters; but what did the crater offer in the way of food? There might be some coconut trees, but the rats would long since have stripped them of their fruit. He could hope and pray for cabbage palms, the fruit of which made a tasty slaw. The men would go into competition with the rats for the birds, a one-sided contest surely. And then of course there were the rats themselves. It was not a flavorsome thought.

It was nearing sunset. Would they make a ceremony of it, on the parade ground of the fort, which structure he supposed would be used as a military headquarters? Half idly, bemused, Ezra looked that way. He got a shock.

The fort was indeed a headquarters, now as before. There would be a major general in charge of so large a force, and his bark, it could be gathered, would be loud. There was a great deal of scurrying down there, the figures looking like toy soldiers, as messages were carried, sentries posted, reports made, back and forth across the very spot where a few short hours ago he and Lady Helen Ashley had stood to be married. Just at first it all

224

seemed exactly the scene he had expected to see. Then he noticed the flag.

It was not the Union Jack but the orange flag of the Netherlands.

Could it be that there was still some resistance, some die-hard handful of bitter-enders who had sealed themselves in a remote part of the fort? No, that was nonsense. The British already ashore outnumbered the entire Dutch garrison, with the militia thrown in, by at least fifty to one. There was no sign of fighting, no sound of firing, down there. Moreover, the flagpole was not located atop some turret or tower difficult of access but right smacketty-dab in the middle of the parade ground, with Britishers passing it all the time.

Could it be that somebody had simply *forgotten* to haul the flag down? or that in the confusion attendant upon the landing the proper order had not been properly given to the proper party and countersigned by the proper officer at the proper time? That wouldn't do either. Thousands could see that flag, and attention would be called to it, caustically. The admiral himself, with his glass, could spy it from his flagship and speak up.

Then it dawned on Ezra that the admiral himself (with his glass) might have *ordered* that this very thing be done.

When you approached St. Eustatius from the west, as Ezra Bond well knew, the first thing you picked up was what sailors called the White Wall. This was a part of the Quill, a whole side, that had fallen away in some old-time earthquake, exposing a stretch of the inner, lighter rock of which the mountain was made. It stood out in any weather, at any hour, a most convenient landfall.

Then, when you had swung around to face Oranjestad full-on, you sought out the fort, which of course was high up. You steered by it, pointing your bowsprit straight at that Dutch flag that fluttered up there, which took you right through the pass in the mole and saved you the price of a pilot.

It would take weeks and even months for word to spread that there was a war between Great Britain and the Netherlands. Ships at sea, and especially those making long voyages, did not always hear things like that until it was too late. Vessel after vessel in the near future, Dutch or French or Yankee, Ezra could foresee, would have her bowsprit pointed at that familiar orange ensign, and would come innocently through the pass in the belief on the part of her captain that he was entering a neutral port. By the time that he learned his mistake, he would be seized. It was a dirty trick, but a technically legitimate *ruse de guerre*. They would sail right into the lion's mouth, dozens of them, scores, conceivably even hundreds.

It looked as if Admiral Rodney was fixing for a long stay.

Chapter

41

In the morning he learned that almost half of his men had left. He was amazed by the number, but not at all by the fact that there *were* desertions. The men knew they could leave at any time they liked, though he had told them that he preferred the night, lest they betray the hideaway. At least those who went, went quietly, leaving their food behind.

The two hands he had taken with him on yesterday's reconnoitering trip had spread the word that this was not, after all, to be a mere hit-and-run raid on the way to Guadeloupe or Martinique, that the British from the looks of things had come to stay for some time. This took the heart out of many of the men, who had looked forward to only a few days in the jungle, at most. If the British were breaking open warehouses methodically, as the hands had reported, it meant a good long stay. It had taken years to pack all that material, and it would take weeks and maybe months to sort it, repile it, price it, sell it, or haul it away.

A greater influence was the rats, which many of the men, despite Ezra's disclaimer, persisted in calling snakes, expecting, it would seem, to be nipped at any moment by a bushmaster, fer-de-lance, or cascabel. Even those who did believe that the noise-makers were rats did not like the ones in the Quill crater.

The night had been hideous, and largely because of them. Pauselessly they had slithered among the ferns, raced up and down the vines, and, worst of all, approached to sniff and sometimes to run across the men who were striving to sleep. One seaman even said that he had been bitten in the chin. He was one of the snakebelievers, and he insisted that he was poisoned and would die if he didn't get down to what he called "civilization." Ezra let him go.

"Imagine mariners being afraid of rats," stormed Ezra.

All the same, he sympathized with the hands. He had heard—as who hadn't?—the story of the seaman who announced that he was shut of the sea and put an oar over his shoulder and started to walk inland. When somebody asked him how far he planned to go, he pointed to the oar and said: "I'll keep moving until somebody asks me what that thing is, and there's the place where I'll stop and settle down." Ezra had chuckled at the story, but he did not believe it. That was not the way seamen were. They might curse it, and frequently did, but they were uneasy and even frightened when deprived of the sight and sound of their own element. He knew these men here, and knew that there wasn't a cowardly bone in any of them. He had watched them ride out, with no expression, blows that would have sent any landlubber to his knees, screaming for mercy—and that, too, while they knew that beneath them there was enough explosive to blow them to Kingdom Come many times over. Yet coop them up in a volcanic caldron, even for only a few hours, and they were rolling their eyes, wiping their mouths with hands that trembled, and in short verging on panic.

Shortly after sunrise a few of the deserters sheepishly returned. They were given back their food. But they would not last long. Ezra knew that. Their nerves were shaken.

They found water, their first consideration. This was a clear bright spring that rose at a point just inside the crater near the part of the lip they had scrambled over, and then meandered, in the form of a brooklet, into the jungle. In a hideaway as high as this one, Ezra had feared that they would be obliged to catch rainwater, and with this in mind he had brought along several spare sails, which now could be used for sleeping.

That first morning was somewhat less depressing than had been the previous night. For one thing, they learned that the jungle was not always as dark as they had found it. The latter part of the morning and the early part of the afternoon the sun found its way through in places, so that the ferns and the trees and the vines were dappled. It was still dim, but at least they could see through to avoid bumping into trees. Only when the sun was low did it become dangerously dark in there.

Not that there was much to see. There were orchids, to be sure, most of them very high, all of them useless; but there were also the huge ugly gray malevolent rats. There were no cabbage palms. The only thing that looked at all edible was a bright red berry, somewhat like a holly berry, reminding Ezra of the barberries in the woods back home, and looking mighty pert in this tropical welter; but when one of the men swallowed a handful of these he reported that they were bitter and stung his throat, and a little later he vomited.

Ezra had given strict orders that there should be no fire, and this was a cause of grumbling. Ezra flared.

"What if you was a British officer down there, and you saw smoke coming out of a volcano that's supposed to have been dead for hundreds of years, you'd come up and take a look, now wouldn't you?"

The sailor scratched his head.

"I guess I'd get away from there."

"And leave a million pounds of loot behind, besides all of those vessels? Oh, no. These boys'll be around here for some time yet."

"That's just what I'm afraid of."

In Orangetown the redcoats were as busy as ants, and as effi-

229

cient. They were not wanton. They did not burn, and they used their battering-rams, it would appear, only when they could not get into a shop, warehouse, or office in any other way. They seemed immediately concerned not with ferreting out those who had fled, or even with classifying and disciplining those who remained, but rather with getting some idea of the extent of their bag. It was tremendous. When Ezra Bond had spoken of "a million pounds of loot" he understated it. There could be three or four times that much. Besides the goods in the warehouses, besides the bullion and the coins in strongboxes, there were all those vessels, well over a hundred, most of them small, to be sure, but some large, and a few, like the frigate *Mars*, were first-class prizes.

More ships were coming in all the time. Ezra had read aright the leaving of the Netherlands flag on the mast at the fort. The navy was as busy down there as the army. Since such an array of warships assuredly would frighten off any oncoming trader, they were scattered in various ways. Some, assumedly the fastest ones, were put on patrol just outside the pass in the mole, so that they could chase anybody who came in close, got frightened, turned, and started away. Others came into the roads and proceeded to man the already-captured vessels with prize crews, and to anchor the derelicts and sink the charred wrecks, and otherwise restore order. Yet others were put on patrol in the waters that surrounded the island. These would anchor when there was any anchorage, or otherwise stand off and on. They all put fast-rowing cutters overside, clearly for the purpose of intercepting any boat that might try to make for some neighboring island with fugitives or with goods. Ezra, peering, believed that this activity would be redoubled after dark. Finally, a fleet of the larger vessels, mostly frigates, made off that first morning for the northwest, probably, Ezra reasoned, to take over Saba and St. Martin, a couple of nearby islands that were also Dutch.

That left the entrance to Statia roads comparatively clear, so that a newcomer could see only the usual forest of masts inside the mole and would have no way of knowing that many of these were on warships. Even while Ezra watched, that morning, two lambs came to the slaughter, being promptly boarded before they could turn and run; and the lookouts he posted there for the rest of the day mentioned five more. Admiral Rodney didn't even have to chase his prizes. He must have been, already, a very rich man.

The two sentries at the lip of the crater, watching the town, Ezra esteemed very important. It was evident that the British would not send a hunting party up the Quill right away, but they might well do so after the preliminaries of pillage had been handled. In any case, in a little while some officers or men—or both—could conceivably organize a picnic up there just to see what it was like. Ezra's own first visit had been on just such a party, which could cause much trouble if the Americans were not warned.

He assigned others to guard duty at the lip, but these were told to circulate. The crater was about three-quarters of a mile from lip to lip, and perfectly round. The floor of it, the jungle, was a little more than half a mile across, Ezra calculated. Between these two was a steep bank of loose rock and rubble, no good for camping but easily scaled or descended. The circulating sentries were told to stick their heads above the level of the lip at different points every now and then, just to be sure that no search party or picnic party came from some other direction but that of the town.

Minding that Satan finds work for idle hands, and troubled too about the way the food was disappearing, Ezra put the balance of the men to work on what he hoped would be a systematic search of every tree in the crater, the object being, of course, bird's eggs. The results were disappointing. In almost every case the rats had been there first, and had done a thorough job.

Three more men slipped away that night, the second night.

"If this keeps up I'll be the only one left," said Ezra to himself; and he wondered what Helen would think when she heard about the desertions. The question of what Helen would think occupied a heap of his own thoughts up there in the crater. He prayed that she would not, after pondering it, decide that he had bolted only in order to save his own skin. It was much more than that, as he hoped she would see. It was a matter of their marriage, no less. Even if they failed to hang him, and even if in time he could desert or perhaps prove that he had been wrongly impressed, what kind of man would he be at the end of another and longer lashing? She must know this. *He* certainly did.

His glass was always with him, and often at his eye. The Governor's residence, the garden behind, the flagstoned court in front, were what he most often stared at; but though there were many scarlet uniforms there—the place clearly had been taken over as an occupation headquarters—it was but seldom that he glimpsed a woman, who then, customarily, was a Negro, a servant of some sort. Twice at a window he did see, briefly, somebody in pink, the color Helen had worn that never-to-be-forgotten morning at the Mariners' Rest. He could not be sure that either of these was his wife, but he allowed himself to think so. He sighed.

The sight of the *Forbearance* down there, anchored so daintily, was excruciating. Why hadn't he waved that torch a little harder? Was another try feasible? or would it be no more than suicide? If anything further was done it would need to be done soon. The sloop was far from shore, and the British, who were going about the business systematically, had not yet reached her for a thorough search, though they had, as Ezra saw through his glass, circled her several times and boarded her for a short while for the purpose of determining that she was deserted. But they would get to her in full force very soon, any day now, and then she would be sent off to England.

Ezra debated this, but only to himself, silently.

Chapter

42

From the beginning the money chest was a cause of trouble. Themselves already paid off, the men resented it as an encumbrance. It was bulky, and it was heavy. It held upwards of £11,000 in coins of sundry kinds, the proceeds of the down-voyage, the most successful that Ezra had commanded; but all this metal would do them no good inside the Quill, for you can't munch silver, you can't masticate gold. It would have been better, the men muttered, if the thing had been filled with biscuit. In vain did Ezra point out that having lost the vessel—through no fault of their own, admittedly—it behooved them to save whatever they could for the owners. They did not answer this out loud, but he could read it in their eyes: That's all right for *you*, with a one-quarter lay, but what about *us?*

The thing constituted a reproach as it sat there slowly sinking into the earth. Ezra wished now that he had done as Abraham van Bibber had—taken along a shovel to bury the box. That would have been easy to do, any night, outside the crater. Then the thing would have been out of view and would no longer persist in reminding them of what a back-wrenching job it had been to tote it all the way up the mountain. But it was too late now.

Late the third afternoon he sent out a hunting squad of three men armed with muskets. It was not easy to find three men of some experience in the killing of animals. It had always amused Ezra Bond the way most foreigners supposed that all Yankees were crack shots, all of America being, in their eyes, one vast wilderness teeming with wildlife. Ezra himself, like most of his acquaintances, seagoing and otherwise, had never seen a bear, a wolf, a fox. He had seen wild goats only at a distance and only down here in the islands; and he was himself a poor shot.

It was wild goats that he sent the men to get. He cautioned them not to stay out long, not to go far, and not to separate lest they shoot one another by accident. There was precious little dusk here in St. Eustatius, but it takes a little while for any man's eyes to adjust themselves to the full coming of night, and Ezra feared that one of these hunters might prove overeager.

They were gone for about an hour and it was quite dark when somebody on watch heard a shot—just one shot, and it sounded far away. For another hour nothing happened. Had the men run into a British patrol? Then there was a hiss, and three figures loomed on the slope, carrying, it looked like, a fourth.

The one shot had been made to count; but what they carried was not the body of a wild goat but that of a pig.

It was a small pig, and it looked weak and tired, as though it had broken out of some peasant's sty and wandered for a long time with very little to eat. It was thin. But—it *was* a pig.

This posed a problem. Back in Connecticut there were old-timers who refused to eat any part of a pig in any circumstances, even as bacon, because they could quote from Leviticus:

"And the swine, though he divide the hoof, and be cloven-footed, yet he cheweth not the cud; he is unclean to you,"

or from Deuteronomy:

"And the swine, because it divideth the hoof, yet cheweth not the cud, it is unclean unto you: ye shall not eat of their flesh, nor touch their dead carcase,"

and ask if anything could be clearer than that?

To this Ezra Bond, like so many others, was wont to reply that Deuteronomy and Leviticus were Old Testament books and so the prohibition applied only to Jews, not to Christians. Frankly, he had never been satisfied with this answer, which smacked of sophistry. In any case, a man who took to the sea couldn't eschew pork. He'd starve if he did. Salt pork—"salt john," they called it, Ezra never did know why—was the principal part of his seagoing diet. The pork barrel was the column that his meals were built around. Bread soon was filled with weevils. Fruit went bad, and so did vegetables, and so did most meats, on a long voyage. Fish that were caught overside could not be counted upon. But the salt john barrel always was there, with its top off.

These men, then, were used to pigs and their meat. Though the cook had gone back to town to give himself up, one of the first, there were many men present who knew what to do with a pig, dead or alive.

However, they also knew that, religion or no religion, New Testament or Old Testament, and personal taste being put aside, pork, to be safe, has to be *cooked*. And it has to be *well* cooked. They might have faced, though surely not with relish, the prospect of eating a goat raw. This was simply not to be thought of in the case of a hog. It would be like eating poison.

This was a night intermittently overcast, the first such, and Ezra agreed to an exception to his no-fire rule. They went to a point just outside the jungle, just inside the lip of the crater, and the side farthest from Oranjestad. There they roasted the pig.

It was a curious scene.

The fire was stodgy and very smoky, for the only wood they could gather was wet. It was in a pit they had dug for the purpose, a pit that could be filled afterward so that both the charred sticks and the fat droppings would be hidden from a possible future scouting party. The pig itself was spitted, and the spit was mounted on two forked uprights and turned by hand. It took a long time because of the poor fire, but nobody left the premises. They watched the process intently, and listened enraptured to the droppings hiss as they hit the flames. It was as though they had never before seen anything like this.

At one end of the pit was a canvas bucket containing the intestines. At the other end a similar bucket held the head and feet. The plan was to bury these with the ashes later, in order to deny them to the rats.

"Goddam' critters just as like to dig 'em up anyhow," said one hand, with a glance at the outer circle of spectators.

"Mind your language, man," Tom Garrettson snapped.

One seaman did timorously suggest that the feet at least be retained, for he said he had heard that Germans not only ate pigs' feet but actually liked them; but he was shushed to silence by the others, who were revolted by the very thought of such a dish.

The rats were fully as interested in this barbecue as were the men, and they were much more numerous. There were hundreds of them, there might have been thousands, that had come swarming out of the protection of the jungle, fascinated by the smell. The circle they formed was not much bigger than that of the human beings, for they were most marvelously bold, and now and then one would dart into the inner circle as well, running up close to the pit itself, easily eluding the cudgels of men who strove to kill it, and then scurry back. For the most part, however, the rats were visible only as eyes, eyes that did not glow like those of a cat but glittered serpentwise, malevolent, and very bright.

Some of the rats moved about a great deal, now in one part of the outer circle, now in another, sometimes edging forward, again falling back. Others remained motionless, their chins against the ground, their eyes gleaming, all hatred.

There were still men who believed that there were snakes in the crater, but now nobody denied that there were rats, and most

236

of the men said that if there ever *had* been snakes the rats would have killed and eaten them long since. With the slanting of a better light, the morning of the second day, the men had found strewn on the floor of the crater a large number of eggshells, undoubtedly birds' eggs, and also many tiny bones. The bones could have been those of birds, but there were few feathers and even a rat wouldn't eat feathers, which in this cooped-up breezeless place would not have been blown away. The conclusion was inescapable. Besides the eggs and an occasional bird, the rats had subsisted on certain roots: there was evidence of this. But they multiplied very fast, as everybody knew, and when there came to be too many of them, and too little food, they fell upon one another, perhaps in organized armies, rat-fashion, and after the war the victors devoured the vanquished.

It was not a pleasant thought. It was not conducive to sleep when you lay on a strip of canvas and heard the little dirty-gray devils rustling in the ferns around you, or when you looked over your shoulder and saw that the darkness beyond the firelight was stippled with tiny bright evil eyes.

"If we was to get took sick and couldn't defend ourself," said Jared Brown, the bosun, "they'd sure have a sweet supper on *us*."

He's thinking of turning himself in, was Ezra's reflection.

When at last the pig was cooked to the satisfaction of all, they laid it out on a sail and went at it with their sheath knives. They ate every scrap of meat and fat, and even sucked the bones, which afterward they buried, together with head, feet, and entrails. Then they drank at the spring, and, except for those assigned to sentry duty, they curled up on the ground and went to sleep.

This night was a quiet one, for the rats did not return to the jungle with the men but instead skittered around the filled-in pit, sniffing, sniffing, their whiskers twitching, while they made small, urgent squeals. They were still doing that at dawn, a few hours later, when the men got up. They were very hungry, those rats.

Chapter

43

A wave of emotion filled Ezra every time he gazed at the *Forbearance* through his glass. He had a real fondness for that sloop. He felt the time rapidly nearing when profane hands would be laid upon her. It was as though he were watching a cherished sister or daughter as rapists encircled her, their fingers twitching for the feel of her flesh, while he, bound and gagged, could do nothing.

On the morning of the fourth day he announced that he couldn't stand it any longer and that he proposed to lead a party down to the beach that very night, take over one or more of a group of gigs he had already spotted, and row out to the *Forbearance*, which he would destroy. He called for volunteers.

There were only seventeen other men left in the crater at that time, including Tom Garrettson and Jared Brown the bosun, who was acting as second mate; and to Ezra's amazement every one of them volunteered. There would be no prize, no chance of gain, nor was any extra pay involved. Ezra had warned them that it would be a laborious and a perilous mission. Yet without hesitation every one of them raised his hand.

For a wild instant he flirted with the idea of taking them all, rigging sail, and "cutting out" the sloop, making for the open sea—and freedom. He quickly dropped this thought. A handful of men, unrehearsed, could never hope to haul anchor, raise sail, and wend their way among all that shipping and out through the pass in the mole without showing a light or making a betraying noise. It was unthinkable. Besides, Ezra was tolerably sure that the British in the course of their preliminary examination of the *Forbearance* had removed every stitch of her canvas. The sloop was too far away for Ezra to be certain of such an act, even through the glass, but the Royal Navy men had done exactly that with all the nearer vessels, the ones he *could* make out in detail, and it was reasonable to assume that they would do it in the case of the *Forbearance,* as a precaution against such a harebrained escape attempt as Ezra Bond had been about to propose.

So instead of beaming at the raised hands, as the men might have expected, he nodded glumly. His eyes sought out those of Tom Garrettson, and he led the mate to one side.

"What do you think?"

"Well, since you ask me, I think every single one of them's offering to go along because they hope that they can slip away in the dark, where they wouldn't have the brass to do it right here in front of you and me and the others."

"That's just what I thought, Tom." He put a hand on the mate's shoulder. "I guess you and I'd better do it alone, then."

"Je*ho*shaphat! When do we start?"

They started at sundown, slipping over the northeastern lip of the crater on a course that would avoid the town of Oranjestad and make instead for a little beach near Tumbledown Bay, where Ezra had spotted the boats. This would mean a long walk and a much longer row back to the roads, but it would involve passing no sentry post. They did not wish to get close to Oranjestad, a place that would ring all night to the boot-clatter of marines and military police.

By the time that they were halfway down the slope it was utterly dark, full night, and Oranjestad was pricked out with lights.

It was curious how the place tugged at them. Even the un-imaginative Tom Garrettson confessed to experiencing this feeling. Neither man had roots in the town or any notable fondness for it, yet it was a harsh physical effort to keep their steps from turning in that direction, so greatly did they crave company, their fellowmen. It was beyond reason, that feeling, a self-destructive impulse similar to the one men often suffer when, perched on high places, they are passionately tempted to throw themselves down.

The urge was still with them when they made the beach and turned their backs to the town, but it vanished when they reached the edge of Tumbledown Bay, being swamped by the shock that there were no boats.

Ezra had spotted those boats well, three of them, and, not trusting his own eyesight, had lent the glass to others, who confirmed this find. He marked it as memorable for the reason that elsewhere along the shore the British had taken care to haul away all manner of boats, even small fishing skiffs, even rowboats, for the obvious purpose of preventing the transfer of booty to other islands. The ones near Tumbledown Bay, Ezra had concluded, belonged to some trusted or specially privileged fishermen.

The boats had been pulled far up on shore and could not have been washed away. Yet they were no longer there. A mite frightened, for the first time, Ezra and Tom ran up and down the beach, scouring it with their eyes; but they found no sign of boats.

Time was pressing. It must have been almost four bells, and they were still a long way from the *Forbearance*. They decided to walk along the beach, not in the direction of Tumbledown Bay, for that would have meant too long a row back, but toward Oranjestad and the Statia roads, in the hope that they might stumble upon some overlooked gig or even raft. When they approached so near to the lights of Oranjestad that every step was fraught with peril, they would turn inland and make for the

Quill, admitting defeat. Meanwhile, they kept their eyes peeled.

They were lucky. They had gone scarcely more than a mile when they came upon a deserted rowboat. It was ramshackle, it was small. It contained only a conch, which suggested that it leaked. Indeed, so contemptible a craft was it that the British quite possibly had seen it—for it was not hidden—and scorned to confiscate it. Who would transport treasure in a cockleshell like that?

There were no oars, not even tholepins, but they were pre-pared for such a shortage. They had dismembered an empty water cask before leaving the crater, and each of them carried a couple of the staves, about two and a half feet long, three to four inches broad, which could be used in a pinch as paddles. It would be a clumsy arrangement, but better than swimming.

The launch took little time, the craft was so light. It proved, as they had expected, a sieve. From the beginning it was neces-sary for one man to bail with the conch while the other paddled, and they did this turn-and-turn-about.

Nevertheless they made good time, for desperation lent them strength, and it was not long after midnight when they slished through the pass and entered Statia roads.

Just at first, and for some time, they were among the "live" vessels—that is, war vessels and vessels maintained by prize crews or by their own crews under British officers. These, despite the hour, were bright with lights and loud with daytime sounds.

The moon would rise late, if it *did* rise, and there were few stars; but being in this crowded anchorage was like being in a city square. For they were not alone. In addition to the large-looming ships, the water was crisscrossed by all sorts of Moses boats, tenders, cutters, and gigs—skippers exchanging visits, offi-cers coming home from parties, trusted hands returning from shore leave, and the ubiquitous marines. The raiders' greatest danger, here, was that of being rammed. If even the smallest of these smartly handled, fast-moving craft was to butt their waterlogged rickle of sticks, it inevitably would sink it. Again, they were lucky. They were often cursed, sometimes jeered, but they were not challenged.

From there, paddling hard, they emerged into what might have been a marine graveyard. These vessels, like the others, were at anchor, close to one another, and they were of all sizes and rigs, but they were dark, silent, blobs of gloom from which no smoke rose. These were the "far out" vessels, the ones that had been abandoned on command but had not yet been occupied by boarding and pillage parties from the Royal Navy. No light showed on any of them, and if there was a man there, anywhere, he was a fugitive, a skulker, who kept out of sight. Nor was there any sound in that drear spot.

One of these dim shapes was the *Forbearance*. She was approximately in the middle of the mass. It took a long time, and their arms were weary when at last they found her.

It was a shock. From afar the *Forbearance*, though a prisoner, always had looked well preened, like some proud bird, a peacock, a cardinal. Up close, undeniably, she showed—well, *shabby*. Her rigging was slack; her sticks were bare; her anchor cables—in the crowded roadstead of St. Eustatius it was necessary to drop two hooks, one forward, one astern—already were slimy with seaweed. Even in the dark of night she seemed discouraged, a craft from which the spirit had flown, a lifeless thing, a hulk. When they had climbed a listless ladder they saw—and winced to see—that the deck was dirty. It hadn't been swabbed in almost a week.

They wasted no time in sadness but went promptly to work, lest daylight discover them. They had brought, in addition to the stave-paddles, a painter, and an ax, only flint and steel. Combustibles they knew that they could find aboard the sloop.

The main hatch was open, the hasty searchers having searched, it would seem, only as far down as the top layer of cargo, the cover, molasses, which they did not esteem worth the trouble of

242

protection. Fortunately it had not rained since the seizure, and the powder below, it could be assumed, still was dry.

Impatiently they rolled aside sundry barrels of molasses, and then, using the ax, they broached three barrels of underlying powder and scattered this at random. All around it, and to some extent on top of it, they placed oil-soaked shavings.

They went topside again. Ezra looked around at the nearby vessels and hoped that there was nobody in them.

Tom took the ax and started chopping the forward anchor cable. Ezra made two torches, using straws yanked out of a besom. They were taking no chances this time. *Each* would toss a flaming torch into the hold.

Tom finished at the bow, which began to swing, and he started for the stern cable. Their hope was that the *Forbearance*, aflame and floating free, might drift against some neighboring vessels and in this way cause even more damage.

Ezra got both torches glowing. Tom finished with the after-cable and the sloop swung about. Tom came amidships, still holding the ax. Ezra handed him a torch. They posted themselves near the ladder that led overside.

"You go first, when we've chucked," Ezra said.

"What's that, a case of age before beauty?"

Ezra grunted.

"Maybe pearls before swine, I don't know," he said.

"Look: I can move just as fast as you can."

"I said, You go first. That's an order."

Tom shrugged.

"Well, you're the captain."

They counted one-two-three, swinging their torches under-handed, and on the "three" they let go.

There was an immediate and very loud, though curiously muffled, "whoom." It was like a gigantic cough, coming from far below. Then flames appeared at the hatchway.

Ezra and Tom spun around and started down the ladder, Tom dutifully first.

Ezra had taken but a few steps when it seemed as though the *Forbearance* lurched out and struck him in the face. Dazed, he was conscious of falling. He hit the water flat on his back. It knocked the breath out of him, and foolishly, still in a daze, he opened his mouth.

There was another and much greater explosion, loud enough to knock a baby's eardrums in, and the water around him was lighted a brilliant red.

What with his clothes and all of the water he had swallowed, he was seared by the excruciating conviction that he would never make the surface. He struggled mightily, his eyes throbbing, his chest thumping.

Suddenly his head popped out, and he blinked in the light of the burning sloop only a few yards away. The heat on his face was terrific, it was unbearable.

He could not see the rowboat—smashed to smithereens, maybe?—but he did see Tom Garrettson, like him just emerged, blinking, spluttering; and he signaled to Tom to make for the shore.

As they set out, side by side, for the town, Ezra began to vomit. He almost choked himself; but in the long run it did him good. He worked his shoes off and let them drop.

The water all around them was red. It seemed itself afire. Things—small things, seemingly—were falling into it, making a thin splatter.

There was another vast "whoom," and Ezra felt as though somebody had shoved the back of his head—it actually pushed his face into the water for an instant; but he never ceased to stroke.

Half an hour later, panting but unscathed, they pulled themselves up on the quay at Oranjestad, where there was so much excitement that they were not noticed. They looked back.

The sloop from Saybrook still was burning, though on a feebler note now, and so were two other nearby vessels. It was a spectacular sight.

There was yet another "whoom," audible even there, and from out of the *Forbearance* rose a giddy column of sparks and smoke. After that she was silent, and dark. It was as abrupt as the whuffing out of a candle.

Ezra swallowed and spat, and what he wiped from his eyes was not all disaster.

"Well," he said at last, "if we're going to get there before sunup we'd better start right now. Come on."

They learned, just before they fell asleep in the steamy fastness of the crater, that in their absence only two of the men had deserted.

"Better'n we might have expected," said Tom Garrettson.

"Aye," said Ezra Bond.

Chapter

44

The pattern of life in Orangetown was changing from day to day, though slowly.

The English in their initial eagerness to compute the loot had done little, at first, to house and feed the civilians, who were everywhere, bumping about, getting in the way. Far from finding their places, so that the crowd of them diminished, the civilians were increasing in numbers as more and more of those who had taken to the hills straggled back into town. When at last the Army did address itself to this problem—and watching from above, Ezra Bond assumed that it was a job for the Army rather than for the Navy or the Marines—it was solved in several ways. A few of the men were assigned to tents in the camp the military had established on the beach, probably because there they would be handy when needed for questioning about the contraband. Others, the more exalted ones, were lodged in Government House or the fort. By far the largest number, though, were scattered among the vessels in the roads—commercial as well as war vessels. And so, with the offices and warehouses at last uncluttered, except by goods, the soldiers along the Street like harassed shopkeepers returned to their stocktaking.

The court at the fort was big enough only for the original

Dutch garrison, or, now, some honor guard or palace guard, a minute proportion of the men who needed exercise on this island. There was no parade ground within the camp, a jerry-built affair at best. This was the reason why, Ezra deduced, after the first landing confusion the British began to send small companies of soldiers and marines out into the countryside. These were surely not foraging parties, for St. Eustatius had nothing to offer but a few patches of sugar cane; and besides, mountains of rations had been brought ashore. The groups took no prisoners, and seemingly sought none, for they did not head for the hills but walked casually along the shore. They were not, then, search parties.

Of *those* there were plenty to the Quill, starting the day after the burning of the *Forbearance,* an act that enraged the British, who thereupon, it was patent, determined to track down and capture the elusive Captain Gunpowder at all costs. Undoubtedly they knew where he was. The deserters, eager to get favorable treatment, would have talked.

The first parties appeared the very next morning. There were two of them, each consisting of a sergeant and seven men. One came directly from the town, the north side of the crater, while the other came from the south. Clearly they had planned to arrive at the lip simultaneously, in order to surprise the skulkers. Ezra's sentries reported their approach, and by the time they appeared he and all of his men were deep in the jungle.

It was ludicrously easy to evade these intruders. Even the clumsiest, the most bovine, of the *Forbearance* hands by this time had developed a feeling for the jungle, a fugitive's instinct, the extrasensory perception of the hunted. They could move like wraiths in the dark tangle, making no sound. They seemed, severally, to be a *part of it,* and could stay motionless for hours on end, "like a bloody crocodile," as one of them said. The redcoats, on the other hand, were visibly awed, as the sailors themselves once had been. At first they failed to enter the jungle at all but only encircled it, peering in from time to time, seemingly

247

in the foolish hope of seeing somebody. When at last they did get up the courage to penetrate the darkness they did so gingerly, in a jagged single line, staring hard but after the blinding sunlight of the crater's edge seeing little. Obviously they were under orders to stay spread out, so as to cover as much ground as possible, but they were human and they tended to sidle together again, moving in small batches that were readily sidestepped by the sailors. The muskets the redcoats carried were regulation Brown Besses, not as long as a homemade squirrel gun back in Connecticut, but they had bayonets fastened to them, which made the going just that much the more difficult. Abashed and conceivably even frightened by the slimy fingers of moss and by the liana vines, they used these bayonets from time to time to slash. This was a noisy business. Also, the soldiers scared the rats, which scurried off before them, yet another loud proof of their presence.

Nevertheless, it was an ordeal, this daily visit. For Ezra at least it was nerve-racking, for he constantly felt the fear that one of his men would break cover and appeal for protection, giving away the location of the rest. None ever did—Ezra kept them together and it would seem that the would-be quitters among them were ashamed to give themselves up right before their shipmates—but the fear remained.

Also, these visits seriously impaired his spyglassed study of Oranjestad, for with the crater crammed with soldiers he could not venture up to the lip except, ordinarily, at sunup and again at sundown, which did not leave him much time.

As before, he used the glass assiduously but in particular to scrutinize Government House and the grounds surrounding it. He hoped, day after day, to get a peep at his wife. Several times he did see a woman, but it might have been Helen or might have been Lady de Graeff, or, for that matter, Lady de Graeff's seamstress up from the town, or some other female: at that distance Ezra could not be sure.

On the morning of the eleventh day he noted a special stir around Government House, always a busy place, and from the nature of it and from the loads on the wains that were being hauled up the Bay Path he deduced that there would be a ball there that night. It was about the right time for a victory ball. Helen would attend. She'd almost have to do so, if only as a duty to her host and hostess. There were few ladies in St. Eustatius, and none at all comparable to Helen, as the fond husband well knew. She would be the center of attention, buttered up by ruttish officers in their dress uniforms, with their bright dress swords, and all the gold braid. Would she dance? He supposed so. Almost certainly.

He turned away with a sigh. He had never learned to dance, himself.

The atmosphere in camp was tense. The men were restless, and complained more brashly than before. Hunger was really pressing in upon them, making them desperate. It hurt. The previous night Ezra had dispatched three more men with muskets to look for wild goats, and they had not returned. It could be that they had bagged a goat, or even two or three, as Ezra pretended to believe. That no shots had been heard might be accounted for by the fact that the hunters had strayed far from the Quill and were reluctant to return in daylight. However, it was more likely that they had deserted.

Without these men there were only fifteen left in camp, including Ezra himself, Tom Garrettson, and Jared Brown.

"They bring back three-four goats, we won't have any way of putting up the extra meat," Ezra told the men that noon. "Nobody thought to bring along some salt."

"Imagine having *too much* to eat," somebody mumbled.

"So what I'm going to do, once it gets dark," Ezra went on, "is, I'm going to climb down the side of the White Wall out there to the beach. There won't be any sentries. It's too isolated.

And I'll take those two buckets along with me and fill them up with seawater. It could help, in case of a big meat supply."

"Oh?" said somebody.

The White Wall itself would be too steep, but the side toward town looked negotiable through the glass, and it might be well to establish it as a possible escape route in case of attack from the town. There might be mussels on the rocks down there. There might be caves, one of which could prove a good hiding place for the money chest, provided his trip established that it would be practicable to carry the chest down there. Such a cave could be a last-resort refuge, in case the band scattered.

Ezra had something else in mind, but he said nothing about this. What they didn't know, wouldn't vex them.

There was no path. He had to make his own way, in the pale moonlight. It was steep, but not perilously so. This was the remotest part of the island, with no hut showing anywhere, and it did not trouble Ezra when his foot dislodged a shower of stones that clacked and clattered on down before him, for the chances of the sound being heard were slight.

He reached the shore unexpectedly soon. It was wild indeed, and very rocky, nor was there any sign that it had ever been visited by man.

The waves slammed in and bridalveiled back, iridescent in the moonlight, but the noise they made, largely smothered among the rocks, was not great: it would not drown the sound of an intruder's approach. Ezra filled the canvas buckets and set them down to mark the bottom of the way he had broken. Then he went exploring. He had heard that there were caves here, and caves he did find in plenty, well above the high-tide mark. Because he had no torch he did not penetrate any of them, but they seemed dry and several were fully large enough to give storage to the money chest.

It was Ezra's belief that the money chest, by its very existence, its unavoidable presence, added fuel to the men's discontent. If it was out of sight it would not offend.

Ezra sought in particular a cave that might have a fresh-water spring or stream. He found none out of which water trickled, but there was one from the mouth of which he could hear a steady drip of water far inside. That might of course be inaccessible. At this hour he could not tell, but he marked the place in his memory, meaning to examine it better later on.

Having satisfied himself on this point, he started for Government House. He couldn't attend that dance in person—he had not been invited—but by God, he at least was going to get right up close.

Chapter

45

He approached the place from behind. It was brilliantly lighted. The fiddlers were playing a lively tune, and dancers flitted past the windows. A minuet? No, it was quicker-paced than that. Ezra didn't know much about these things. Fascinated, he edged closer. He slipped into the shadow of a wellhouse.

He did not remember much about the back of Government House, except that there was a narrow garden bordered by a low vine-covered stone wall—a wall that did not for an instant remind him of the stone walls of Connecticut. The slave quarters, he knew, were far to his right. They would be deserted now anyway, for this was not a plantation and the slaves were all house slaves, personal attendants, who would be out in full force for the ball. Between the slave quarters and Government House itself, to which it was connected by a covered walk, was the kitchens kiosk. *That* would be a highly busy place, he knew, but it was far enough away so that he did not worry about it.

He couldn't account for the wellhouse. What was a well doing out here on a bare rocky slope several hundred feet from the outer edge of the garden? Could it be that the garden once had been larger, including this spot, and the well was dug for the watering of it? The wellhouse was a square wooden structure, about four feet on a side, painted white, and with a loose little roof. It looked old. It smelled musty.

Ezra wished to get closer. He knew that he was being foolishly romantical, featherbrained, but if he could catch even a fleeting glimpse of Helen in one of those ballroom windows it would instill him with a strength he might otherwise not have: so he argued with himself.

He stepped out of the shadow and made at a quick dogtrot for the garden wall. It was altogether possible that there was no sentry on duty in the back garden. Why, after all, should there be, unless it was just in order to keep the men busy doing something?

The wall was very low, only ornamental, not meant to keep anybody out. It was topped by a curious cactus-like plant that bloomed only at night: Ezra did not know the name of it. This plant had spikes, and he stepped very carefully over the wall, avoiding them.

He took refuge behind an hibiscus bush.

Almost at once he saw her as she swept past a nearby window, a vision in pink silk, her bare arms and shoulders agleam in the candlelight. Then she was gone. He leaned forward, his heart hammering. Already he felt rewarded. How long would it be before she appeared again—Helen, his lovely bride?

She swept by, a vision of loveliness. He could not see her face this time, and all that he could see of her partner was an arm. A trembling seized him, and he was all-over sweat. For a mad instant he thought of plunging through the window—it was low enough—and knocking down that anonymous officer who dared to lay a hand on Helen. He shook his notion off. The dancers disappeared.

A stronger and much more sensible emotion tugged at Ezra, urging him at least to poke his head through the window and shout to Helen that he loved her. He wanted to make sure she understood he was hiding because of *her*, and how else could she learn this except from his own lips? Again and again he had thought of wild plans for getting word down to her in the town or at Government House, but he had dismissed these as too perilous. Now he crouched behind a bush within a few feet of his beloved, and still he could not tell her.

Once again she showed briefly at the window. It was torture. Gasping, his forehead cold and wet, Ezra Bond leaned out for a better look.

"Halt! Who goes there?"

Ezra did not move, except to crouch a bit, preparing to dash off. But he made himself look away from the ballroom window. If he were to see his wife just once more, howsoever briefly, he would gawp as an idiot gawps and they'd take him like taking a child. He must keep his wits about him.

The voice had come from his left, and not far away, nearer the house. Ezra could not see the man.

Suddenly, from that same spot, there sounded a musket explosion. It might have been a cannon going off, so severely did it shatter the stillness of the garden.

Ezra saw no flash, heard no ball. That meant—unless this was a nervous new recruit who had fired by slip of the finger—that the guard was being summoned.

Oddly, the music went right on, the fiddles. Loud as that shot had been in Ezra Bond's ears, those in the ballroom, it would seem, had not even heard it. Dancers still swirled past that window up there. The feet still shuffled rhythmically.

The sergeant of the guard, however, had heard it. He appeared from around the south corner of the house, two redcoats at his back. They ran right past Ezra to the sentry Ezra couldn't see. There were hasty whispers.

Ezra reasoned that he must have stepped on a stick, love having rendered him clumsy. He stooped, and sure enough, there at his feet were the two broken parts. He threw them against the house. Then he whirled around, sprang over the garden wall, and raced for the well.

254

He did not care whether the sentries actually *went* to the place where those sticks had struck the house, so long as they *looked* that way for a moment, giving him a chance to make this cover. On the one hand, the sticks would confirm the sentry's assertion that he had heard something. On the other hand, when they fanned out to search the garden, and found nothing—and there was no reason why they should search beyond the garden, for the slope on which Ezra crouched behind the wellhouse was open to the moonlight, treeless, for half a mile or more—the soldiers would put it all down to a prying pickaninny and return to their posts. They would not spread the alarm, which would only serve to make them look skittish. There must have been many a major and colonel in that ballroom, not to mention a general or two. You kept as quiet as you could when suchlike personages were abroad.

He did not steal a peek. He reckoned that he was safe here, and he wouldn't risk being seen and having to run for it. Cramped as he was, his leg muscles sore, he wouldn't have been able to run fast anyway.

What a near thing! Poor Helen! If ever the dance had been interrupted to have a prowler dragged in, and that prowler proved to be her own husband, his coat torn, his hair tousled, and not even wearing a sword—his sword was in the money chest, no doubt gathering rust at this very moment—how ashamed she would have felt!

How elaborate a search was made he didn't know, but he heard nothing. He gave them ample time, maybe an hour. It was a small garden. At last he prepared to heave himself to his feet. He would walk slowly away from the house toward the beach—a fast movement might catch in the corner of somebody's eyes—and if he were seen and hailed he would break into a run.

He rose, facing the garden.

Two soldiers were coming toward him. They weren't thirty feet away.

255

He ducked behind the wellhouse again.

He was sure that they had not seen him. They were not out here on a search, for they had not been alert, but walked carelessly, their muskets in their hands held low, while they chatted.

The only explanation could be that they were thirsty. But— a British soldier drinking water?

There was only one place where Ezra might be safe—*in* the well.

It was like a large doghouse. The roof, an inverted V, was fixed a foot or so above the walls, to allow room to put in and take out the bucket. The bucket itself was not in sight, but the wheel was, and there was a rope.

Feet-first, belly-down, he wriggled over the top of the side, just under the roof. He grasped the side with both hands and let himself go.

He dangled free, swinging a little. It was a temptation to feel about with his toes for a niche in the stones that lined the well, so that he could take some of the pressure off his hands and arms but the well was old and the stones down there might be loose. A splash would betray him. So he simply hung.

The soldiers were beside the well now. Had they passed around it they could not have failed to see Ezra's gripping fingers; but they did not. They were talking, an inconsequential conversation from the tone of it. Ezra did not try to make out the words. These men were Londoners and used a language of their own, a language unintelligible to an ordinary person. They said "ax" for ask, for instance, and "bison" for basin, and "voman" for woman, and contrariwise "werry" for very, a curiously ugly whine.

A couple of hands began to run the rope over the wheel, hoisting the bucket: Ezra could hear the sucking sound as it came out of the water and then he could hear it drip as it rose. Those same hoisting hands, on the downstroke, must have come within an inch or two of the back of Ezra's head. He hardly dared to breathe.

He heard a cork pop unobtrusively, and then he smelled the sharp odor of rum. That was it! The stuff had been stolen from the wet canteen before cutting. It was not meant to be taken straight; it was much too strong for that. Laced with water, it constituted what British sailors sometimes called grog. And these men were about to lace it with water, to have a drink. That was why they had come out here.

The bucket in passing *did* graze the back of his head. It felt like a chunk of ice there.

The bucket was not replaced but left on the ledge of the well house, and in a moment the men turned away, their voices dribbling off in the direction of the garden.

Ezra yielded to temptation and felt for a toehold. He succeeded only in loosening a stone, which fell into the water with a great plop.

To him, inside the well, it might have been a bomb; but there was no break in the bumble of the soldiers' voices nor in the receding crunch of their boots. Soon he heard them no more.

Getting out, in his weakened condition, was harder than getting in had been. He lay for some time in the shadow of the wellhouse, hoping to regain some of his strength, and when at last he did rise he noted that many of the Government House windows now were dark. It must be late. He hunched up his shoulders and started for the shore.

By the time he reached the White Wall and the two canvas pails the sky was streaked with the pastels of dawn, and he could see a ship in the offing. There would be a skipper and perhaps a mate or two on that ship, each with a glass at his eye, lining up the vessel with the White Wall, as Ezra himself had done so many times. He, Ezra, would assuredly be seen if he started up the side. There was no law against climbing the Quill, to be sure, but the sight, at daybreak, in this wild place, might well be something that the captain or mate would comment upon in port

257

—once they had recovered from their astonishment at finding themselves and their ship under arrest.

There was another vessel after that one, and Ezra, while waiting, fell asleep; so that it was the middle of the afternoon before he really started up the slope. It was rugged going.

When he gave the agreed-upon whistle from the lip of the crater, Tom Garrettson and only Tom came out of the jungle to greet him. Tom was cursing and weeping at the same time, like a young skipper who has just lost his first command—as, in a sense, he was.

"Every one of 'em! Every last tarnation dratted one! When you didn't show up by sunrise they said you'd quit."

"They ought to've known better than that."

"So I told 'em, but they wouldn't listen. They were bound-and-determined to go. They took their guns and knives with them, and the only reason they didn't take their rations is because there weren't any rations left *to* take. I held 'em up for hours, talking, and I did at last get 'em to go down on the east side, so's they wouldn't be seen from Orangetown. That was the best I could do."

Ezra Bond put a hand on the man's shoulder, and shook him affectionately. Tom in truth was older than Ezra by some ten years, but Ezra always thought of him as a boy, a boy not very bright perhaps but dogged and with a doglike devotion to his master.

"But don't you worry, sir," Tom cried. "*I* won't walk out on you! I'd have waited for you here till Hell froze over."

Ezra gave him a grin.

"I'm sure you would," he said.

Chapter

46

Tom Garrettson never had had much schooling, having been at sea since he was a boy, but he could read and write some. Not that this mattered on St. Eustatius. What was more notable was that, though short, he was of a powerful physique, with long arms and massive muscle-bunched shoulders, and at any kind of work he was virtually tireless. He was not a man with many varied interests. When he undertook any task he just put his head down and charged into it, like a bull; and he did not let up until the thing was done. He was not remarkably good company, for he had no wit and little small talk of any sort, but he could be a mountain of strength when the road got rough.

So they faced one another, these two. They were old friends.

"I don't know about you, Tom, but the way I figure it right now it'd be a good idea if the first order of business was a prayer, which we sure need."

"We sure do. I reckon you're right."

They knelt, then, one on each side of the money chest, and they prayed quietly and well, without even moving their lips.

Ezra was the first up, and he promptly started to take stock.

The deserters had left a few odds and ends, but nothing of moment, except the money itself, no food. The two who remained had one musket and two pistols, six flasks of powder containing in all about four pounds, and a three-pound chunk of lead together with a mold for cutting balls, besides a box that held about twenty spare flints. They had the two collapsible canvas buckets. Each had flint and steel. They had no tobacco or rum. They had the clothes they stood in, which were in good condition, but they did not have the means to repair these when they got torn or began to fall apart. In addition, Ezra had his Book, his glass, and his sword.

The sword certainly was the least important of these items, and indeed it had no place at all on the Quill, to which it had been brought in a fit of absentmindedness. Ezra quite naturally had worn it when he quitted the *Forbearance*. This was only fitting. Thereafter, in the excitement at the town, in the work of the climb, he had forgotten it. Here in the crater it was of no use at all, and he had put it into the chest on top of the coins simply to get it out of the way.

He unsheathed it now, when he and Tom Garrettson went over their precious possessions, and learned, to his amazement, that it had not collected any rust but was as bright and supposedly as sharp as ever. He still could think of no function for it. He wouldn't know how to fight with it: that required special, expensive training. He probably could not even hold it correctly. Sighing, he sheathed it and put it back into the chest.

"That's about as useless as tits on a tomcat," he mentioned.

Garrettson giggled.

They were achingly hungry, but they agreed that before they went hunting for goats they had better conceal the money chest down near the west shore.

"Those men ain't going to keep quiet, once some officer gets to talking to them. A man in prison, he'll do a lot for a little favor."

"Just what I figured," said Ezra. "It's not that the lobsterbacks would want *us*—you and me—but—"

"Oh, I don't know. To say that he had captured Captain Gunpowder, that would be a rosette in anybody's hat."

Ezra stared in astonishment at him. He had not supposed that Tom Garrettson knew the nickname. But he shook his head.

"Oh, no, Tom. You and I don't mean anything, when they've got prisoners by the thousand down there. No, it's this"—and he kicked the chest—"that will draw 'em here like flies to a manure heap."

"They got plenty of coins down there too, besides the prisoners."

"I know, but even for men like that, eleven thousand pounds is no small punkins. No, they'll be up here pretty soon, and they'll be slavering, their fingers all one itch. Suppose we go below and look for a good dry cave? Give you a chance to learn the way, too."

"Aye, aye, sir."

Ezra noticed, on the trip down, that Tom was a poor mountaineer. He showed uncertain of himself in this alien environment, and several times he slipped and fell to his knees. It might have been in part weakness and even dizziness brought about by hunger. At the base of the mountain, near the sea, *his* sea, he was more spry.

They found the very place they sought, and with little trouble. It was dry, and it was far enough back from the high-water mark so that it would be safe from spray even in the most violent blow.

They found the water Ezra had heard, and it was clear and cold, if hard to get at. They examined five other caves, all of them high and dry, though not roomy. Any one of these, like the one with the water, like the one in which they planned to stow the money chest, would have made a good emergency hideout, a good shelter from rain, but not a good permanent camp.

They left the musket in one of them, meaning to return the next day. It would be difficult enough to carry the money chest down the side of the Quill without being encumbered with a six-foot weapon.

It was after dark when they got back to the crater, the jungle, and they slept that night with the rustle of rats around them, but not, blessedly, amid a sea of assorted snores.

"Some of 'em, it's a wonder they didn't get heard down in Orangetown," said Tom Garrettson.

In the morning when they started to move the chest they realized how flabby they had become from lack of food. They could scarcely lift the thing, and getting it up on the lip of the crater drenched them in sweat and had them gasping like a couple of fish out of water.

It wasn't a very good chest. It was oaken and had iron studs and a brass hasp. There was a rope handle at each end. Four men had carried it up. Two were to take it down.

Beyond the lip it was easier. There was no vessel in sight, so they did not lose time. Now they did not have to carry the heavy thing but could slide it along the ground, the slope was that steep. Indeed, the difficulty was not to get the chest to move but to keep it from moving too fast, from slipping out of their control to smash itself on the rocks far below. In order to do this, one of them went ahead, facing the sea, the chest pressed against his back and shoulders, while the other gripped it from behind, paying it out inch by inch.

At first Ezra was the front man, while Tom Garrettson followed up in the rear, but halfway down the hill they switched positions, not because one was easier or harder than the other, but simply for the sake of change.

They could not have been more than twenty feet from the bottom when it happened.

Tom had been slipping. A stubborn man, he refused to stop and take a rest, as Ezra had proposed, but insisted that he was as strong as ever, and as steady. For this reason Ezra had been especially careful and had been trying to bear more than his share of the weight from behind, though he was obliged to do this very gently, lest he hurt Tom Garrettson's feelings. The final slip, however, caught him unawares.

The chest lurched forward, the rope tearing itself out of Ezra's sweat-slippery hands. It struck Tom—on his knees after his fall—in the small of his back.

Ezra dove headfirst for the thing, but all he got was a shower of dust and small stones in his face. For an instant he could see nothing at all.

He heard a scream. He heard a splintering crash; then a vast clacking and clinking; then silence.

He half-fell, half-ran the rest of the distance.

The chest had flown open, and Tom Garrettson, on his face on the beach, his limbs starfished out, was literally buried under a pile of doubloons, guineas, joes and double-joes, pieces of eight.

Ezra tore into the currency with both hands, and soon had his mate uncovered. Tom was motionless, his eyes squinched shut, but he still breathed a mite, and he had some faint pulse. His ribs had been crushed like sticks, perhaps his spine as well. He was bleeding, very slowly, at the mouth. That meant a hemorrhage, probably in the lungs. And *that* meant a surgeon—or death.

Ezra hesitated a split second. He did think, fleetingly, of running to Oranjestad, rather than of carrying Tom there. He was weak, and Tom Garrettson was a heavy man.

He tossed away this thought. They would doubt him in town. There would be delays. The soldiers might well smell a trap, and conceivably there would be forms to fill out, orders to get counter-signed . . . whereas if Ezra appeared with an obviously wounded man in his arms he would get immediate attention.

He worked Tom over his left shoulder, head down behind. He would have preferred to have that head up, but he could think of no way to do this. A litter or an improvised chair of some sort, in the circumstances, was unthinkable. There wasn't time.

There wasn't time anyway. Ezra had not staggered half a mile when he realized that Tom was dead. He couldn't have said how. There had been no cry, no cough, or throat-rattle; but it had happened.

He lowered Tom tenderly to the beach. He opened and closed the eyes several times. He worked a thread out of his shirt and put it across the open mouth; but it did not waver. He held the wrists, feeling for the pulse, which wasn't there. He placed his ear against the heart. Nothing.

He wept for some time, as he knelt there.

He carried Tom back to an inlet he had half-circled on the way. In a cave the body might attract carrion crows, and the breakers of the open ocean could throw it back upon the beach. With strips of linen torn from his own shirt he fastened rocks to the ankles and the wrists. He read from Job, his favorite book:

"Let the day perish wherein I was born, and the night in which it was said, There is a man child conceived.

"Let that day be darkness; let no God regard it from above, neither let the light shine upon it.

"Let darkness and the shadow of death stain it; let cloud dwell upon it; let the blackness of the day terrify it."

He read for some time, aloud. It wouldn't bring back his mate, but it did help Ezra a little to bear the pain. At last, sobbing still, he pushed at shoulders and hips, and the body slid into the water. It sank instantly, and he could see it no longer.

Thomas Garrettson had returned to the sea.

Chapter

47

The first time he ate a rat he had to do it in the dark. He was so hungry that his head ached, and he was dizzy most of the time, and stumbled and staggered like a man dazed by a blow.

He would sit on the floor of the cave, his back to the money chest, head between knees, trying to keep out of his ears the air-filling *thunk* of explosions on the mole before Oranjestad. Even there, and though they were muffled, those sounds stung him. He seemed to have no resistance left. He, who would start at the click of one pebble against another, winced whenever there was an explosion on the mole. They were not regular, those explosions, which made it that much worse. He could not tighten his nerves in anticipation. They were likely to come at any time.

It might have been a month after they had descended upon the island, or it might have been six weeks or even more—Ezra had lost all track of time and there were not even seasonal changes to note on St. Eustatius, where one month was much the same as the last—that the British, seeing that no more innocent skippers steered into the trap they had baited with a flag of the Netherlands, replaced that flag with a Union Jack. It was then, and not until then, that they started to dismember the mole.

Admiral Rodney, it was clear, was bound he would destroy

this "nest of vipers" once and for all, so that if in the exigencies of war it slipped from British hands it would no longer be of any use to such vipers as might elect to return to it. Squads of sappers would mount the seawall that had been so carefully and laboriously built by the Dutch. At intervals undoubtedly calculated in advance, they would hack holes in the top pavement with pickaxes. They would rip out stones and toss these into the sea. They would fill the holes with gunpowder, attach long fuses, and stuff in dried seaweed, weighted down with broken mortar, for wadding. Then they would light the fuses and depart.

Ezra had watch the process many times from the rim of the Quill crater.

There was never any way of knowing which batch of gunpowder would go off first. Sometime they would proceed almost rhythmically from left to right, sometimes from right to left, and at other times the middle ones would be the first to explode. Each threw up a tremendous column of shards and smoke, while it shattered all peace and sleepiness for miles around.

If one of the batches did not explode, then Ezra would know that he could count on quiet for the rest of that day and for the night that followed it, for the British always allowed that much time to elapse before they went back on the mole, being wary of temperamental fuses.

They must have used a prodigious amount of powder each time, enough to keep General Washington's army going for a month.

Now and then a single series of explosions would be enough in itself to wreck a section of the wall so well that sappers in cutters, armed with long poles, could finish the job by pushing what remained into deep water. More often the sappers had to go back for another try, at least once. The Dutch, a thoroughgoing people, had built well.

When he stopped to think of it (which was not often), Ezra Bond reflected that there was little wonder that he jumped at every jar. The wonder was, rather, that he was alive at all.

266

He had heard the expression "gnawing hunger," and he had always accepted it as just so much poetry, a figure of speech. But now he knew it literally. His insides felt as though some animal were eating them, masticating them, munching them bit by delicate bit. He knew now how that Spartan boy felt who hid the stolen fox under his tunic and was eaten alive because he wouldn't admit it, a feat that until this time Ezra had esteemed almighty foolish. He felt as if the sides of his stomach were rubbing together, which maybe they were.

Reading the Book brought some solace, but he could not keep it up long at any one time because his eyes throbbed and watered. He was furious, as though some hand had refused to obey one of his orders, for in the past his body had never failed to do whatever he demanded of it.

His memory, blessedly, was made numb by the hunger. He seldom thought about Helen, though he reproached himself for this negligence. He did not crave her physically, as he should have done. She didn't keep him awake; and indeed he would doze off at any time, and this was one of his worries—that he would sleepwalk straight into a patrol. When he did remember any of his past it was more likely than not about his boyhood in Saybrook, especially in winter—sledding, throwing snowballs, making a snowman. These were half thoughts and half dreams, he supposed, and some of them were so realistic that he would find himself (there in the tropics!) flapping his arms or holding his hands over his tingling ears to protect them from the cold. But most of his thoughts were about food.

With strips torn from his shirt he had improvised a fishing line, to which he attached a hook that he had made from the smashed hasp of the money chest, but he had no bait and he caught no fish, though he cast for endless hours at different points along the beach. Twice fish came to *him*, as it might be said. They were tossed up on the beach, still alive, and he scooped them into his hands before they could flop their way back. He cooked these and ate them, afterward licking the bones.

He never did find any mussels on the rocks that he could keep down. It was the same as with the berries in the crater.

Three times only, in the course of many full nights of roaming, did he get a shot at a goat. Twice he missed completely, and the third time he had to chase a wounded animal for at least a mile before overtaking and dispatching it. The goats were lean, the light poor, and Ezra an inexpert marksman at best. In his weakened condition he thought that the beast, when he carried its corpse back to his cave where he wasn't afraid of having a fire, was the size and weight of a small horse; and in truth it did produce an unexpectedly large supply of meat, enough to last him for three days. Gorged, then, he had hurled the head, feet, and intestines into the sea, an act he was later to regret.

It was the remembrance of this that led to the rats. He was in his favorite cave, the one with the money chest, his head between his knees, staring stupidly, unseeingly, at his sword, which lay upon the floor. He fell to thinking, by association, of the similar parts of that pig they had cooked just inside the lip of the crater. Would they still be good? It was not a fragrant conjecture, but when a man's starving he is not finicky. But—how could they be dug up? Well, how was the hole in which they were buried dug in the first place? One of the men had brought a cutlass, a thick broad blade. That was gone now, but here was Ezra's dress sword. It wouldn't serve as well, but it might do the trick. He rose, strapped it on, and went outside.

This was the middle of the day—*what* day, Ezra had no idea— but he did not fear that he would be seen climbing beside the White Wall. Few ships were putting into St. Eustatius these days, where once there had been so many. The sea, today, was clear.

He was sure that he could remember where they had barbecued that pig, the exact spot. He was panting when he reached the top of the Quill, and he was sweating profusely, something that happened to him these days at the least exertion.

Also, he trembled. He was overeager. He had to pause a moment, to get control of himself. He drew the sword and swished it several times. Then he went on, slowly, feet widespread, like a man who wades through water.

The pit was a pit again. He saw as much from a distance, but he resisted the inclination to run to it, approaching instead with that agonized, wide, shuffling tread.

There was nothing left but a cluster of well-sucked bones. Those tarnation rats had somehow smelled the stuff and dug it up. One of them was there even now, sniffing, hoping that a scrap of food had been overlooked. When Ezra appeared, it gave a curiously mouselike squeal and started to skitter away. Ezra, with a curse, slashed at it. The rat dropped in its tracks.

Ezra Bond stood staring down at it for a long while. At last, gingerly, he picked it up by the tail. It was dead all right.

He sheathed. Holding the beast at arm's length, he made his way back down around the edge of the White Wall.

He washed the rat in the sea. He spitted it on his sword and roasted it for a long while over a fire, turning and turning it. He took it to the back of the cave, behind the chest, and there, crouching like an ape, he ate every bit of it.

After that first one it was never as hard.

Chapter

48

To a dog (goes the saying) all the world is a smell. It was getting to be thus with Ezra. His sense of touch surely had coarsened, thanks to brine and sun. His taste? What taste would he have left after a diet that was predominately rodential? His hearing was impaired, he believed, because of the headache that racked him continuously. His eyes often smarted and they would water when he stared hard at anything. This troubled him, for he had previously been a sharp-eyed man. Even with the assistance of the spyglass he saw many things blurrily. But his sense of smell grew keener every day.

He supposed that this was the most primitive of the senses. Coupled with it, in Ezra's case, was a sense of peril, of urgency, or warning. An old red-haired Scottish sailor once had told him that where he came from, folks said that if your nose itched it was a sign of danger. Ezra's nose did not itch, and he might be more than half asleep, when something would suddenly and pushingly tell him to take cover. He was not sure but that this was tied to his increasingly keen sense of sniff. Perhaps he really *did* smell the coming of an enemy?

This instinct, or sixth sense, or whatever it was, was especially useful at this time, when the British, having cleaned up the truly important work of counting and computing the confiscations and shipping these Home, had turned to the lesser task of ferreting out Captain Gunpowder.

Most of the many vessels that had been anchored in Statia roads when the British pounced were gone now, as were most of the warships, for there would be no safe anchorage when the mole had been demolished; but a few of the latter, patrol frigates, stood off and on, and every day some of the barges, laden surely with treasure, were rowed out to these. There were fewer soldiers too, and now that the looting had been completed there was less for them to do. An idle soldier is a bad thing; so they were sent forth in search parties with instruction to nab, somehow, the last holdout of St. Eustatius.

Ezra had no doubt that they knew who he was. As Tom Garrettson had said, some of the hands were sure to talk, if only in the hope of getting better food. The fact that Ezra had a nickname and was a highly successful smuggler of gunpowder would lend zest to the hunt. In himself he was not significant; yet, knowing the English as he did, Ezra had no question that they looked upon this as a form of sport. He could imagine the officers—some of the enlisted men too, risking their rum rations —laying bets on just where and when this notorious Captain Gunpowder would at last be run to earth. By being so sly, and so stubborn, he was affording a great deal of entertainment to men who would otherwise be bored. He felt no gratification whatever.

He only hoped that they weren't putting pressure on Helen down there in the belief that she knew where he was. It was largely because of this possibility that he had refrained from making any attempt to get in touch with her. It would be better, he reckoned, for her *not* to know where he was, or even if he still lived. That way, there was no chance that she might be tricked or frightened into betraying him, something for which he was sure she would never forgive herself.

The picnic he had so confidently expected never did show up;

271

and indeed, once the British had finished with the warehouses and the mole there was, unexpectedly, a falling-off of the search parties, precisely when these might have been expected to increase in size and number. Wary, suspecting that this was bait to lure him out, Ezra moved around as furtively as ever, going nowhere until he had first looked, twitching his nose, it could be, like any hound.

When they did come again they were not Army men but Marines. This was as it should have been. Ezra, after all, was the Navy's pigeon, not the Army's. And Marines too, like soldiers, needed exercise.

This time, also, there was an officer in charge: previously it had been but sergeants. Ezra was gratified; though he feared that the search would be more diligent.

It wasn't. It was hardly a search at all, but rather a summoning party. On the rubble-strewn slope between the jungle and the lip of the crater the Marines lined up in due order, and the officer, a lieutenant, facing the jungle, called: "Captain Bond! Please come out!"

How courteous of them! Ezra noted the "captain" with even more wry emphasis than he took the "please." Was this a case of wishful flattery? or did they think that solitude and the sun had addled his wits? He did not, of course, stir. He conceded in his mind that he might be somewhat crazy—"touched," anyway—but he was not so crazy that he would walk into the loving arms of the Royal Navy.

The party started to encircle the jungle, clockwise. This made hard walking, and they moved slowly, cumbrously, loosening many stones, so that Ezra, flitting like a ghost, even when he could not see them could hear them. Every now and then the lieutenant would call: "Please come out, Captain Bond!" It was like a chant in church. Ezra smiled lopsidedly.

They did not leave until an hour before sundown, and Ezra remained in the crater for that whole hour, fearful lest they had left somebody behind with orders to shoot him if he broke cover. As a result, when he did make his way down to the shore he was ratless.

Next morning, hungry, he climbed the Quill before dawn. He started his hunt in the part of the jungle that was nearest to Oranjestad, so that he could keep watch on that portion of the crater. The search party of the previous day had come that way, and something warned Ezra that they would return.

They did—and he almost ran right into their arms.

Squatting like any savage, hunkered down on his heels, Ezra waited, His patience, these days, was amazing.

The sun was fairly up but the air in the crater still was steamy when he thought that he heard a faint rattle of stones. He had expected that. Coldly he stared at the spot where the men might emerge. He knew that he could have imagined the sound, just because he *did* expect it.

Soon somebody appeared. It was Helen.

Had Ezra been standing, his knees might have buckled under him. Even so, he swayed. It was as though he had been clubbed with a club. His eyes misted. There was a pounding in his ears.

When he had recovered, at least a little, it was only with a tremendous effort that he refrained from leaping to his feet and rushing to her. What held him back was that same mysterious sense of impending peril that he had felt before, that atavistic instinct to distrust everything and everybody. Truly he was a beast now.

Helen paused, teetering on the ridge. It seemed to Ezra that she looked behind her for an instant, though in that light he could not be sure. She must have been out of breath after the climb.

She started toward him, walking with an uncertain step. It was almost as though she could see him squatting there, though he was sure that she couldn't.

He saw something behind her, on the far side of the lip, something black that bobbed for an instant and then went down out of sight. Might it have been the black felt top-hat of a marine? He could not be sure.

A moment later, near that same place, he caught, briefly, a glint of something bright. It might have been a bayonet.

Helen began to call, coaxingly, caressively, in a curiously high voice, as she approached.

"Please come out, Ezra. Everything will be all right."

She extended her arms toward him.

It was too much. Marines or no marines, trap or no trap, it was more than Ezra's flesh could stand. He would seize one kiss, one swift passionate embrace, and then run. Gone was his instinct, his sense of fear. He sprang to his feet.

Instantly Helen's voice was lowered.

"Don't show yourself," in a whisper that trembled with urgency. "Stay down. Ezra, they're following me."

She did not enter the jungle but turned to the right, a few yards away, and resumed that oddly high, unnatural chant, her arms still outstretched. She might have been in a daze, a stupor. She might have been walking in her sleep.

"Please come out, Ezra. It's all right. I want you so much."

He froze, half-erect. He looked back to the lip of the crater.

Seven marines appeared, one by one. They said nothing. They crouched a little, hunched forward, walking as quietly as they could over the loose stones, seeming to try to tiptoe, and making no effort to overtake Lady Helen, whom, however, they must have been able to see: Ezra himself could still hear her.

Their bayonets were fixed, and the officer held a bare sword. They passed, as Helen had, within ten or twelve feet of the place where Ezra stood in slime. They too turned to the right.

Ezra allowed them a full minute in which to disappear, and then he spun around and scampered into the very heart of the jungle, where he waited, trembling, sweating profusely. As Ulysses stopped his ears with wax and caused himself to be lashed to the mast when his boat neared the island of the sirens, so did Ezra Bond refuse either to look or to listen to his beloved.

How long she remained out there calling, or whether she moved about a bit or stood in one place, he did not know. He heard nothing; and he did not leave his hideaway until night had come. Once again he was without a rat when he went down to the cave. He remained there for three days.

Thereafter for some weeks or maybe a month there was scarcely a day when a search party did not comb the crater, occasionally calling his name. They sure wanted him. They searched other parts of the island as well. At least three times—and they might have come often when he was asleep, for he slept most of the daylight hours now—a party of redcoats passed along the shore. Seemingly they believed—the fools!—that if he was alive and heard them he would come out. He of course did not budge.

Chapter

49

It had always been difficult to kill the rats, swatting them with the sword, for they were fast movers. It called for great patience and there were many misses. But that was in the daytime. At night it was simply unthinkable; and under this new arrangement Ezra Bond did not dare to venture out of cover in daylight, or to have a fire then; he had become completely nocturnal, like a skunk.

He did not let this faze him. He was tired of rats anyway, and he had discovered another, less noisome food. With the glass, when the crater was still his, uncontested, he had surveyed all of the island that he could see—which was almost every foot of it. He had noted a dozen or so small cane fields, each with its small peasant's hut. The distance denied him details, but from his acquaintance with the West Indies he knew each such hut in all probability would be sided by a banana tree and perhaps backed by a melon patch or a bean patch. And there was the cane itself. Sugar cane wouldn't fill the stomach, but if you had strong teeth you could chew a heap of nourishment out of it.

He felt mean even to think of such sneaky raids. The peasants were crushingly poor. Yet Ezra himself, though he ate off a chest that held £11,000 in cash, was even poorer. His conscience might tell him that he was doing wrong, but his belly instructed him to go right ahead.

He did determine that he would steal only a little bit from each place, but that was less out of pity for the peasants than out of fear that if they learned they were being systematically robbed they might complain to the military, who would set a trap for him.

These places were all on the far side of the Quill, a considerable distance from his cave. They were scattered, too, each far from the others. Between dusk and dawn Ezra had to cover a great many rugged miles.

When he saw a man he slipped behind a tree. When there was a dog, and it barked, he backed silently away. He could not afford to be chased. In his condition he could not run fast or very far. He no longer trusted his legs.

Yet the operation, if tiring, was absurdly easy. Each night he carried an armful of food back to his cave, where now he actually had a surplus. This was mostly bananas, beans, and melons, as he had predicted, but occasionally he would get other things as well. He had one bunch of grapes, and two ripe coconuts, great finds.

When the fever hit him he did not know it. He did not remember falling, or collapsing, nor yet crawling into the cave, though his knees were scratched and bruised.

He emerged not slowly but abruptly. It was like coming out of a fog into a lighted room. He was dizzy and pitifully weak, and his face still was burning, but his mind was clear. He knew instantly that he must have been unconscious for a long time. He was startled to see that there was no food, not even a peel, not a rind, except the empty husks of the coconuts. There had been enough there, he'd reckoned, to keep him in eating for a week.

He was very thirsty, and as he made his way to the cave where the spring was he felt his face for fever—and learned that he was heavily bearded.

His hair was long, but he had kept it neatly clubbed, and he had been scrupulous about his daily shave. But now there was at least a week's growth of stubble on his face.

It gave him a creepy feeling to think that he had been virtually dead for so long a time. He had eaten, he might have crawled about, and he had certainly messed his breeches, without knowing a thing.

This was late afternoon, from the sun, but though there were several ships in sight none was near enough so that he had to fret about being seen.

It took him a long while to clean himself and to shave, and his hand was so unsteady that he cut himself again and again. His bones ached.

He decided that he would go into Oranjestad for a little while. This was not a new idea. Several times before, when his spirits were low, he had contemplated it. It had seemed to him then, for a little while, that unless he heard human voices, he would go mad. Each time, in the past, he had resisted this urge. Now he deliberately succumbed.

He would not enter any house or shop. He would not accost anybody, and he would not answer if anyone spoke to him. He would move slowly, so as not to attract attention, and he would keep as much as possible in the shadows.

He made himself as trim as he was able to do, though he knew that he must look grotesque, a scarecrow.

The thing he had most to fear was an encounter with a military patrol. These patrols, of three or four men each, would roam the streets of St. Eustatius every night, to pick up drunks, to stop fights when called upon, to start them when bored. The patrolmen would have no regular beat. They would always be on the lookout for deserters or for waifs who could be accused of desertion. They wouldn't carry pistols, only clubs; but they would be quick to strike.

Nevertheless, he would risk it. In all sobriety he did fear that he might go mad otherwise.

However, he was hot: his face was hot. Perhaps he still did have a touch of fever, a wispy tendril of it? He would go again to the cave where the water was and get another drink before he set out.

This cave had a wide mouth, but it narrowed sharply, and to reach the tiny shallow pool into which water dripped so doggedly it was necessary to get down on hands and knees. This Ezra did, as he had done many times before; but this time, unexpectedly, he slithered straight down on his face and chest, stretched flat. Nor could he get up again. He simply didn't have the strength. It was with a terrible effort that he turned over on his back, and the floor of the cave seemed to be rocking like a boat.

He knew that he was fainting, but he felt no fright, only wonderment. *More* sleep?

Then it was broad daylight, and silhouetted against the opening of the cave were three figures, one of whom knelt before him and stroked his face with soft hands.

"Darling, darling!"

He must have moaned or made some sort of sound, for the other figures stirred, jabbering excitedly.

"*C'est le Capitaine Poudre!*"

"*Ah, oui! Enfin le Capitaine Poudre! Vraiment!*"

"It's all right, darling," Helen kept saying and she stroked his cheeks. "They're friends of ours. They're French and they've taken over the island and everything's going to be all right."

279

Chapter

50

She told him of many things, astonishing him. It was confusing at first, and he scowled as he tried to grasp it. The physician, Governor de Graeff's own, cautioned him against too much conversation "until you get your strength back," but Ezra was insatiable and kept asking for more news.

He was always aware when she was present. His eyes were the hardest hit, and a good deal of the time he lay with a wet cloth over them; but even so he could tell, without hearing her, when she came into the room. He just *knew* it.

"Hello," he'd call.

"Now remember, you must be quiet, dear."

"Until I get my strength back."

"Yes, until you get your strength back."

"And then—*whee!*"

That France had taken the island of St. Eustatius away from the British did not amaze Ezra Bond. France understandably would gather up as many of the West Indies as she conveniently could, in order to be in a better bargaining position when peace negotiations were started. It had all happened while Ezra was tossing in fever in the cave on the west shore—most of the British occupation force had gone by then—and it had been a duplication of the earlier seizure: a weak garrison, overwhelming force, an immediate surrender. With the warehouses emptied and the mole shattered, the place was not the prize that Rodney got, but it did have a certain nuisance value as a threat to the nearby St. Kitts.

Helen, her husband learned, had climbed the Quill on three separate occasions, in the hope of at least catching a glimpse of him. She had not wanted the Marines to accompany her. On the contrary, she had tried to sneak away without them; but they were watchful.

"They said I had to have protection. They couldn't tell what you might do. They regarded you as a madman."

"Well, I reckon I was, more or less. But I only saw you the one time. I *would* have been mad, for sure, if it had been more."

But why, he asked, had the Marines persisted, on their own, for days and even weeks?

"Because Admiral Rodney offered fifty pounds out of his own private purse for the one that first flushed you. He felt very strongly about it."

"I'm touched," murmured Ezra.

"It was hard, climbing that hill. After all, I'm a woman—"

"I'm sure of it. And once I get my strength back—"

"Sh-sh!"

"Well, I can anyway think about it, can't I?"

"But that wasn't why I stopped. It was because of the Marines. I was afraid the sound of my voice might have been too much for you."

"It would have been, in a little while."

The coming of the French had solved everything, except the question of Ezra's whereabouts. The French had heard of the gallant Captain Gunpowder, whom they much admired, and they were most co-operative.

"But—you're English!"

"I'm not English. I'm American now. I'm their ally."

"Eh?"

"If I'm married to an American, that makes me American, doesn't it?"

"Well, I suppose it does, when you look at it that way."

"And besides, don't you remember that old saying that all the world loves a lover? The French especially."

"Ah!"

"I don't even own any property in the British Empire any more. Everything I've got is in the form of Amsterdam guilders."

"Good investment," Ezra said. "I've got a heap of them too. By the way, could you ask Van Bibber to drop in on me, next time you're down in the town?"

"Talking business might be bad for you."

"Talking business has never been anything but good for me."

The agent had been cleaned out, and his mouth fairly watered when he heard of Ezra's hoard, the only one, it seemed, that had survived. Ezra, who trusted him implicitly, gave him detailed instructions about how to find the money chest; and when Van Bibber brought it back, and when Ezra had counted the coins and had established that not a one was missing, he lent Van Bibber five thousand pounds—at twelve percent interest, which was generous the way money was on Statia at that time. Ezra did not have the authority to do this; but he believed that he was still a captain, even though he no longer had a ship, and a captain must make decisions. This was *Forbearance* money, and Ezra Bond owned almost a quarter lay in the *Forbearance* venture. The five thousand would make a good stake, here in St. Eustatius, the basis for future credit; and Ezra still had enough left to send back to Connecticut any of his men who might have survived the British press gangs.

Helen's story of how she at last found him delighted Ezra.

"To go on visiting the crater every day would be to chase you away or maybe even cause your capture, but when the French came I went up there for the fourth time, of course. I talked two officers into going with me. It wasn't hard."

"I can believe that."

"I wanted you to see their uniforms and then you'd realize what had happened and you'd come out."

"I wasn't there."

"I know that—now. So I went to Governor de Graeff and asked him who knew the island best—geographically, I mean. And said a man named Peter van Braam, a mulatto. D'ya know him?"

"Yes."

"He's a boatman."

"Yes."

"So I sought him out and I asked him where he would hide if he had to hide and couldn't use the Quill, and he said in one of those caves on the west shore, near the White Wall. So I went there. And I heard the drip of water in one of them, and I knew you'd certainly need water, so I went in—and there you were, thank God."

He touched her cheek lovingly.

"And she's even intelligent too," he whispered.

"A little white house in Connecticut is what I want for us," he told her. "With a little white fence in front of it."

"I'd want a garden," she stipulated.

"You'll get your garden. I'll be away at sea a lot of the time, and you'll need something to keep you busy. But you'll like the folks in Saybrook, and I'll warrant they'll take to you."

"As long as you do, dear."

"You don't have to worry about that."

They talked this way. All they could *do* was talk; but it was pleasant and passed the time.

The real jolt she saved for the fourth day of his recovery, when his head was clear and his eyes were better.

"When this tarnation war is over—" he had started to say.

"It is over."

"*What?*"

"For all intents and purposes, dear. At least, nobody's shooting at anybody any more."

So engrossed in his gains had Admiral Rodney been, as Helen explained it to Ezra, that he lingered too long at Statia, giving a great French fleet under De Grasse a chance to break out of Fort Royal and make for the North American mainland.

"The money, yes." he said. "Plus the fact that you were here, I'll bet."

She blushed a mite. She blushed easily these days.

"I think it was mostly the money," she murmured.

De Grasse had sailed to Chesapeake Bay, where his fleet cut off all water retreat on the part of Lord Cornwallis, who was holed up at Yorktown, Virginia, with Rochambeau's French army and Washington's Continental army blocking the land side. Washington, for the first time, had plenty of gunpowder. Cornwallis had done the only thing that he could do—he had surrendered. And peace was simply a matter of arrangements.

"So it looks as if we'll get there sooner'n we could have hoped for a little while ago, eh?"

"To that little white house in Connecticut."

"With the little white fence in front of it."

They were holding hands, tight. They grinned at each other.